THE FOURTH LEVEL
BON VACANCES
BOOK EIGHT

I0452343

NICHOLAS HUNTLEY

.

"We, Walloons, enjoy the splendor of French civilization; this wonderful fruit, ripened by centuries of labor and glory, we bring to our teeth every day; it nourishes in us what is most human."

– Léon Degrelle

Act 1, Scene 1

The black-painted oak casket with its golden handles on either side was lowered into the ground before the many grievous onlookers. The casket that carried the deceased subject of the mourners was approximately two-meters in length, over half a meter in height and three-quarters of a meter in width. The women were in sorrow, the men held a scowl on their faces, and a little boy was emotionless. The boy had long, light-blonde hair that could be compared to the light sand of the beaches beyond the shore behind the grave. The light blue eyes were like the English Channel beyond. His skin was a bitter white, but smooth as the child was young and as short as an eight-year-old could be. He, like the many in the crowd, was dressed in black formal attire.

"We all knew Derby for the part he played in all of our lives. He was a father, a brother, and a friend, and a war hero who saved us all from a terrible tyranny," a priest addressed to the crowd. "Twenty-five years ago on this very beach, our Derby marched with his comrades in the fight for freedom and to liberate the people of Europe. It is a great tragedy that his life could be cut short for all of his service and by such tragic means as a car crash. May God bless his soul and let us all remember to pray for our dear Derby."

The sound of bagpipes played by servicemen began to draw in a low pitch around the crowd. The boy flinched at their sudden start, but he continued to stare straight and towards the casket as it became out of sight and a part of the earth.

Suddenly, the boy's jaw began to tremble as the casket reached the bottom of the pit with a thud. The boy looked over to the tombstone that read, 'Derby Martel de la Cabernet, 10 August 1920 – 4 March 1969.'

The boy's father, a young man in his early twenties with a medium-build and fair skin like his son, held onto the boy's shoulders from behind. He looked at the grave of his father with sharp medium-blue eyes and regret. His own hair was medium length, but a slight darker blonde than his son. Next to him was his wife, the boy's mother, who had an elegant appearance surrounding her. She was dressed in black dress with a veil over her young white face. Her hair was akin to her son's, but her eyes were a bluish-green, and like her husband, she was in her early twenties. Her hair was tied in a bun, and she wore a feminine derby hat.

Next to this couple was a woman similar in appearance to the boy's father, but shorter and wearing glasses. She had longer hair than the woman next to her and was slightly younger as well. On the other side was an older lady in longer black dress and veil over her face. Her eyes were puffy from her tears and she had light brown hair tied back and underneath a similar hat to the boy's mother. Her skin was fair, and her eyes were blue. She was with three other females, one older and the other two roughly the same age as her (in their forties) who kept their heads down in reverence. They were with an older gentleman with white hair in an English naval officer outfit. The man had a long nose that came down his long face. His fair was brushed back and neat. The man kept his right hand in a pocket and looked towards the tombstone with half-open eyes and a disciplined face.

Next to these people was an older man in his late thirties. The man had blonde hair and blue eyes. His hair was combed to the side, and he had a beard at his face. He was with his wife who had medium-brown hair and blue eyes as well. She wore a pillbox hat with a net over her face. In front of them was their daughter, a young girl less than a year older than the boy. She had medium-brown hair like her mother and blue eyes. She also wore a beret atop of her long brown hair and had rosy cheeks.

The boy looked down, hiding the fresh onset of tears that flowed from his eyes. The father sensed the shift in energy and looked down, but it was too late. The boy had pushed away from his father's grip and trudged past his mother and father. Through the crowd, he ran over the natural green grass atop the cliffs of Normandy and away from the burial.

"Charles!" his father shouted in his deep Canadian accent.

"Charles, sweetie!" the mother pleaded in her Austrian accent. "*Bitte komm zuruck!*"

"*Charles!*" the young girl yelped in her French accent.

Charlemagne didn't listen to those that cared for him. Instead, he ran away, far away from the misery that surrounded him. He ran up the hills and down to the meadow. Charlemagne then crossed the dirt track road and continued onwards until he found himself in a broad forest with deciduous trees that had rustling leaves from the light coastal wind.

The voices of his parents echoed behind him. He didn't listen, however, as he continued to sprint until tripping over a protruding root. Charlemagne slammed onto the ground on his side. He pushed himself up from the ground and sat down. Charlemagne then began to look around the quiet forest before twitching his hand as he felt a tingle atop.

A black-spotted beetle had climbed up onto his hand. Charlemagne looked at and breathed quietly. He brought his other hand to shield the bug from falling over. He then stood up and looked around the forest where he was, turning in each direction as if he was lost. Charlemagne looked around and then stopped.

Charlemagne flipped his hand and brought the beetle to his palm. He then walked over to let it down by a tree. Charlemagne wiped his eyes with the cuff of his blazer. He gave a weak snuffle until he could begin to hear his parents again.

Instead of turning and responding to the noise, Charlemagne ignore them and focused on the early spring breeze tracking through the forest, rustling the newly formed leaves atop of the trees and sending a pleasant chill as it blew across Charlemagne's hair. The green glow above him with sunlight pouring through created a refuge within the forest for him.

"I wonder…" Charlemagne murmured to himself as he looked forward, observing three mice at the base of a tree.

One of the mice had fled from Charlemagne as he approached, but the other two, bickering over a piece of fruit that had fallen from the tree above them, stood their ground.

"Who is the fittest?" Charlemagne whispered to himself. "Who is the strongest? I'm going to guess Mr. Beige Mouse because he's more aggressive than Mr. White. The strongest usually survive – that's what granddad told me…"

Surely enough, the beige mouse came out triumphant and began to flee from the other mouse. Charlemagne watched the mouse run off when a hawk flew down, giving a terrible screech as it grabbed the mouse by its claws and then rushed upwards and away. The piece of fruit that had been fought over was left on the dirt for the white mouse to collect. Charlemagne had jumped backwards from the sudden appearance of the hawk. His face had become flushed, and he gave off sharp breaths.

"The strongest came out overtop," Charlemagne muttered in his English accent. "Strong – granddad would want me to be strong."

"Charles," a voice cried out from behind him.

"Granddad?" Charlemagne questioned, turning around with happy eyes.

"Charles," Mr. Cabernet, Charlemagne's father, said, stepping forward from behind the other direction. "Charles, don't ever do that again."

"Oh, Charles!" Mrs. Cabernet, Charlemagne's mother, said in her accent.

Charlemagne's mother walked over to him and embraced him.

"*Meine Junge…*" Mrs. Cabernet said, kissing her son on the cheek before bringing her hands to each cheek. "*Was ist passiert? Geht es dir gut?*"

"*Mir geht ist gut, Mutter*," Charlemagne responded, keeping his eyes down. "I'm fine."

"*Gut.*"

Charlemagne's mother smiled at him.

"*Du habe seinen Akzent, wisst du?*" Mrs. Cabernet said.

"I miss him," Charlemagne confessed, eyes watering before hugging his mother again.

Mr. Cabernet watched from behind, crossing his arms and looking at his watch.

"Vienna, dear," Mr. Cabernet groaned in his urban Canadian accent. "Come on – we should return to the attendants. We left my grandmother with her parents and the Dumas family."

"*Sei mutig, mein Sohn*," Vienna told Charlemagne, ignoring her husband. "*Das Leben deines Grossvaters lebt in dir weiter.*"

Charlemagne nodded to her. Vienna stood up from where she was knelt and took Charlemagne's hand. She then walked over to Mr. Cabernet who began to lead them out of the forest.

"I know that you miss your grandfather, Charles, and it is tragic what's happened, but your mother and I have been talking before we flew over here and we've decided it's time to take you back to Canada," Mr. Cabernet explained. "What do you think of that?"

"What about grandnan?" Charlemagne questioned. "Will she come with us?"

"Your grandmother has family here in England and they'll look after her," Mr. Cabernet explained. "It's time for all of us to return to Allabrese once and for all."

"I don't want to…" Charlemagne pouted. "I don't want to leave."

"Charles," Vienna said, putting her arm around Charlemagne, "don't you want to be with mother as well? I've missed my little boy so much – if it wasn't for your father…"

Mr. Cabernet looked at Vienna with an annoyed face.

"Listen, Charles," Vienna instead said. "We can compromise – yes? How about we let you go to a boarding school here in England and then you come back to Canada to go to a high school there? In the summer time, you can return to Allabrese and spend your summers with me and your father. Does that sound good?"

Charlemagne didn't respond.

"Your father and I also have some good news we have to share with you," Vienna said. "We wanted to share it with you once we returned home, but maybe it will cheer you up instead."

"What news?" Charlemagne questioned, looking over to his parents.

"You are going to be a brother, Charles," Vienna announced. "Isn't that exciting?"

"Why?" Charlemagne simply replied.

"Because I'm pregnant, Charles," Vienna responded. "I'm going to have another child and you will be an older brother."

"I don't want to be an older brother," Charlemagne instead said, shaking his head.

Vienna looked to her husband. Mr. Cabernet rolled his eyes. The two simply sighed as they walked with Charlemagne, returning him to the funeral where armed soldiers were firing shots over the English Channel in memory of Derby Martel de la Cabernet.

Act 1, Scene 2

"At a time when the old demons of the far-right are rising again, it is important that we remember the heroes that liberated us and gave us the freedom we now have," the French President stated at his podium. "However, on this date, we do not only honor your grandfather, Mr. Cabernet, but the entire Cabernet family for all of their contributions in both humanitarian and economic matters. The Cabernet family has become a shining example of good moral character, which we can only expect to have been inherited by Derby de la Cabernet. For the late Mr. Cabernet was a patriotic man that helped us defeat the evils of nationalism."

The hands of those clapping behind the family could be heard in the ballroom. Charlemagne nodded and blushed towards the crowd as he stood next to the president. The large room of the Versailles Palace had every chair occupied, all five-hundred, for the occasion by politicians, investors, businessmen, entrepreneurs, and media representatives. Charlemagne stood straight next to the president in a fine pressed black suit with his steel grey hair neatly combed to the side and moustache stretched across his upper lip as always.

An older woman with golden blonde hair in a blue dress opened a velvet case with the Legion of Honor medal inside. The medal had a red ribbon atop that went down to an oak wreath, which connected to a larger laurel golden wreath behind the white Maltese Asterisk. In the middle of the star was a circular golden emblem of Marianne, the national personification of France, surrounded in a blue border with the words, '*République Français*,' in gold print.

The President of France took the box and then walked over to Charlemagne for them to pose with the award. The media representatives immediately consumed Charlemagne and the president, flashing their cameras at them before the president turned to Charlemagne, took the medal from the box, giving the box to the attendant, the First Lady of France, and then inserting the medal into the left breast of Charlemagne's blazer, leaving the medal suspended by the ribbon. The two then shook their hands, triggering the journalists to flash their cameras again. The audience clapped and Charlemagne gave a shy smile as he nodded.

The children, Diana and Tristan, watched from the front row with Judith Lambert and Richard Huxley at their side. Dr. Lambert was dressed in a white dress with her blonde hair tied back, giving a proud smile as she looked to Charlemagne and clapped. Tristan had neatly trimmed hair and was dressed in a black suit with a red tie. Diana wore a burgundy spring dress and had her hair straightened.

After a long five minutes of basking in the light of the media, Charlemagne was brought over to the podium to speak to the crowd. The President of France and First Lady stood at the sidelines.

"*Merci*, President Macron, for this award and your kind words to my family. My one regret, today, is that it had to be myself receiving this reward and not the most honorable member of the family, my grandfather, Derby Martel de la Cabernet. However, as a head of the household, I am gracious nonetheless to accept this award in his place and in his memory. My grandfather was indeed a man of morals and principles as you said, and it is with these principles that we conduct ourselves in our everyday lives. My grandfather taught me the importance of certain values: truth and self-sacrifice being the primary ones. Had it not been for the sacrifices of my grandfather, I would not be the man I am today. The world does not owe any debt to the Cabernet family and never will. We are a simple family of

France, and we have done our duty only to help the people of France, our people, and by helping France we have been able to help the rest of the world as France has. The same is possible with any other family – that is what it means to be French – it is to be part of a family. However, 'you must help yourselves and your family before you can be able to help others' is what my grandfather used to say, and each family has within in them the capability to help others. On behalf of my family, my children, my ancestors, and myself, I thank you, President Macron and your wife just as I thank all of France, my countrymen and women. *Vive la France pour que le reste du monde vive.*"

The audience gave another round of applause as Charlemagne moved from the podium to shake the hand of the president again. The journalists took another round of photographs and the crowd then moved on to stand up. Charlemagne smiled at the attention and then the president moved away from him as the assembly ended.

Charlemagne walked over to Judith and the children, linking arms with Dr. Lambert so that they could go with the rest of the attendants to the reception in the ballroom. The walls of Versailles were as bright and colorful as gold.

Diana and Tristan walked with Judith and Charlemagne into the ballroom and looked around themselves. The room had quickly filled with the same people who attended the ceremony. Servants moved around with plates of appetizers and flutes of champagne. An ambience of classical music emanated through the room.

"Oh, Charles," Judith said, taking Charlemagne's hand. "Come, dance with me."

Charlemagne didn't object and melted into the crowd of people, disappearing from the sight of the children. Charlemagne smiled as he brought his hands to the hips of his girlfriend, looking to her in her elegance. The couple looked to each other, Charlemagne tilting his head down and Judith tilting her head up as they began to go at a slow pace with the others.

"You gave a beautiful speech, darling," Judith remarked in a quiet voice.

"Do you think so?" Charlemagne questioned. "I wanted to be concise, yet effective – I feel like I wanted to say more but couldn't."

"It was perfect," Judith assured him.

"I must confess," Charlemagne remarked, "I truly do wish that my grandfather was here to have received this reward. The world could be so much more different than it is had he lived."

"Yes, but you told me that because of his death, you were motivated to become who you are, Charles," Judith replied. "You told me that the spirit of your grandfather lives on in you and that with every effort you make, it is his effort as much as yours."

"I don't truly know who I would have become had he lived, but under his guidance, I'm sure I would have at least been… good."

"You are great, Charlemagne," Judith said to him, kissing him. "Never forget that."

Charlemagne nodded to Judith. Diana and Tristan looked at the couple from the distance.

"Do you think it's going to happen?" Diana questioned. "Do you think he's going to propose before we leave?"

"The last time Charlemagne proposed to a woman, he told me it was in Paris," Tristan responded. "It's possible, but I have my doubts that he would want to do that again, exactly as it was."

"Charles proposed to a woman?" Diana questioned. "When did this happen? How come I was never told of this?"

"I asked Charles about his personal life last year before we were dating," Tristan responded. "He told me that he knew a childhood friend, the one that used to travel with him. They dated for four years, and granted, he never actually proposed to her, but he planned on it – atop of the Eiffel Tower."

"What happened?"

"He stood her up," Tristan responded. "Charles said that he went to Switzerland for something more important and then they never spoke to each other ever again."

"Ever?"

"Never," Tristan affirmed. "Not even to get closure or to officiate the fact that they were no longer a couple."

"Wow," Diana reacted, brushing her arms as if she had a chill. "I didn't know any of that."

"Yeah, well, that's all I have to tell," Tristan remarked, looking back to her. "I'll be right back. I have to go use the washroom."

"Sure," Diana replied, nodding to him.

Tristan walked off and left Diana alone. Diana looked around the ballroom at the couples dancing and then over to Tristan as he disappeared.

"*Bonjour*," a man said from Diana's left-side.

Diana jumped and turned. She saw a young man next to her – possibly slightly older than her by one or two years. He was tall, approximately six feet or so, and he was dressed in a slim black suit with a black tie. He had thin blonde hair that was even thinner at the sides and back. At the lapel of his blazer was a distinct gold pin. The top of the pin was shaped like a nine-millimeter cartridge, but with the top bullet flattened and smushed. The bottom portion was shaped like two opposing fangs and amber-colored with a golden border. It was shaped like a bug or possibly a bee. The boy had fair skin like Diana and bright blue eyes. He spoke in an unknown French accent.

"Are you Mr. Cabernet's daughter?" the boy asked.

"Adopted-daughter," Diana corrected, "but yes. Who are you?"

"My name is Léon Bauer," the boy stated. "What is your name?"

"Diana," Diana remarked.

"Like the princess or the goddess?" Léon questioned. "You are beautiful enough to be of English royalty, *ma chéri*."

Diana blushed. Tristan re-entered the room and looked over to Diana with the boy. He instantly frowned and made his way over.

"Have you been out to see the sights yet? How long have you been in France?" Léon queried.

"Not long," Diana replied. "I just arrived last night and I'm still really adjusting to the time difference to be honest."

Tristan walked up to Diana and took her hand.

"Hey," Tristan said to the both of them. "Who's this?"

Léon looked down at their held hands and then over to Tristan.

"My name is Léon Bauer," the boy replied, extending his hand. "Are you Tristan?"

"Yes," Tristan replied, shaking his hand.

"I was just talking with your girlfriend about whether she's seen much of France."

"No, we haven't," Tristan replied. "Why?"

"It'll be a worthy look," Léon said to them. "If it's alright with you, do you want to come and see a movie I'm showing in one of the rooms? It's not very long and quite informative. It's a tourist film, really."

Diana and Tristan looked at each other. Diana shrugged and the couple walked with Léon out of the ballroom and down the hall outside towards a darkened room. There were various seats pointed forward towards a screen. At the start of the aisle was a cart with a film projector pointed towards the screen.

"Take a seat," Léon offered, prepping the projector.

Diana and Tristan sat down in the back of the room. They looked forward and waited for the film to start. The film projector started to trickle, and a light shined at the front. The film jittered and then began to play. The title screen of the film simply displayed the word, 'France' in artistic font before going into colored footage of the streets of Paris in the sixties. Diana smiled as we watched. The streets of Paris were dark but lit by neon lights in this particular district. The footage then changed towards a more traditional area before showing the Eiffel Tower in the daytime alongside some more streets with the traditional architecture of the buildings on the side. Vehicles drove in either direction and there was a simplicity to the city. The footage then changed again to the view of some pedestrians, or locals, in coats walking by. There was a view of some children, smiling.

From here, the film changed to a view of the Arc de Triomphe and then a plaza with a fountain. There was a long mall that stretched along from the fountain and was surrounded by trees. It led to an obelisk of sort. The film then showed various stone statues before going into a view of some traditional French cafes. Locals sat outside of the cafes in total peace. From here, it then showed an exterior view of the Notre Dame and then a park with some artists attempting to sell their art on the side. From here, the footage focused on a park where various people could be seen enjoying themselves, lying down, sitting by a large fountain, and children playing on the grass.

The film then changed to a different location distinct from Paris. The space was more tropical and showed footage of a road by the oceanside.

"This is Nice in Southern France," Léon commented.

"It's beautiful," Diana remarked.

"Yes," Léon affirmed. "It was."

••

Charlemagne and Judith continued to dance to the pace of the music until the two were simultaneously interrupted by a man about the same height as Charlemagne, but with a slightly larger build. He was older, in his sixties, and had slicked back grey hair. He had dark brown eyes and a jovial appearance. He was dressed in a grey suit and handkerchief in his front pocket. He also held a cane despite having a good posture and ease in walking.

"*Monsieur Cabernet,*" the man spoke in a deep accent. "*Pouvons-nous parler?*"

"Sorry?" Charlemagne questioned, turning to him as he separated from Judith.

"A word," the man asked again in English.

Charlemagne looked to Judith and nodded. Judith stood back and walked with the man through the crowd. Charlemagne picked up a glass of champagne as he walked with the man.

"Monsieur Cabernet, my name is Marcel Maurras, *député de la deuxième circonscription des Ardennes,*" the man introduced himself, "*et le chef du Parti populaire français.*"

Charlemagne shook his hand. The man stopped as they walked and took his hand with both of his to greet him.

"It is a pleasure to meet the grandson of Derby de la Cabernet," Maurras said, "let me express what a sorrow it was to lose your grandfather."

"Thank you," Charlemagne responded, "but that was over forty years ago."

"A tragedy, nonetheless," Maurras insisted, "but you are right. Let us not talk of that tragic accident in the past, but instead focus on the present. Congratulations on your award – *la Légion d'honneur* is not just any other medal, but one with a rich history behind it from the Napoleonic times."

"I do realize that," Charlemagne admitted. "It will become a treasured family heirloom."

The two of them came to a balcony that looked out to the expansive Versailles broderie gardens of box hedges and plant beds separated by paths – a *parterre*. The skies were orange with a streak of cirrus clouds that stretched across. Maurras led Charlemagne outside for them to talk by the balustrades. He produced a carton of cigarettes and lit himself a smoke.

"Good," Maurras admitted, "I know you are a man of great intelligence, Monsieur Cabernet, so look inside the ballroom and tell me what you see."

Charlemagne looked into the ballroom and to the attendants in their formal attire. There were still guests dancing to the music, while others stood around drinking champagne, eating luxurious foods and conversing with laughter.

"I see people having a good time," Charlemagne confessed. "Nothing extravagant."

"Three hundred years ago, the scene would be quite similar," Maurras said. "*La Chateau de Versailles* has not changed in all these years, but the people inside have, or so it may seem. From the Bourbons who ruled under a divine right of kings to a more corrupt plutocracy under the supposedly divine rights of man and citizen. The French Revolution – the liberal revolution, Monsieur Cabernet, was a grave mistake. The tyranny of one man was replaced with the tyranny of many. France is in her worst state yet, and yet you claimed in your speech that she is well?"

"France *is* well," Charlemagne argued. "She is thriving. I'm sorry, but while I consider myself to be apolitical, I cannot agree with this far-right rhetoric. France, as a country, has never been better."

"Better? In what aspect? What France, may I ask, is thriving?" Maurras asked with an annoyed face. "Monsieur Cabernet, you are smart; what misconception of France do you see to be well?"

Charlemagne rolled his eyes and scoffed.

"For you, France may be thriving, because your enterprise, Cabernet Industries and her holdings in France are doing well. France as an economic machine is thriving, but that is liberal conception of the state – a dystopian one, Monsieur Cabernet. France used to be a nation-state where the nation was not just ruled by the people, but the nation was the people and the people the nation. I am more than just a politician, Monsieur Cabernet, I am but a man – *un homme du pueple francais de Wallonie, de Normandie et de Bretagne. Du golfe de Gascogne aux Pyrénées et à l'Occitanie. Des Alpes à la Meurthe.* This is what the French nation is. My people, Monsieur Cabernet – our people, are not thriving, but are in misery and on the brink of a fate worse than death. To disappear, be replaced, and forgotten. Our culture. Our history. All appropriated and lost. The government disregards our people in favor of the economic and political interests of the bourgeoise elite. This trend is not unique to the French realm, but to the entire liberal world. You might not understand this, Monsieur Cabernet, but I'm sure you grandfather would have.

He was, as you said, a man of strong morals and principles, as well as one that did not spend his time in palaces."

Charlemagne looked to Maurras with a frown.

"What do you want from me?" Charlemagne questioned.

"I came to you in search of support, but I can see that you do not understand," Maurras stated. "I pray that one day you might understand."

Maurras put out his cigarette and then left. Charlemagne looked to him as he left. He then finished drinking from his flute and set it on the balustrade.

• •

Diana and Tristan continued to watch the film to its end. Léon quickly turned off the projector once the footage had ended and turned on the lights.

"That was so beautiful," Diana remarked, leaning into Tristan. "It just makes me want to go out and see it all for myself."

Léon nodded. Tristan was looking at him and slightly suspicious. The doors then opened with Charlemagne entering.

"Mr. Cabernet," Léon greeted. "It is a great honor to meet you. Congratulations on your award. Your grandfather was a great man who will never be forgotten."

"Thank you," Charlemagne responded, looking at the boy. "Children, I believe it's time we left and returned to the hotel."

"Okay…" Diana said, standing up with Tristan.

The couple walked over to Charlemagne while Léon prepared something.

"Here," Léon said, handing over a circular package. "A gift from me to you, Diana. A reminder of how France was."

"Thank you," Diana replied, taking the package.

"Monsieur Cabernet," Léon then said, turning to him. "Again, congratulations and best regards."

The boy bowed to Charlemagne and then left. Charlemagne turned and watched the young man leave before turning to the kids.

"Who was that?" Charlemagne questioned them.

Diana shrugged.

"I think he was a tourist agent of some sort," Diana guessed. "He showed us a lovely film of all of France."

"Really?" Charlemagne questioned, sighing. "Alright then, I believe it's best if we return to the hotel. I have to be at Cabernet Energy in Paris for a meeting early in the morning and I'm sure we're all still adjusting to the seven-hour difference."

"Sure thing," Tristan agreed, yawning. "Let's go."

Act 1, Scene 3

Charlemagne, Judith, and the kids exited from the side of the Versailles Palace and waited on a lit street for their ride into Paris. It was now nighttime. A luxurious black car drove down the road and pulled up the sidewalk. The driver then got out and opened the door for the family. Once inside, the man closed the door and went back to the driver's seat. The windows of the car were tinted, but the inside of the limousine was spacious.

Charlemagne and Judith sat together with Diana and Tristan at the other side. Each couple faced each other in the small limousine. Judith held onto Charlemagne's left arm while Diana and Tristan sat apart. Charlemagne was quiet during the car ride, looking into the darkened window and away from the others. The car drove them from Versailles into La Défense of Paris, which was the financial district home to the ancient city's skyscrapers.

"Wow, are we in Paris or in Harlech?" Diana questioned, squinting through the tinted windows before simply opening them.

Diana looked out and stared at the designer stores and boutiques. She maintained her smile as they drove along with a wind brushing in. The glass structures were tall and bright.

"Oh, Diana," Judith said, "please close that window. You're bringing in an awful chill. Isn't she, Charles?"

"Sorry?" Charlemagne questioned as if he was waking up from a dream. "What was that?"

"Oh, nevermind," Judith remarked as Diana closed the window.

"Diana, tomorrow you'll have plenty of time to see the town after we're finished at Cabernet Energy. Even then, we're here for the entire weekend."

"A weekend, but we have an entire two weeks of spring break," Tristan remarked.

Judith frowned at Tristan.

"Charles and I are very busy with work at the moment, and we can't afford to lose precious time," Judith explained. "Isn't that right, Charles?"

"Sorry?" Charlemagne questioned again, looking to her. "I do apologize, my dear, but I'm simply not paying attention to the conversation."

"Oh, this is what happens when you drink, Charles," Judith complained. "You get all drowsy and senile. Nevermind – we're almost at the hotel."

The car brought them to a tall skyscraper belonging to the Windsor Hotel five-star hotel chain. The chauffer opened the passenger door for them to exit and they stepped out onto the streets for another brief moment to make the transition from the car to the hotel.

The family entered the hotel lobby and walked to the elevators to go up to their suite. Charlemagne inserted the key card into their suite door and then opened to enter into the large, spacious modernist apartment suite. At the side of the entrance was the family's luggage set down from the airport.

In front of them was a living room that looked out to a patio balcony stretching around their half of the top floor. Windows covered every exterior wall and looked out to Paris. The couches were rectangular, white, and the dining table surface was made of glass. Everything was clean and simple, and there wasn't an absence of fake plants in smooth black cubes by the windows. On the walls, there was abstract artwork – simple streaks of dynamic and contrasting colors.

"Right, I believe we have three bedrooms, one master bedroom suite for myself and Judy, and two other bedrooms for the two of you," Charlemagne remarked, pointing to either side. "I hope that works for us?"

"Yup," Diana replied, taking her things.

Tristan grabbed his luggage and went to the right-side with Diana while Charlemagne stayed on the left with Judith. Charlemagne took his and Judith's bags and went into their bedroom, closing the double door behind them. Diana and Tristan split paths to go into their bedrooms.

Diana set her luggage and the film atop of a loveseat and looked out of her window to the rest of the city. She took a deep breath and then turned around as Tristan entered her room.

"Isn't it beautiful?" Diana questioned. "All of Paris before us."

"Yeah," Tristan replied, walking over and grabbing hold of Diana gently from behind. "It's too bad we can't stay until our anniversary."

Diana sighed.

"I'm going to get changed," Tristan said, kissing Diana on the cheek. "I'll be back in a bit."

Tristan walked off to go back to his bedroom. Diana span around.

"Are you going to sleep on your own tonight?"

"No?" Tristan replied, turning back to her. "Unless you want me to."

Diana shook her head. Tristan left her on her own for a brief moment while Diana went into the bathroom. Tristan returned to his room, opened his luggage and took out some sweatpants. He then removed his suit, piece by piece, returning it into its cover bag before setting it into a closet. He then finished changing into some black soccer sweatpants and a grey hoodie before taking his toothbrush and toothpaste to go into the bathroom as Diana opened the door. He then started to brush his teeth with her.

From there, Diana left first to go into her bedroom to get changed while Tristan finished off in the bathroom by washing his face. He then returned his toiletries to his bedroom before walking down the corridor to Diana's bedroom, closing the shutter doors that looked into the living room and then knocking on Diana's room.

Tristan entered and looked over to Diana, organizing her things. She had set a Bible on the end table with a bookmark an inch from the end. She had changed into a night gown, which was something Judith had talked her into. Tristan smiled as he looked at Diana. Her hair was still straightened from when Judith helped her in the private jet and her fair skin was smooth. The bed had its covers pulled back.

"You know, it's pretty risky if someone knocks on either of our bedroom doors in the morning," Tristan remarked as Diana sat down. "Maybe we should sleep in separate beds…"

"Fine," Diana shrugged, smiling at him.

"But maybe I don't have to go right away…" Tristan then added.

"If you say so," Diana replied.

Tristan gave a playful frown.

"Or maybe I'll just sleep here and risk it."

"Turn off the light," Diana said, turning on the end table lamp.

Tristan turned off the light and then walked over to the other side of the bed as Diana got in. Tristan got into the bed, removed his hoodie, and then went over to hold Diana as she turned off the lamp. The couple had left the blinds open to the city beyond behind Tristan. They went quiet for a moment as Tristan held onto Diana with both of their eyes open.

"You know, I can't stop thinking about that movie we saw," Diana confessed. "If that man was some sort of tourist salesman, he did a really good job."

"Yeah…" Tristan remarked.

"You don't sound so convinced as I do," Diana responded. "You didn't like the movie?"

"I – I don't know what to say. It was beautiful, but… it seemed a little bit mythical and unreal."

"Of course it was real, Tristan. It was a live movie – it wasn't an animation or even CGI."

"Right," Tristan replied. "How silly of me."

"I want to stay longer," Diana said. "Promise me that when we're older, we'll visit again and see all of France."

"To travel sounds nice," Tristan sighed, "especially Europe. St. Petersburg and Reykjavik were breathtaking and there's so much more to see."

Tristan then gave another sigh.

"What's wrong?" Diana asked. "I'm thinking about the movie, but you're thinking about something else, aren't you?"

Tristan didn't respond. Diana turned around to face him.

"What is it?"

"I'm worried about getting caught," Tristan confessed. "All it'll take is for one of them to knock on your door, for example, and for you to say the usual that you're – naked or something, and then whoever knocked will go to my bedroom and see I'm not there. There's no bathroom connecting the two bedrooms like in the manor, and we're just setting ourselves up."

"So what if they catch us? Let them," Diana teased. "I'm tired of hiding."

"We have to though," Tristan insisted." Who knows what they'd think of it – I mean, who knows how they'd feel about us sleeping together."

"We'll have to tell them eventually," Diana reminded him. "You know that – we can't hide forever. You and me, Tristan, we're as God intended and there is nothing morally bankrupt about what we have between us. We're not related. We're not of the same sex. We're a man and a woman whose union is a mirror of the beauty of God."

Diana held a hand at Tristan's chest, over the amulet attached to his gold chain necklace. Tristan smiled at her in the dark.

"What would Charles think of us?" Tristan questioned.

"He'd be happy for us."

"What would Judith think?" Tristan then asked with greater hesitance.

"She'd be happy for us too."

"Hm, I don't know. I don't think she would – I don't think she likes me that much."

"Oh, nonsense," Diana replied. "Of course she likes you. She has to."

"I always get a vibe like she's stricter with me for whatever reason. She's nice with you – hell, she treats you like you're her own daughter, but when it comes to me, it's like I'm a bad dog."

"Are you jealous?"

"No, I'm pissed."

Diana frowned and brought her hand from Tristan's chest to his cheek.

"I'll talk to her for you," Diana said.

"No."

"Yes, I'll talk to her, but I'll make it seem casual. I'll just ask her if she has a problem with you and sort it out. If there is a problem, I'll do my best to solve it and that'll be that."

"And if that doesn't work?"

"Then I'll tell Charles."

Tristan looked at Diana with uncertainty.

"It'll be fine," Diana said, kissing him on the lips and then hugging him. "It'll all be fine."

"How have you become the optimist?" Tristan questioned.

"We're rubbing off on each other."

Act 1, Scene 4

The next morning, Diana and Tristan woke up without a problem and went downstairs with Judith and Charlemagne for breakfast at a restaurant in the hotel. The family was seated with a view outside and of some televisions. There was some footage of the award ceremony being played in French. The family sat down and looked at their menus until a garçon came to take their order.

"Can I take your order?" the garçon asked in a metropolitan French accent, opening a pad with haste.

"Coffee with cream to start, please," Charlemagne requested. "For the two of us."

"And for the children?" the waiter asked, shifting his attention to the kids.

"Orange juice, please," Diana asked.

"Same," Tristan said.

The waiter nodded.

"If it's alright, we've all agreed to have the buffet this morning," Charlemagne said.

"*Bon*, when you are ready, you may go," the waiter replied, not making eye contact with them.

The waiter nodded and wrote down in his paper. The waiter then took the smaller plates on the table and left. The family then stood up and left to go to the buffet where there was an array of selection as well as various cooks arranging crepes, omelets, and other delicacies hot.

Once Diana was ready, she returned to the table where glasses with juice had been set for the kids alongside round mugs of coffee for the adults. Judith was already at the table and preparing her coffee with sugar.

"Oh, what have you got there?" Judith questioned.

"Crepes with strawberries," Diana replied. "What about you?"

"I haven't the greatest appetite, so I've simply fetched a croissant and this bit of fruit here. I also have a bit of a headache and need to prepare myself for the press conference and meeting up ahead. How did you find the party last night?"

"It was okay," Diana replied, drinking some juice.

"Any cute boys?" Judith questioned. "Surely at least one."

Diana didn't reply and simply blushed.

"Honestly, dear, nobody?" Judith questioned.

"I wasn't looking."

"Is there someone at home then?" Judith asked.

"What?" Diana questioned, dropping her smile a bit.

"Anybody in Allabrese? Perhaps a boy in school?"

"No…" Diana replied. "There's not a lot of boys my age in my class. Well, there was Arturo, but he left Allabrese last summer."

"Arturo Medici? What happened to him?"

"He transferred to a private school in Harlech because it was the best hope for him to get into a good university. He didn't have the best grades and needed the prestige of a school to give him some opportunity."

"Interesting," Judith replied, looking over to Tristan as he returned with French toast on his plate. "Is there anyone else?"

"No," Diana replied, shaking her head.

Tristan sat down.

"You know," Judith carried on, "I went to an all-girls school in Harlech when I was your age. I enjoyed it immensely. How would you like the same? You could use the same as Arturo – the chance for opportunity."

"I don't even know what I want to do after high school," Diana replied. "I don't think it'd be right for me."

Tristan held a worried look on his face as he scanned his eyes from Judith to Diana.

"You must decide on something soon, my dear. Is there nothing in the world that interest you as a career?" Judith asked, pausing for a moment. "You like to read, do you not? Reading is a great skill and could put you in something interesting and lucrative, for example, scholarly research."

"I don't know," Diana remarked.

"It's time to start thinking about the future, Diana," Judith warned. "You're going to be going into Grade Twelve next September and applying for university before the end of this year."

"I think Diana's happy where we are – at Lord Phoenix," Tristan interrupted.

"Well, that's fine for you, Tristan, but it is Diana's decision and future we're talking about," Judith replied in a firm tone. "A woman needs to find herself a career – she can't be relying on a man."

Neither Diana nor Tristan replied. Charlemagne soon returned with a hearty plate of scrambled eggs, hash brown, bacon and grilled tomatoes alongside a croissant to the side. The family ate in quiet for almost twenty minutes. Judith, unsurprisingly by her small breakfast, was the first to finish and sit drinking her coffee as the others finished. One by one, they all concluded their meals and sat back.

"Alright, we have quite a day planned ahead of us and will need to be at Cabernet Energy in an hour or so for the meeting. Then, there'll be a press conference on the announcement of the Fusion Reactor and such…" Charlemagne remarked, wiping his mouth. "Afterwards, we'll have lunch with some executives and then have time to go explore the city as you wish, children."

"Yeah, about that…" Tristan replied, crossing his arms. "Diana and I were talking about this this morning and have a proposal. How about we let you adults go and take care of your Cabernet business and let Diana and me explore the town. We can then meetup for lunch and spend the rest of the day together."

Charlemagne looked at both the kids and didn't immediately reply. He started to scratch his head.

"I'm not sure about that, Tristan…" Charlemagne confessed. "It's not safe to let you both wander the city on your own. Neither of you speak French and there are a lot of people that *will* exploit you."

"Oh, don't be so protective, Charles," Judith interrupted. "If the children want to go out and explore, then by all means they should. It'll be better than being stuck with us in all honesty. Look at them, they're sixteen each – going on to seventeen soon."

Charlemagne crossed his arms. He then sighed.

"Very well," Charlemagne said, taking his wallet out from his blazer, "but be careful."

Charlemagne and handed the children some euros.

"Enjoy yourselves and be sure to contact me, Tristan, if you need anything," Charlemagne said. "Understood?"

"Yes, sir," Tristan affirmed.

From the restaurant, Charlemagne paid for their breakfast and then they went back up to the penthouse for some more preparation before meeting their private limousine at the front of the hotel. The skies were grey, and it was neither warm nor cold. Tristan wore his hoodie and had a backpack. Diana wore a simple raincoat and also had a backpack. Judith wore a grey coat over her black dress while Charlemagne simply wore a beige overcoat over his traditional grey suit.

"Can I offer you children a ride into town in the least?" Charlemagne questioned, turning to them as he went to the limousine. "I'm going eastbound and will be passing through."

"No thanks," Tristan replied. "We want to ride the metro and go straight to the Eiffel Tower."

Charlemagne nodded and said, "Very well," before turning to go into the limousine. "I'll see you for lunch then – twelve sharp. Take care."

The kids waved to Charlemagne and then saw the limo off. Charlemagne sat down and took a deep breath. Judith looked to him and smiled.

"Relax, darling," Judith assured him. "They'll be fine."

"I hope you are right," Charlemagne replied, sighing. "You seem to be very confident in their abilities to take care of themselves."

"They're almost adults, Charles – if anything, they're young adults," Judith argued with a smile. "You need to let them take care of themselves. I'm surprised you're being as protective as you are."

"I've been far too careless and ever since what happened at the start of last September – the fright I had over Tristan possibly dying – I don't want to relive that terror. I do care about them, Judy."

"Nobody is saying you don't, Charles, but you can't be so overprotective to satisfy yourself," Judith warned.

"Well, you are the one that let them go to the Arctic behind my back..." Charlemagne grumbled, "but you do have a point."

"Yes, and on the topic, there's something else I need to talk to you about. It's in regard to Diana," Judith remarked. "I've talked to her, and I believe it would be best if we sent her to a boarding school of some kind. Preferably in Harlech."

"A boarding school?" Charlemagne questioned. "What on Earth for?"

Judith explained to Charlemagne the conversation she had in regard to Arturo. Charlemagne didn't reply and sat in thought for a few minutes. He then crossed his arms. The limousine continued to drive the couple through La Défense and into the heart of Paris along the N13. The car had just passed over the Île de Pont at the River Seine.

"What did she think of the idea?" Charlemagne suddenly asked.

"She hasn't decided," Judith honestly answered, "but we might need to push her if we believe this is the best for her. Even then, it would only be fair to support the idea given that you went to one. I went to one. She'll be open to so much more opportunities than at her current school. She might even find her vocation before it's too late."

Charlemagne sighed.

"It'll be what's best for her – for her future. She isn't like Tristan. Tristan will be able to go to any university he likes based on his extra-curriculars and high grades. Diana won't have that privilege."

"Right…" Charlemagne nodded, looking out the tinted window. "Perhaps it could be good for her."

Charlemagne continued to stare out the window and looked out to town. The visor between the limousine passenger seats and front of the car then began to open. Charlemagne looked over to the chauffer who was looking into the rear-view mirror.

"Monsieur Cabernet," the chauffer spoke in a deep and thick accent, "I am sorry to interrupt, but I am afraid I am going to have to make a little detour through the city to get to Cabernet Energy. You see, there are some ongoing protests against the government past *l'Avenue de la Grand Armée* and towards *l'Arc de Triomphe*."

"Protests?" Charlemagne questioned. "I didn't realize there were ongoing protests in France. I, at least, never heard of such thing. Have you, Judy?"

"No."

"What kind of protests?"

"Ah, *les Gilets Jaune* is a weekly protest on Saturday when people come to protest against the president's regime. It has been ongoing since last November."

"A little protest is disrupting traffic? How *drôle...*" Charlemagne grumbled once more. "Very well, we left early anyways."

"*Tres bien, monsieur*," the chauffer replied, closing the visor between them. The limousine began to drive around a large roundabout at the end of *Avenue de Charles de Gaulle* where there was some construction in the middle. Charlemagne opened the window so he could look outside, looking ahead to *Avenue de la Grand Armée* to see hundreds upon hundreds of people ahead, dressed in yellow vests. Charlemagne's eyes widened as he saw the chaos of people up ahead and along the entire causeway towards the Arc de Triomphe at the end.

"Good Lord," Charlemagne remarked, turning his neck as they drove away. "Go back. I want to see more!"

The car did not stop. Charlemagne rose from his seat and banged on the tinted visor.

"Stop the car!" Charlemagne demanded.

The limousine slowly came to a stop as the chauffer pulled into a parking lot between two directions of the road. They were on Boulevard Pereire. The chauffer lowered the visor.

"What is wrong?" he asked.

"Nothing," Charlemagne insisted, "it's just that I thought the protest were small! There were thousands of them out there!"

"Ah, it is fairly big!" the chauffer remarked.

Charlemagne opened the door of the limousine.

"I am going to go take a better look," Charlemagne remarked.

"What?" Judith questioned. "Are you insane?"

"It's a protest – I'm not going to join them. I'm just going to poke around and see what it's all about."

"What about the meeting? The press conference? Charles, what if the media sees you at this protest? You don't even know what they're really protesting about – upsetting the President of France after the award he gave you last night isn't the best idea…"

"Bah, I won't make a scene of myself," Charlemagne assured her. "I'm incognito – nobody will recognize me. It'll be fine! Take care of the meeting and press conference on your own. I'll be back as soon as I can."

Charlemagne then walked off and cross the street to get to the other side. He then started to walk south and back towards the roundabout so he could get to the start of the Avenue de la Grand Armée.

From the entrance of the avenue, Charlemagne saw the large crowd of over a thousand people ahead, all wearing yellow safety vests. Charlemagne proceeded to walk down the avenue with caution. The protesters ranged in age, but all seemed to be locals. A lot of them had banners, signs, and some held flags on poles: French flag, a red flag with two stretched leopards (the Normandy flag), other regional flags, and some other distinct ones that varied. Some of the protesters were dressed in outlandish costumes.

"*Macron est un idiot, une mauvette!*"

Charlemagne continued to walk down the avenue, noticing some protesters were pointing at him. Another shouted his name. Soon, almost everybody was looking at him as he walked down, slowing his pace until he saw a group of three protesters run towards him.

"*Charlemagne! Charlemagne!*" a protester shouted. "*La marionnette chevalier de Versailles!*"

"*Charlemagne!*" another protester said, rushing towards him. " *Êtes-vous perdu, mon vieux?*"

"*Sors d'ici!*" a third protester said to the other before turning to Charlemagne. "*Monsieur Cabernet, bienvenue aux manifestations.* Welcome!"

"*Merci,*" Charlemagne replied, nodding.

"*Rentrez chez vous, sales mondialiste!*" someone shouted to him.

Charlemagne frowned as he saw some people with smartphones filming him.

"Monsieur Cabernet," the protester who greeted him said, "ignore these people. Let us talk. Tell us, what are you doing here in Paris?"

"I came here for business," Charlemagne responded in English. "I saw the protests and decided to see what was happening."

"Monsieur Cabernet, let us talk about your speech at Versailles last night," the protester asked, walking with Charlemagne. "Are you a globalist?"

"No," Charlemagne denied. "I'm largely apolitical. I'm a simple Christian man, and my intentions in my speech last night were not political. I believe in simple values of truth and self-sacrifice as well as the need to help those in need who are in a worse state than I am."

"And Mr. Cabernet, you said that French is in a good state?"

Charlemagne swallowed his breath and then looked to the people filming him.

"Well, enlighten me on the state of France if I was wrong – I have not been here in almost twenty years, so I cannot say much. Tell me, what is it that all of you are protesting? What are you demands from President Macron and the National Assembly?"

"Mr. Cabernet, we are movement of people and we demand our government to represent the interests of the people instead of the bankers and oligarchs as well as the media moguls."

"Right, and what are your propositions then?" Charlemagne asked as they continued to walk to the Arc of Triomphe. "I will offer you my opinion on them."

"Mr. Cabernet, we want a re-establishment of the republic – a Sixth French Republic – and new constitution with an emphasis on direct democracy and value of opinions of the people. We want all matters to be settled through referendums – matters such as the French membership with the European Union – we want that gone -- and in the immigration of migrants from the Middle East and Africa – we want them gone. All of these matters of which have been approved by these politicians without the consideration of the French people."

"Well, I can certainly agree that the opinion of the people, especially the people of this country, are more important than those of the elite," Charlemagne responded, "and from what I remember from the 2005 referendum on the European Union constitution, President Nicholas Sarkozy betrayed the French public opinion when he signed the Treaty of Lisbon into law two years later – a treaty which was more or less the same as the constitution the French people rejected."

"You do understand then," the protester responded. "We, as a people, are tired of the French bourgeoise overlooking and ignoring us."

"What else?"

"We want the establishment of a higher minimum wage," a girl shouted from nearby, "and a higher minimum retirement pension."

"In my opinion, the importation of people results in the reduction of a minimum wage as the immigration results in the supply of labor keeping up with demand instead of demand keeping up with supply," Charlemagne responded. "It is also my opinion that some companies, and by extension, these oligarchs you speak of, would be motivated to continue paying a low minimum wage instead of keeping up with inflation and cost living to save themselves money. I am not a fan of either of these, and it is has been my action through Cabernet Industries to ensure that nobody is paid an unfair wage."

"And these wages as well as all salaries and other wages should be raised with inflation!" the woman jeered.

"Yes," Charlemagne agreed, "they should."

"And do you agree that larger companies, such as your own, should be paying more in taxes than they are than individuals or small businesses?" the man asked.

"I'm not aware of how much Cabernet Industries pays the French government for our operations here, but something that should be understood is, in this 'globalized world,' Charlemagne said with air quotes, "in order to keep businesses in certain countries, a small business tax needs to be employed otherwise these companies will leave along with the jobs they provide. Small businesses and the common people do not have this option and are considered to be inelastic when it comes to taxes. Large corporations, like Cabernet Industries, can come and go as we please – we are elastic to changes in taxes. However, it is not only my firm belief that a company should still pay more, especially more than the common citizen and small businesses, but that certain businesses should be nationalized and their profits put towards social and government programs instead of in the hands of a few. The businesses that should be nationalized are ones having to do with valuable resources, such as oil and gas, and other dangerous industries such as banks."

"And French properties, such as the airports and power plants," the man said. "You do not like privatization then?"

"I believe that certain industries should be privatized, such as small businesses or ones that produce consumer goods – they don't need to be controlled, while others should be centralized for the good of the people, especially ones that need motivation to thrive. You see, corporations are like wild dogs – you need to incentivize them and tame them in order to control them. You can't and should not let them control you or else they will ravage you."

"What about the protection of French industries? We want *our* industries to be protected over international ones," the man stated. "Do you agree?"

"I believe that as a people, you have the right to protect yourselves and the interests of your own people, which includes your own industries," Charlemagne responded.

"What about an end to the carbon taxes and rise of gas?" the man asked.

"The carbon tax is nothing more than a con to get you, the people, to pay more to your government, who as I have learned at this moment, has not cared for you," Charlemagne responded, "and taxes like these not only virtue signal for politicians, but result in the rise in the prices of petrol at an unnecessary cost. Look, the production of carbon dioxide has no causation in the rise of temperatures, and even if it did, the hypocrisy of elites to promote 'zero emission' policies while they emit one-hundred times more than the common citizen, is shameless. The emission levels of countries like France or the United States are nothing compared to that of countries in Africa, India, or China."

"Mr. Cabernet, we also want more funding for medical care, psychiatric care, and the care of the elderly. Do you agree on this?" the woman asked.

"Your elders, no matter their sins of the past, should be cared for," Charlemagne responded. "They are your kin as well as your fathers and mothers. In terms of medical care, a healthy society and people, is a thriving society, and that is what I want for all people. The same is true for psychiatric care – healthy mind, healthy people."

"And what about affordable housing?" the man asked.

"Cabernet Industries does not deal with real estate, but it is my opinion from what I have seen in Harlech in Canada, the rise of oligarchs who control rent prices as well as the foreign investment in the real estate market has become problematic. However, Canada is a large country with plenty of room for growth in its own people with the right social programs. France is a concentrated society like Britain. You do not have much room, and with that in mind, I would point to foreign investment as being a major problem. You remove the foreigners (these investors who can go to their own countries but come here in seek of profit) you remove the problem."

The crowd began to mumble amongst themselves. The man then looked to Charlemagne as they arrived at the roundabout of the Arc de Triomphe.

"You agree that asylum seekers and migrants should be removed from France?" the man asked.

Charlemagne sighed and then nodded, saying, "France is a small country and these people serve only the elite and their desires. They are objects to them. We have no business taking them from their countries and depriving their own people. We have no business in any foreign country. What I said last night, when I said, France helps the world, was not in regard to foreign intervention, such as in wars of diplomatic crises. I meant in what France had to offer to the world – the innovations, ideas, scientific progress and cultural wonders. I am a man of all these things. I am not a politician. I am not a warmonger. I am not a globalist. What on Earth would cause people to say otherwise other than their own twisted worldview? If help is the cause, then send help to these people in their own nations, but instead countries like France and the United States destabilize these nations – look at Syria for example and the civil war there. Also, look at Poland – Poland does not take migrants, but they do send the most financial aid out of any European Union country to help the people who are in need of assistance. This is a model that can be looked to."

"Did your grandfather not intervene in a foreign war?" someone asked.

"My grandfather, as a Frenchman, intervened in a war of his people, which he had the right to do," Charlemagne responded. "Whether it even was a war of his people, or as it seems, a war for the oligarchs who have constructed this New France, is something I am now questioning, but is beside the point."

"Lastly, Mr. Cabernet," the woman said, "what is your opinion on the financial aid for the parents of children?"

"I am very supportive of financial aid programs that assist parents," Charlemagne responded. "The family is the core unit of any healthy society and should be supported, not replaced, demonized, or destroyed. In fact, the procreation of children should be supported as an alternative to these pro-immigration policies as an investment into the people. The fact that politicians support the latter is a sign that they truly do not care for the people, which should not be surprised. Altruism is not a definition of these people. It is a mask they hide behind."

Charlemagne stopped and looked over to the Arc de Triomphe. In front of the monument were a row of navy blue vans alongside of a line of riot police armed with weapons and body gear. They also riot shields and helmets

"So, Mr. Cabernet," the man said, "in general, you are very supportive of our policies. You agree in almost everything, but yet you do not do much for us?"

"I do what I can," Charlemagne replied, turning back to the people, "through my company, I do what I can. The benefits of my leadership with Cabernet Industries is that my work is honest work through an honest heart – it is charitable at the same time as being responsible. I wish I could do more, especially for my French brothers and sisters, and our conversation now has left an impression on me that I won't forget. All I can say is that you have my attention and support – *Vivez les français!*"

Act 1, Scene 5

Diana and Tristan watched as Charlemagne's limousine drove off before Tristan let out a sigh.

"Alright, let's get out of this place and towards the real city of Paris," Tristan remarked.

"Which way to the train station?" Diana asked. "Left or right?"

"Let me get out my phone so we don't get lost," Tristan responded, taking out his smartphone.

The couple waited in front of the hotel for another minute before Tristan put his phone away.

"Okay, we're not too far," Tristan replied, "it's right."

The kids proceeded to walk right and come around the base of the hotel skyscraper. The two of them then crossed an intersection and went along a narrow road to see a set of wide stairs going upwards. Along the sidewalk on the opposite side were some slim trees. In front of the stairs were there flag poles, one with the regional Île-de-France flag, another with the French flag, and the third with the European Union flag.

Diana and Tristan crossed the road to get to the staircase and then went up them. The stairs were not only wide, but long – at least twenty meters in length before reaching the top plaza. The couple turned at a slight right angle before coming to the center of the plaza. A promenade continued in either direction for pedestrians, of which there weren't that many at this time in the morning.

Tristan took Diana's hand, and they started to walk southeast along the promenade, looking down at a freeway below, the N13, which they walked over. Ahead of them at the end of the promenade was a unique structure that almost resembled a modern sports stadium. The face of the structure from where they were walking was almost triangular. Upon closer examination, they realized it was noticeable to be a shopping mall by the window displays on the ground floor and logo above the main entrance doors.

Tristan led Diana right again so they could go up a ramp. Ahead of them was a large rectangular arch structure, the Arch of the Defense. Behind this monument was a tall and simple building, but behind this structure was a large sphere that was part of another structure. In front of the arch monument was an open plaza or a large promenade that went along south for the entire stretch of the metropolitan area. The couple stopped to look up at the large arch.

"Wow, it's pretty fitting for this place," Tristan commented, "but still pretty monumental."

"Well, it *is* a monument," Diana replied. "Come on, take a picture of me in front of it."

"You want your picture taken in front of it?"

"I'm not even sure if I can get it all – we need to step back a bit."

Diana and Tristan walked south for a couple of meters. Tristan pointed to their right at another modern glass structure.

"What's that? A news station?" Tristan questioned

"A news station with window displays?"

"It is France," Tristan argued.

"I think it's another shopping mall, genius."

The couple stopped to take their picture before taking a selfie together in the center of La Defense. From there, they returned north to where they had spotted a large circular staircase to the left of the arch. Diana and Tristan walked down and came to the tall metal post in the middle with some advertisements. They then turned right again to go down a pathway over a bridge that led to some stairs and escalators. The kids then went down these to go into a long tunnel that led into a larger commercial corridor with shops on either side as well as entrances into the respective malls on either side. There were a lot more people in the subterranean tunnel than above. Ahead of them on both the left and the right were two circular ticket or information booths with machines around them as well.

Diana and Tristan went to the machines to pay their fares for the train. The machine's screen was yellowish and had multilingual options including English. Tristan selected English and was brought to a screen asking if they wanted to purchase tickets or reload a pass.

"Tristan, we don't even know what train to take to get the tower," Diana cautioned. "Maybe we should find a map or something before we buy tickets."

"Are there more than one train? Don't they all go the same way?" Tristan questioned.

"If they're anything like the trains in Harlech, then no. I'm sure they've got individual and multiple lines. Come on, let's find a map or something," Diana replied, dragging Tristan away from the ticket machine.

"I don't see any maps," Tristan complained.

"Then let's go talk to the ticket booth," Diana replied. "Come on."

Diana and Tristan stepped behind someone waiting in line to speak to the man in the ticket booth. Once the person in front of them was done, they stepped forward to talk to the man in a turquoise polo. He was a large man with balding hair.

"*Comment puis-je vous aider?*" the man asked.

"*Nous voulons aller à la tour Eiffel,*" Tristan responded.

"Please, speak English," the man replied, "your French is 'orrible."

Tristan's face sunk.

"To go to the Eiffel Tower, you want to take the Line 1 going east and get off at Charles de Gaulle – Etoiles. From there, you take Line 6 toward Nation until Bir-Hakeim."

The couple paid for their tickets and then went off towards a series of gates. They inserted their tickets separately for the gates to open and then they went forward towards another set of escalators that went further beneath the earth to reach the concrete platform where they would wait for their train. The platform was small and above them were LED lights that shined down and created a bright atmosphere. On either side of them were trenches where the rails were for the trains. In the middle of the platform, spread across the entire length were concrete pillars. The walls behind the trenches were composed of white tiles with an array of different advertisements that promoted a selection of different products, events, and more, such as ones that showed two hairy and burlesque men kissing each other, another that showed a group of Middle Eastern migrants in impoverished conditions at a dock, or another that had a muscular black man kissing and groping a white woman.

Around the couple was a modest crowd of people of different races and sex. In fact, there were very few white people around them in comparison. The people of different races ranged from Africans, North Africans, Middle Easterners, Central Asians, East Asians, and Southeast Asians. Before the trenches, there were barriers that protected pedestrians and citizens from falling or being pushed onto the tracks. The couple waited for their train under the sign that read, 'Chateau de Vincennes' alongside an estimated wait time of five minutes.

Within five minutes, a squared train arrived and slowed down. Once the train had stopped, the doors opened on the train and at the platform for people to board. The space on the train was limited and small. There were less than twenty seats around the couple, and they were quickly taken. Once everybody had boarded, the train doors closed and the train set off eastbound.

Diana and Tristan stood near the doors, watching them open as people exited and boarded at the stops they made. The tunnels ranged from being narrow to being shared by other trains passing the other direction. The couple saw one other train as they made their journey. In addition, the tunnels had circular bulbs dotted along the tunnels. In total, they made about five stops before finally reaching Charles de Gaulle-Etoile. The train came to a stop, and before the couple could exit, they were pushed and shoved by the people that were exiting. Diana and Tristan waited for a moment before exiting and stepping onto the narrower platform. The rail trench was wider at this station and situated in the middle instead of on the sides.

The platform at Charles de Gaulle-Etoile was smaller than at La Défense. The walls displayed similar advertisements but were yellow-tiled and curved. The couple looked around for an exit and decided to simply follow the people out before following some signs that led them to Line 6.

Diana and Tristan reached the Line 6 platform and waited for the next train to take them to the Eiffel Tower. The platform they were at was similar to the one they had gotten off of, but the trench in the middle was smaller. The opposite side exited for people to exit, while the side the couple were on existed for people to board. There were less people around here than on Line 1. Within another five minutes, the train arrived and the couple boarded with the other people. They even managed to find a seat by the window this time. Once everybody had boarded, the train doors closed again and the train set off once more.

Tristan kept his eyes set out the window, looking out to the tunnel, which interchanged from being cavernous to carved out.

The train made approximately four stops from Charles de Gaulle – Etoile to Bir-Hakeim. However, upon exit from the last stop before Bir-Haikeim, the train transitioned from underground to being outside. Tristan looked out at some of the windows of some traditional buildings before seeing through some trees to see the Eiffel Tower across the River Seine.

"Look!" Tristan remarked, nudging Diana.

Diana looked and saw the Eiffel Tower for a split second before a train going the opposite direction passed. The train slowed down and the view of the tower was blocked again by a building in front. Within less than a minute, they were also stopping as they arrived at the cagey station that was Bir-Hakeim. The train doors opened, the couple stepped out and walked down some stairs to reach the ground of Paris.

Diana and Tristan walked forward along the pavement to reach the road that ran parallel with the River Seine. They then looked around for some crosswalks that would lead them towards the Eiffel Tower. The couple walked north, stopped at a crosswalk, and then walked across to pass a pizzeria beneath a hotel. From there, they stopped at another crosswalk and waited before crossing over. The Eiffel Tower was within their sights.

The couple came to a park along the riverside and proceeded to walk north towards the Eiffel Tower. The parkway path eventually led to a larger intersection in front of the looming tower. There was a carousel nearby as well as various people. Diana and Tristan waited at the crosswalk to pass and then walked over to the other side, stopping in front of a glass wall that blocked them from walking underneath or even going anymore nearer to the Eiffel Tower.

"What the hell," Tristan complained, scanning the wall on either side.

Tristan looked ahead and could not see people on the other side. He then pointed over to a gate. There were also letters on the glass wall that pointed to the left. The couple proceeded to walk leftwards. Tristan looked into the wall again and could see secondary walls near the base of the foot of the tower. The walls displayed a mural of people, tourists, except they weren't real and just printed off. Diana began to notice some armored police officers with assault rifles standing around. The couple continued to walk, coming around to a path that led to a gateway with more police officers.

"I don't think the tower is open today…" Tristan reported, looking over to the cops.

"I don't think I want to go into the tower anyways with all these cops around…" Diana remarked, sighing.

"What then?" Tristan asked.

"Is the park still open?" Diana questioned.

"I'm not sure."

"There's an entire city of culture around us – you got to pick something or else I'm going to pick."

Diana was silent.

"Let's go to the park then," Tristan responded. "You can take pictures of the tower and pose in front of it at least."

"I wanted to go up to the observation deck and take a selfie with you…" Diana responded. "It doesn't matter. We can come back when it isn't closed."

"I'm not sure when that might be, but okay."

"Let's go to the Louvre," Diana said. "Maybe the sun will poke out and then we can go to the park."

"Sure," Tristan responded, taking Diana's hand.

The couple walked back across the street and decided to continue along the riverside pathway. Tristan checked his phone for directions to the Louvre and they continued their course, stopping only at the Bridge of the Concorde so they could cross the Seine and reach a plaza of an obelisk. Diana took some pictures, and then the couple admired the view of the Arc de Triomphe in the distance.

Tristan noticed there to be quite a lot of people with yellow vests, but instead of looking at them, the couple instead disappeared into a large park where there were less protestors and more tourists. Diana and Tristan maintained their hands together as they slowed down and enjoyed each other's company. They stopped in front of an octagonal pond with greenish water and then continued along a path surrounded by hedges and trees. Tristan could notice the promenade wasn't as clean as it was in the film they watched last night, and there was a distinct amount of tourists from countries outside of Europe and North America. All Tristan could do was get out a sigh as they reached another fountain.

The Louvre was ahead with the glass pyramid of the museum in the center. They walked along to a road past a smaller version of the Arc de Triomphe. There were some buses unloading tourists and a larger crowd of people than anywhere else. The couple crossed the street and went towards the entrance gate in front of the glass pyramid in the center of the plaza. Tristan noticed a small presence of armored police officers around like at the Eiffel Tower.

The structure surrounding them was large and traditionalist, which paid contrast. Diana and Tristan stood in line to pay for tickets to enter the museum, and then they passed through to enter under the glass pyramid and stand at the balcony that looked down towards the sublevel of the museum. There were a set of staircases to their left that went below as well as an escalator to the right. The space beneath the glass pyramid was large and spacious with smooth beige-white floor tiles and various corridors at each side and corner for them to choose from.

"Which way?" Tristan asked Diana.

Tristan looked at the various banners that displayed Egyptian antiquities, Hellenic / Roman antiquities, and then another with artwork.

"How about we skip Egypt for now – I'm still hungover from our summer trip," Diana sighed. "I want to see the Mona Lisa."

Diana and Tristan decided to follow a banner with the Mona Lisa into a corridor that led them to the Denon Wing. From here, the couple walked with the tourists.

• •

"This one makes me miss Zephyr…" Diana grimaced, looking at a painting of a frightened white horse in a storm.

Diana and Tristan continued to walk along a simple corridor with a glass ceiling. On either side of them, planted on the walls, were framed artworks from throughout the ages.

"It takes a different mind to paint," Tristan remarked, looking at some of the paintings.

"You're sounding like Madonna," Diana replied.

The couple reached the end of the corridor where the Mona Lisa was holstered on its own face of wall. There was a large crowd of tourists in front of this artwork. The couple moved away from the painting and towards the others on the beige walls. Tristan held a light smile on his face as they looked at the vibrant colors, the extreme detail, and the precision and accuracy of each person, face, man and woman.

The paintings that the couple gazed upon include 'Oath of the Hortatii' by Jacques-Louis David from the 19th century to 'The Arcadian Shepherds' by Nicolas Pouissin in the 17th century. They also saw Eugène Delacroix's 'The Massacre of Crois' and the better known 'Liberty Leading the People by the same painter. The couple also looked at 'The Education of Achilles' by Jean-Baptiste Regnault' and a featured painting titled 'The Torture of Prometheus' by Jean-Louis-Cesar Lair.

There were also a selection of other European painters from outside of France, other than Da Vinci, including Caravaggio's 'Death of the Virgin' and Caspar David Friedrich's 'Seashore by Moonlight.' Tristan looked to Diana as they held hands, but he frowned as he saw a sunken look on her face.

"What's wrong?" Tristan questioned her. "Do you not like this?"

"No, I think what we're seeing is beautiful – beyond beautiful – breathtaking, but... you know, perhaps that movie raised my hopes up, but Paris isn't really what I expected it to be."

"Cheer up," Tristan replied, "you're just having a little culture shock. I read about it on the flight over, and that's why I was a little cautious with the movie we watched – I knew this would happen. I knew you would be a little disappointed with the actual Paris of today."

"I'm hugely disappointed."

Act 1, Scene 6

Charlemagne, Judith, Tristan, and Diana stood in the Notre Dame Cathedral in front of the wooden chairs they had sat in for the last hour. An organ played and the procession of the Mass walked down the nave, or central aisle of the church. The Notre Dame was a large cathedral with a long nave. Immediately in front of them was the transept of the church, or arms in the crucifix form of a church which diverged from the nave into nooks that branched off from the center aisle. The arms were symmetrical in appearance, and on the larger face looking to the outside were enormous circular stained-glass windows, or rose windows, at the very top. Below this window were smaller stained-glass windows, which themselves were above a large door going to the outside. In the center crossing were steps that came upwards to an altar of sort with four figures on the front. Next to this was a podium where the readings and the homily were delivered from.

The family looked forward, past the transept and towards chancel of the church, or aisle that led towards the altar with benches on either side for the choir to sit. In front of the chancel was the main altar, or high altar with a statue behind of the Virgin Mary holding Jesus Christ with angles to the side. Behind this statue was a gold crucifix before the arcade of the apse that connected to the arcade of the chancel. At either side of the statue were black statues of angels atop of pedestals and larger statues of Louis XIII and Louis XIV kneeling before Christ.

The floor of the Notre Dame were light grey and dark grey tiles. Behind the pews were chairs stretching along. On either side of the nave was an arcade with thick cylindrical pillars forming the pointed arches that were almost four meters tall. Atop of these arches were smaller arches, the triforium, which was an inner gallery on an upper level looking down into the church and above the side aisles. Above the triforium were clerestory stained-glass windows before the ribbed vaulting of the ceiling. Below the pointed arches were chandeliers.

Once the clergymen had exited, the family left their seats to leave and come out to the front of the cathedral. The entrance of the church was protected by an iron fence with gates at the entrance ways. Each of the three doorways into the cathedral had arches around with tympanums, a semi-circular decorative wall surface over the entrance containing sculpted depictions of the Last Judgement.

Above the main entrance of the cathedral were statues in recesses. Above the center doors was a circular tracery, a stonework that supports the stained-glass window on the other side. On the right and the left of the tracery were arched windows. On the level above, before the dual belfry were lancet windows.

Outside of the cathedral, Charlemagne paused for a moment where he had his arm linked with Judith. His phone was going off inside his blazer jacket. The family was dressed in formal attire, different from what they wore at Versailles. Tristan wore a blue suit, while Diana wore a white dress. Judith wore a dark red dress and Charlemagne wore his simple grey suit.

Charlemagne brought his phone to his ear and listened.

"Hello?" Charlemagne questioned.

"Charles, it's Richard," an anxious Richard replied. "We need to talk. What the hell were you thinking?"

"What on Earth are you talking about?" Charlemagne questioned, walking with the kids to the left. "What did I do?"

"What did you do? It's more in regard to what you said – the media is tearing you apart, Charles. What else? What else did you expect to happen after you spoke to those protesters?"

Charlemagne tilted his head and turned away from the family. The sun was out and it was mildly warm. Next to the cathedral was a pathway going to a park next to the River Seine. The pathway in front of the cathedral went to a simple bridge. Charlemagne took them along the side of the river, through the park next to the cathedral. There, they could see the spire atop of the transept and the buttresses alongside the clerestory windows of the nave. From outside, the rose windows could be seen behind a tracery above the doors leading inside.

"What have they done? Did they manipulate the footage?"

"What? No," Richard responded. "They published the footage on social media and it's gone viral! Every major news network in the West is talking about you right now, and it's not good!"

"What are they saying? Hello?" Charlemagne brought his phone away from his ear. "Richard, what are they saying?"

"It'd be better if you saw for yourself. Where are you?" Richard questioned.

"I'm in front of the Notre Dame with Judy and the kids," Charlemagne replied. "Listen, I'm going to return to the hotel and speak with you there. How about that?"

Richard hung up on Charlemagne. He put away his phone and then looked to the others with a frightened face.

"What's wrong, Charles?" Judith questioned.

Tristan and Diana looked to Charlemagne.

"I'm sorry, but I'm afraid I'm going to have to return to the hotel – something bad has happened, according to Richard."

"What's happened?" Judith asked.

"I'm not quite sure – something I've done, I'm afraid. Children, don't let us bore you – go along if you must."

"No, I think I want to return to the hotel too," Tristan replied, looking to Diana with a worried face.

Charlemagne returned to the hotel with Judith and the kids. From the limousine, they went straight to their suite where Charlemagne took off his blazer jacket and immediately fetched the television remote. He turned on the TV and then switched to the BBC. Along the bottom of the news footage held the tagline, 'Is Charlemagne de la Cabernet a racist?'

"Oh, good Lord," Charlemagne remarked, taking out his phone.

"Wait, what?" Tristan questioned, looking at the footage that was playing.

Charlemagne was surrounded by those protesters he had seen yesterday. Tristan looked to Diana who was looking at the TV. Footage from Charlemagne's comments were being played with the concluding remark, '*Vivez les français.*' Charlemagne, in the hotel room, sat down and held his phone in his hand.

"Is Charlemagne a racist?" a newscaster questioned. "You know, with remarks like these, you might as well think he is."

Charlemagne switched the channel to another news network. It played a press conference held by the President Macron with an English dub. The president was speaking.

"It is with great regret," the President said, "that Mr. Cabernet attended those protests and gave his sympathies to those vandals, especially after our meeting the night prior. It is my recommendation that he withdraw those comments at once – he has been misguided by these peddlers into the situation of France, which is understandable given that he is not even a resident or citizen for that matters."

Charlemagne changed the channel to yet another newscast.

"If you look at the history of the Cabernet family," an American scholar on the TV stated in an interview with some newscasters, "you see that the Cabernet family is not even French to begin with."

Charlemagne's face went red.

"Oh, then who are they?" the female journalist questioned.

"They're English – I mean, beyond the fact that Charlemagne, like his grandfather, speaks in an English accent. Derby de la Cabernet's wife is English – a daughter of Louis Mountbatten, who is a descendant of Queen Victoria and therefore related to the Queen."

"You're related to the queen?" Judith questioned, looking to Charlemagne.

"Technically," Charlemagne remarked, crossing his arms, "I try not to think about it."

"And what about Derby?" the newscaster questioned.

"My research into the Cabernet family concluded that the Cabernet family came to Canada from the United Kingdom. There are immigration records that support this claim. Listen, you look at who Derby de la Cabernet was, and you can see that he was not a nice man either. Yes, he fought in World War II, he stormed the beaches of Normandy and liberated France, but that is the pinnacle of his accomplishments – accomplishments of which he came to regret later in his life. The man was a racist and a fascist sympathizer by the time of his death. Good riddance he's gone."

Charlemagne threw the remote control in his hand at the TV, cracking the screen.

"What an absolute load of rubbish!" Charlemagne shouted, standing up. "Do you believe this?"

"Charles, calm down," Judith responded.

"No! I will not calm down while my family legacy – my family name and my grandfather are smeared by the dredges of society!"

"What are you going to do then?" Judith questioned. "Fight them? Charles, you can't."

"I'll prove to them…" Charlemagne remarked, tapping fists together. "I'll prove to them that my family is of French origin."

"How?" Judith questioned.

"There is one man that'll know," Charlemagne said. "Judy, I'm afraid we'll have to extend this vacation until further notice. You can return to Allabrese if you wish, but I'm staying. I have work to do."

"No, Charles, I'm staying, with the kids too. Tell me, what are you going to do?"

"I- I have to see an old mentor, it seems," Charlemagne said, sighing. "Someone who I haven't seen in a long, long time. We'll have to rent a car. We're travelling to *Vals de Loire*."

Act 2, Scene 1

Charlemagne drove a family sedan into the countryside of Centre-Val-de-Loire, driving along a narrow road with open farms on the left and right with offshoot dirt roads spouting off. The sedan was luxurious, well-made, and a medium-blue color. In the distance were some forests of deciduous trees and the sight of some houses. Charlemagne held his cellphone to his ear as he spoke with Richard.

"Charles, put the phone down," Judith complained.

Charlemagne looked to her with annoyed eyes and put the phone on speaker. He then put the phone on the dashboard.

"Listen, Charles," Richard said, "my main concern isn't your remarks, but the reaction its drawing from other people. It's been a hell of a Monday here in the office, especially for public relations. We've been receiving constant hostile remarks and death threats from anonymous persons on social media – hostile threats against not only the company, but key figures like me and your sister, and there are hundreds and hundreds of news articles popping out from all over the Internet."

"Well, get Ian to prosecute these people," Charlemagne simply replied.

"And what am I supposed to do about all the people on social media demanding our partners to cut ties with us?" Richard questioned. "Joseph says what they're doing is called 'cancel culture,' or something like that."

Charlemagne sighed and then said, "I don't know. I'm sure you'll figure something out, and if you're concerned about the safety of yourself and the family, then the Protection Squad is there to protect you. We didn't spend the last year organizing them for nothing."

"Fine," Richard replied, sighing, "okay. I'll take care of the fire here. I'll see you in as soon as possible."

"Cheers," Charlemagne said, turning off the phone.

Tristan looked to Diana as she held her camera as though it were film camera.

"What are you doing?" Tristan questioned.

"I'm making my own video," Diana replied. "I want to film France as it is today. If we're going to be staying here for another week or two, that means we're going to be doing some travelling."

Diana then changed her view from Tristan to outside the car as they passed some neat rows of some vineyards.

"Are you sure Dr. Dumas is still living here?" Judith questioned. "I'm skeptical of trusting an address that's over twenty years old."

"I'm sure he is," Charlemagne responded. "The winery is a family home and they would never abandoned it."

Charlemagne continued to drive along the countryside as they came to some rolling hills with acres of occupied space by the same neat rows of grape vines. There wasn't a cloud in the sky this late morning and the sun was shining down. The road continued along for another few kilometers until they turned left onto a dirt road going towards an estate up ahead.

The Dumas estate was an old, but well-kept traditional structure with smooth beige stone walls. The house was L-shaped with a large front courtyard made of mossy flagstone. There was also a cross-shaped fountain at the far corner of the house with a causeway that went around to an annex barn of some sort. There were various cars parked on the property and a site of a half dozen people, single couples and one family.

"Oh good," Judith remarked, "we're not the only ones here, which means this is a wine tour."

"Dr. Dumas doesn't do wine tasting…" Charlemagne grumbled.

Charlemagne parked the car by the other cars and then the family got out. They walked over to where visitors were looking out to the plantation of grape vines that spread out around the property. There was a young blonde toddler boy out exploring as well while a male explained to them in French about the process of viticulture.

The man had medium brown and short length hair. He appeared to be in his early fifties or late forties. He had fair skin and a stubble. He also wore jeans, high boots, and a light blue dress shirt tucked in as he talked, making motions with his hands.

"What's he saying, Charles?" Judith questioned as the family joined the tour.

"He's going over the plantation of grapes, the optimal geography and climate. He is saying that hills are better and that Val de Loire is optimal due to warm temperatures. He is now saying that once the plants are ready, they're harvested and taken to the winery."

The man explaining to the crowd made eye contact with Charlemagne. He then ushered the crowd to continue into the winery while he gave a bright smile and walked over to Charlemagne.

"*Bienvenue, mon frère!*" the man greeted Charlemagne, taking his hand and hugging him. "*Ça fait longtemps! Ça va?*"

"*Ça va, Jacques,*" Charlemagne responded. "*Comment vas-tu?*"

"*Bien, mon frère. Bien – et ces belles personnes? Qui sont?*"

"*Jacques, voici ma petite amie, Dr. Judith Lambert, et mes enfants, Tristan et Diana.*"

"*Bonjour,*" Jacques remarked, shaking Judith's hands before moving towards the kids. "How are you?"

"I'm good," Judith replied.

"Wow," Jacques remarked, bringing his hands to his hips. "I did not expect to see you, Charles. What brings you to the Dumas home?"

"I'm here to see your father," Charlemagne responded. "Is he here?"

"*Ah, mon père... non. Il n'est pas là.* Sorry, in English. He is not here. My apologies, Charles, but let us have a word before you go – yes? I am in the middle of a tour of the winery. Come join us – I will explain everything once it is over and we can have some wine. Good?"

"Yes, good," Charlemagne replied, walking with Jacques towards the winery annex.

The family went with Jacques around to the annex behind the house, which had an open garage door that allowed people to enter. Along the sides of the annex were large metallic tanks. Towards the entrance of the winery was a sort of conveyor belt that led to a rectangular machine.

"From the fields, the grapes are sorted, de-stemmed, and then pressed," Charlemagne remarked before turning around to look down the aisle.

Charlemagne gave a sentimental sigh as he looked down. Judith and the kids looked over to him.

"Charles, what's the matter?" Judith questioned, walking over to him and embracing him by the side.

"I'm only feeling a little nostalgic," Charlemagne replied. "I'm having flashbacks to when I was a kid and I used to play with Manon around here."

The kids looked over to Jacques as he broke off from the tour and left them with some workers. He then returned to the Cabernet household and smiled.

"Sorry, but I couldn't leave the tour without a tour guide. Come, Charles, let us share a fine bottle of apple cider and talk. Let me just go fetch a bottle from the cellar. Come."

The family followed Jacques Dumas outside and towards some cellar doors. Jacques opened the doors and then went down the stairwell, turning on a light at the end. Charlemagne took Judith's hands, helped her down while the kids lagged from behind. The Dumas winery cellar was large with various barrels lined up against the perimeter walls as well as locked cabinets.

"Let's see," Jacques said, going towards a cabinet and taking out a ring of keys. "I stored a bottle for this occasion – when I would see you again, *mon frère*. Let me see if I can find it."

Tristan looked around the basement with Diana. The ground was a dusty wooden floorboard and there were multiple beams and wooden pillars in a gridwork across the shape of the house and annex, a T-shape. A workbench at a corner of the room had a display of gas masks as well as a few bolt-action rifles stacked in the corner like a broom or shovel.

"Ahah!" Jacques proclaimed, pulling out a greenish bottle and blowing off the dust. "Here it is. Let us go upstairs to my kitchen and share this. I will introduce you to my wife, and we can talk."

Charlemagne and Judith followed Jacques upstairs while the kids remained behind.

"I don't suppose we're invited to the wine tasting," Tristan grimaced.

"You don't even drink wine or alcohol for that matter," Diana remarked. "Besides, look over there."

The kids went over to the rifles. The ends of the guns were fitted with bayonets. Tristan tried to pick one up, but it caused the rifle to tip over and slam a wooden chest before hitting the ground.

"Woops," Tristan replied, picking the rifle up and leaving them.

The chest in the cellar seemed to be ancient. It had French letters on the side in an army-like font. Diana stepped towards it and opened the chest, but instead of munitions, there were simply a bunch of family heirlooms.

"Hey, look," Diana remarked, picking up a photo and showing Tristan. "It's Charles."

"So what? There are a dozen pictures of Charles as a kid in the manor basement," Tristan replied, looking at the picture.

"But look," Diana said, pointing at the girl with Charles, "also look at the location."

Charlemagne appeared to be at least seven-years old in the picture. He was posed with a female around the same age who had medium brown hair like Jacques as well as medium blue eyes. She was dressed in a white dress with buttons at the top and a splinter along the bottom half, or fold. Charlemagne wore khaki shorts that began at the top of his knees along with a white polo. The duo were standing in front of the Great Sphinx in Egypt. Diana turned the picture around and read what was written in cursive writing, 'Charlemagne et Manon, 1967.'

Diana set the photo back where she found it and then pulled out a pictured frame. She blew off the dust from the glass and looked at the people in the frame. Charlemagne was in front of a couple while the same girl from the picture was with a boy about the same age as Charlemagne, but these two were in front of a different couple. From the couple with Charlemagne, the man wore a white dress shirt with the sleeves rolled up tucked into some baggy brown formal trousers. He had blonde hair like Charlemagne and a moustache across the top of his lip. His cheeks were flabbier than Charlemagne in his present and his face was more squared. He also medium-length hair that was combed to the side. He was with a woman who wore a white summer dress and hat. She had her arms around the man in the picture and had dark blonde to light brown hair. Charlemagne was dressed in grey trousers with a black sweater and did not look too happy in the picture. The couple next to them were dressed in formal casual attire. The man wore a sweater vest over a crème dress shirt and brown baggy formal trousers. The wife wore a darker dress with stockings. The girl in the picture wore a navy blue dress and bonnet. The top of the dress went right to her neck. The boy in the picture wore a short-sleeved dress shirt with sleeves that went to his elbows. Like his father, he wore baggy dress pants. The entire group was posed outside of the Dumas estate.

"So, I'm guessing the couple with grumpy little Charles is Derby and Ophelia," Diana said, pointing. "The girl is Manon and the boy next to him is Jacques. The couple with them is Dr. and Mrs. Dumas."

Tristan kept looking at the picture in silence until he said, "Geez, losing Derby for Charles must've been like losing his dad."

"I don't think I can relate to that," Diana remarked, putting the picture frame down.

"I can," Tristan replied with a frown.

Charlemagne and Judith were brought to the kitchen of the Dumas house where they met with a woman in white capris and a fashionable blue shirt. She wore an apron in front of her clothes and turned to the couple as they entered. The kitchen was a colonial kitchen with white tiles and cabinets.

"*Ma chérie, voici Charlemagne et Judith Cabernet.* Charles, this is my wife, Helene."

"*Bonjour,*" Mrs. Dumas greeted, curtsying to the couple.

Jacques set the bottle on the center of a round table in the corner of the kitchen. He then turned around to fetch four wine glasses from a cabinet, bringing them down and setting them on the table.

"Sit," Jacques insisted, opening the bottle. "Tell me, what are you doing in France?"

"I was here for some official business, but got sidetracked," Charlemagne replied as Jacques poured cider into Judith's glass. "I take it you've heard of the scene I made in Paris."

"Sorry? Paris? No," Jacques responded, pouring into Charlemagne's glass. "I don't keep up with the news or with what is happening in the capital. I am a busy man that sells wine. I do not watch TV or listen to the radio."

"Charles, you need to drive us back into town," Judith warned as Jacques filled Charlemagne's wine glass.

"Ah, do not worry," Jacques remarked. "Please, stay the night and have dinner with us. We have the room and you can meet my children. We are always welcoming of guests!"

Jacques proceeded to pour for himself and his wife.

"What about your father?" Charlemagne questioned. "I hope he has not passed on."

"My father is in Orleans, Charles. He lives in a small apartment in the city, which is better for him. He has been lonely since my mother passed away… sometimes, I go with the children to visit him, and sometimes Manon visits him. Have you seen Manon? What happened with you and her? I never learned."

"You know what, Jacques," Charlemagne instead said. "I believe we might just stay for the night. We were going to return to Paris, but if your father is in Orleans, then it appears that we'll have to make arrangements to travel there tomorrow morning. A night here won't hurt us. What do you think, Judith?"

"*Oui, c'est bien!*" Jacques remarked, toasting with the couple. "*A nos retrouvailles.*"

Act 2, Scene 2

The next day, by noon, Charlemagne parked the family sedan he rented along the curb of a quiet, but crowded road in downtown Orleans. The road was narrow and had cars parked on either side. To their right was a white stone wall with trees behind and on their left were rowhouses constructed in the last century or so. The apartments were bright colored in white and beige brick with balconies on the second and third floors using black steel railings. The windows were rectangular and slightly arched at the top. The roofs were a dark cyan color and in the style of mansard roofs.

Charlemagne led Judith and the kids down the sidewalk and towards one of the apartments. He came to a black steel gate, opened it and then entered into a small foyer. Charlemagne looked at the apartment listings near some mailboxes and then proceeded to up to the stairs to the third floor.

"For someone who is aging, Dr. Dumas does seem to have quite a lot of stairs for him to climb," Charlemagne remarked, reaching the top.

On the third floor, Charlemagne walked a short distance towards Apartment #3. He knocked on the door and waited for a response with the others. No response came. Charlemagne looked to Judith and then knocked again. No response came again.

"Perhaps he's not home," Judith remarked, looking at her watch. "Let's try again later."

Charlemagne did not respond and knocked once more, harder. His knocking was immediately met with the response of a voice saying, "*Quoi?!*" from the other side. Charlemagne held a smug look on his face and waited for the door to open.

Once the door opened, Charlemagne looked to the man on the other side. Dr. Dumas had aged drastically and had also grown a slight hunch. He also seemed to have lost some height as he was at least two to four inches shorter than Charlemagne. Dr. Dumas was dressed in a brown plaid suit with a bow tie, similar to Charlemagne. He had a thick and dark grey beard across his aged face with thick gold-rimmed glasses. He was balding and only had short hair to the sides of his head. He also used a cane to help hold himself up.

"*Qu'est-ce que tout ce bruit ici?*" Dr. Dumas questioned. "*Qui êtes-vous?*"

Dr. Dumas spoke in a raspy voice.

"*Docteur Dumas, c'est moi, Charlemagne de la Cabernet!*" Charlemagne greeted. "*Avec ma copine et mes enfants!*"

"*Quoi? Charlemagne?*" Dr. Dumas reacted, adjusting his glasses with doubt. "*Mon Dieu, c'est toi! Mon fils, je ne t'ai pas vu depuis si longtemps! Entrez, s'il-vous-plait!*" he insisted, motioning them inside before turning to Charlemagne and whispering, "*Est-ce qu'ils parlent français?*"

"*Non,*" Charlemagne responded.

"*Oui,*" Tristan muttered, resulting in Diana elbowing him in the stomach.

"*No,*" Diana whispered.

"*Ah, je regrette,*" Dr. Dumas responded, moving out of the way as Charlemagne entered and bringing a hand to the top of his balding head. "Please, come in. Come in!"

"Dr. Dumas," Charlemagne said, turning to Judith and the kids.

"*Mons fils, Jean, s'il vous plait,*" Dr. Dumas responded. "*Et qui sont ces gens?*"

"*Ceci est ma copine, le Dr. Judith Lambert, et ce sont mes enfants adoptifs, Tristan et Diana*," Charlemagne introduced. "Judith, Tristan, and Diana; this is my old mentor…"

"Dr. Jean-Baptiste Cyril Dumas," Dr. Dumas introduced himself, extending a hand to either of them. "*Je suis si heureux de vous rencontrer tous*. I am so happy to meet you all! Please, call me Jean."

Dr. Dumas turned to Charlemagne.

"Come, let me prepare some tea for us to share," Dr. Dumas stated, leading the family into his small apartment.

Dr. Dumas led them down a brief corridor into a small, but beautifully decorated living room. He had Charlemagne sit in a green armchair and Judith with the kids in a long green couch. He then turned off the TV and went around to a second armchair where he stood behind.

"Do you children want anything? Or is tea okay? I do not have much to offer… perhaps some juice?"

"Tea is fine," Tristan replied with Diana nodding.

"Ah, *bien*," Dr. Dumas replied, leaving and going into the kitchen behind.

"Please, let me help," Charlemagne remarked, standing up and going into the kitchen.

"*Non, je suis vieux, mais je n'ai pas besoin d'aide… pour le moment*," Dr. Dumas responded from the kitchen.

Tristan sat with Diana and looked around the living room. Behind them were a set of French windows that went out to a patio looking into a courtyard. There were several other patios belonging to neighbouring apartments. The French window was slightly open, letting in some warm air from outside. At their feet was a red-gold Arabic rug beneath a handcrafted coffee table with a glass top. In front of the coffee table was a white brick fireplace, and atop of the fireplace was a moderate-sized flat screen television.

On Tristan's left was the armchair where Dr. Dumas had stood behind. Behind this chair was a narrow table with picture frames. Behind the chair that Charlemagne had sat on briefly was a large bookcase next to the corridor leading towards the front door of the apartment. In the corner next to the bookcase was a desk with a computer and office chair. Outside was a small, but crowded garden consisting of potted plants and flowers.

Charlemagne helped arrange some teacups on a tray while Dr. Dumas filled a kettle with water and set it to boil.

"I take it you've heard of what happened in Paris yesterday evening…" Dr. Dumas said in a frightened voice.

"Yesterday?" Charlemagne questioned. "No, I was at your son's house – the family residence."

"The Notre Dame… she was set on fire and left to burn sometime last evening… attempts to extinguish the fire were useless and the spire was lost."

"My God," Charlemagne reacted, "how could this have happened? Who?"

"I am not sure, but the authorities are saying it was an accident."

"The Notre Dame has withstood centuries of havoc… only to be burned to the ground now…. Is the fire still going on?" Charlemagne questioned.

"I am not sure…"

The water finished boiling before Dr. Dumas poured it into a teapot. He then loaded the teapot onto the tray and set a separate cup with cream and another with sugar. He then carried the tray out of the kitchen with Charlemagne behind him. He set it down on the table and then proceeded to pour some tea into each cup. Once everybody had a drink, Dr. Dumas sat in his chair and looked at everyone with smiles.

"Tell me, Charles, what have you been doing? Tell me about your latest adventures," Dr. Dumas insisted. "Tell me about these kids and your beautiful wife. Tell me about your involvement with the Gilets Jaune."

Charlemagne held an awkward face as Dr. Dumas finished his last sentence.

"I would rather not talk about the protests… but I suppose you know what I said," Charlemagne replied.

"Of course," Dr. Dumas responded, "and all of France. Why do you look so embarrassed, *mon fils*? Do not apologize and do not hold regret. Do not listen to these journalists and their opinions – they are the opinions of a few."

"The media is saying that my family never came from France. They are saying that I'm a bigot and a racist for wanting the best for the French people. What am I to do?"

"Charles, be proud of who you are and where you came from. You, *mon fils*, are French and should be proud of the fact. More so, we are European! The media attacks you because they feel they are threatened by your words, and they should feel threatened, because you go against what they seek – the destruction of France and all her beauty. Your words at *Versailles* were well spoken, but a bit outdated. France is not well, *mon fils*. She is dying, and at a time like now, one should not take spite in one's ancestry and their lives, but pride, especially in the cultural and scientific achievement of which her collective body – all of France and all of Europe have given to the world, as you said."

"I don't even know who I am anymore," Charlemagne urged. "The man on the TV seemed to know more about my family history than me. All I know is that my mother was born in Austria and my grandmother was English and a daughter of Louis Mountbatten. I never had the chance to talk to my grandfather about our family history. He didn't leave anything behind for me either."

Dr. Dumas set his cup of tea down and brought his fingers together. He nodded.

"All that I know, *mon fils*, from the conversations I have had with your grandfather, is that the Cabernet family started with your great-great-great grandfather Sennett Cabernet. From Sennett, you have Lycidas Cabernet, who led to Pepin Cabernet and then Derby Cabernet. From there, you have your father, Everest, and then yourself, Charlemagne de la Cabernet. Your forefather, Sennett, came to Canada in the 19th century, alone…"

"The man on the TV said they migrated from the United Kingdom… There are documents from the Canadian archives that support this claim – his name, Sennett Cabernet, signed on immigration slips from the United Kingdom!"

"Bah, that is not conclusive!" Dr. Dumas replied. "I know, Charles! I know, in my gut, I know that you, Charlemagne, and the Cabernet family, is French in origin. I know that!"

Dr. Dumas sat back and paused for a moment.

"Your household name, Cabernet, originates from the type of wine, Cabernet Franc. I have no other knowledge of any other household with this name – and your household found their wealth at the start of the last century… it would be hard to trace them any further back."

"I want to know, though," Charlemagne replied. "I want to know where we came from. I want to prove to the world that I am French."

"Do it then," Dr. Dumas replied. "Do what you must and let the world know. I challenge you, Charlemagne, to prove your ancestral background – it should be fairly easy with a simple genetic test of the Y-chromosome, but there is a problem."

"What problem?" Charlemagne questioned.

"Genetic testing is illegal here in France, and because of that, third-party organizations that do these tests find their French samples in England, so if you go to them, they will most likely conclude you to be English and validate these experts' opinions."

"What then?"

"You must investigate your origins yourself, *mon fils*, and collect DNA from various locations throughout France, going into cemeteries and crypts to do so and create a wide palette so that you can determine your ancestry through them. If you match, then you are French, and if you do not match… well, that will not be the case," Dr. Dumas replied, laughing. "To start, I suggest that you travel to the place where it all began: Brittany and the Carnac Stones. There, you will find an untampered burial tomb and find Celtic DNA belonging to the Gauls of Celtica."

"Very well," Charlemagne replied, "I will do that then."

"Charles," Judith interrupted, "a project like that will take weeks."

"We have the time… the kids don't need to go anywhere and if you need to go, then go."

Judith frowned and then sighed, saying, "No, I'll stay."

"Good," Charlemagne responded.

"Ah, there is one more thing – something that will help you," Dr. Dumas remarked, standing up and going around to his bookcase. "Let me find it."

Charlemagne, Judith and the kids waited as Dr. Dumas rummaged around his bookcase. Diana looked around the living room as they waited, looking out the window into the neighbouring patio to notice a shady figure crouched behind the railing. They were dressed in all black, in the middle of daytime, with a hood over their head. They also had a backpack and a notepad in hand. Diana made eye contact with the figure and frowned at them. She then nudged Tristan.

"Charles," Diana said, looking at the figure still, "we're being eavesdropped on."

"What?" Charlemagne questioned, turning around and looking outside.

The figure stood up and proceeded to run off, tripping over a table and falling to the ground. Diana immediately stood up and went out to the balcony, causing Tristan to go after her.

"Diana!" Tristan shouted as she jumped over to the neighbouring balcony as the figure stood up and ran off. "Diana, wait!"

The figure jumped off of the neighboring patio and onto a rooftop. Diana followed after the figure while Tristan followed after Diana. The figure ran forward, turning around a corner and then jumping down onto a lower roof and across.

From the lowered roof, there was a space between two rooftops at a small alleyway. The figure jumped across the space and onto the roof on the other side. Diana jumped after the hooded figure with Tristan behind her.

The hooded figure ran towards a corner connecting two separate rooftops at a chimney. They vaulted over and continued along with the kids behind them. The rooftop ended at another chimney step, requiring them to jump over before reaching the end of another rooftop. From here, the figure jumped down atop of a chimney and then onto a lower elevated roof. The kids followed and saw the hooded figure jump across another small gap and then turn right onto the continuing rooftops, which ended with a ladder going upwards two levels.

Atop of the roof, the figure went to the end and then slid down a slanted portion to the right that came to another patio balcony connecting two buildings. The hooded figure came to the edge of the balcony and jumped over to a rooftop next to the former building they had climbed up to. The chase then continued along different elevated rooftops, coming to a steep roof where the hooded stranger began to skip atop of the roofs of dormer windows before jumping down to a lower dormer window of another building and then continuing along.

From this rooftop, the hooded figure jumped to a structure behind on the right, running along and then coming to a larger jump between two structures. The hooded figure then turned right. The kids followed and saw the hooded figure jumped down a level. Diana followed after, jumping down atop of a dirty concrete column and then going around to some terracotta rooftops. Tristan followed Diana to the top of this rooftop, which they followed to the end before coming to three jumps over the separate chimney stacks.

The hooded figure stopped at the end of this rooftop where he had nowhere else to turn. He took a step back and went to a hatch, opening it and then jumping down. Diana went first, coming into a crowed corridor of an apartment. She followed the hooded figure around a circular staircase, reaching the bottom where the figure pushed out and came to a pedestrian promenade where there were no cars. The construction of the road was similar to the road Charlemagne had parked on and was a neat, squared stone, but with an addition of a neat cobblestone-like double aisle in the middle with rail tracks. There were also lamp posts on the side and pedestrians walking either direction on either side. The hooded figure went down the street in a hurried pace, shoving past people.

Diana and Tristan continued after the individual, passing shops and pedestrians along the road until they reached a large rectangular plaza. The rails went rightwards, but the hooded figure went straight through the middle of the plaza and past some palm trees in moss green boxes. The central plaza was made of a rectangular stone in differing shades and there was a statue to the right center of the plaza of a figure on a horse. On the left corner of the plaza was a carousel. A building ahead of them wad decorated with the flag of Orleans, flag of *Centre-Val de Loire*, and the French flag five times between each window.

The hooded figure continued down the road on the right, which had banners of the flag of Orleans, red and yellow, at the side of every window to the end. There were no cars driving along this road, but there were cars parked on the side in front of an arcade beneath the structure on either side with pedestrians walking under the cover.

By now, Tristan was right behind Diana, and Diana was nearly able to tackle the hooded figure by her speed. Tristan's ears poked up as he heard a bell. He turned to the right and then over to Diana as the hooded figure came to the end of the road and was about to cross the street. The streetlight on a post was red. The figure stepped off onto the larger street, over some railings. Tristan immediately grabbed Diana as she was about to cross after him.

A large golden tramcar ran into the hooded figure. The kids stood back as the tram passed. They then saw the person they had been chasing, a male, on the ground with blood pouring from his head on the concrete floor. Tristan immediately went over to pull him off the street, but he soon realized the person was dead and backed off with Diana.

A small crowd of people watched around and a woman shrieked. The contents of the person's backpack had erupted, and a dozen papers and items were flying everywhere with the wind. Tristan could hear an ambulance in the background approaching. Diana stepped forward and picked something from off the ground – it was a press ID. She showed it to Tristan.

Tristan then looked up and over as the family car arrived with Charlemagne and Judith. The ambulance then soon arrived. Charlemagne took the kids away from the incident and towards the car.

"What on Earth happened?" Charlemagne questioned to them.

Tristan explained. Diana then showed Charlemagne the press badge. Charlemagne took it into his hand and showed Judith.

"This is deeply concerning…" Charlemagne remarked, "but that fellow didn't deserve to die… Children, never do that again – you almost gave me a heart attack when I saw you off – both of you."

"Sorry," Diana whispered.

"Come on," Charlemagne remarked," let's disappear before the police get involved."

• •

Once the family had returned to the Dumas apartment, Charlemagne explained what had happened to Dr. Dumas.

"Anyways…" Charlemagne remarked, sighing. "What is it that you wanted to show me. Did you find it?"

"No… and perhaps for the better…" Dr. Dumas remarked, avoiding eye contact with Charlemagne as he stood up and went to close the French window. "However, I did find something else, which was mine. It might help you with where you are going next – *à Bretagne*."

Act 2, Scene 3

The next morning, Charlemagne, Judith and the kids set off from Orleans and westwards towards Brittany. Charlemagne drove along a country road, reaching a meadow on their right where there were various stones atop of the grass.

"Hey, Charles," Tristan remarked. "Isn't that where we want to be?"

"No," Charlemagne replied. "On our right is the Carnac and Menec alignments. We want the Quiberon alignments over at the peninsula of Quiberon not too far from here. I'm going to take us to the hotel and then set off for the stones tomorrow morning. I need to do a little bit more research and pick up some more tools before I start to collect my samples."

Charlemagne continued to drive along, turning left and going down the road to come to the small seaside village of Carnac on the Atlantic coast. The village was smaller than Orleans and its roads were winding and narrow, resembling a seaside English village. Charlemagne drove down a road in which there were various small local businesses. The weather was fair, and it was warm enough to open the windows and let in the smell of the sea and sound of seagulls.

"Charles, are you lost?" Judith questioned.

"No, I'm just trying to find the hotel."

Charlemagne turned right and went downhill, turning left onto a beachside road. To their left was roadside parking while on the right was a parking lot directly in front of the beach.

"Well, doesn't this look nice," Charlemagne expressed, looking to the right towards the beach.

Ahead of the parking lot was a promenade before the beach that stretched down across the coast of the town. On their left were various houses before branching off into moderate-size hotels with balcony views of the ocean.

"Ah, here we are," Charlemagne remarked, turning into a parking spot on the curbside. "Perfect."

The family got out of the car and proceeded to unload their baggage before going to the hotel. Charlemagne picked up the keys and they then went up to the top floor to a suite reserved for them. The suite and rooms were smaller and less luxurious than the ones in Paris, and like in Orleans, the family were confined to two bedrooms in which Tristan and Charlemagne would have to share a bed while Judith and Diana would have to share another.

Once they were settled, Charlemagne proceeded to study the notes that Dumas had given him at the kitchen table. He concentrated on the notes before looking over to the kids, Diana wore a white top, and some shorts and Tristan wore a polo with some shorts.

"Where are you off to?" Charlemagne questioned.

"We're just going for a walk on the beach," Tristan replied, "are we allowed to do that?"

"Sorry, yes, of course. Go ahead," Charlemagne remarked, "just take a key with you. I might go out with Judith in a bit."

"Okay…" Tristan responded, going over to the kitchen counter and picking up a card key.

The couple then left out the door where in the hallway, Tristan looked to Diana. The couple looked at each other in agreement and then went down the corridor a set of stairs going down.

"Charles really has become overprotective," Tristan finally said in the lobby. "It's starting to really annoy me."

"It's just something we're going to have to live with," Diana sighed, "and he could be worse. Lucky for us, we have Judith acting as the voice of reason."

"I thought mothers were supposed to be more protective," Tristan replied, "at least that's how it was with my folks."

Diana glared at Tristan as they walked down the path exiting the hotel. They then came to the beachside street, crossing it and reaching the beach on the other side.

Meanwhile, Charlemagne continued to look at the notes, studying them before looking over to Judith who had showered and changed into a new set of clothes. She now wore a white blouse with a black skirt. Her hair was tied back, and she wore black sandals. Charlemagne was stood at the kitchen table with his reading glasses on, tapping a pencil on the desk. He continued to look to Judith and then down to the notes.

"Honestly, Charles, give it a rest for a moment and let's go out and enjoy the sights," Judith insisted. "You spent all evening looking at that paper."

"I'm weak on the subject…" Charlemagne replied, looking at the doodle of a hill on the paper. "My own country's history and I'm a pillock on the details…"

"Stop obsessing over it – I'm sure you know more than I do. You don't need to be an expert on everything in the world, Charles."

Charlemagne looked at her and then turned back to the table.

"Perhaps I could use some fresh air and some exercise… we can go into town and look around. Maybe they have a bookshop, and I can find something on the Gauls."

Charlemagne left to go into the bedroom while Judith rolled her eyes. He then returned without his blazer or vest or even his bowtie and had replaced all three with a red sweater vest.

"Let's go out and see the town, shall we?"

Diana and Tristan walked down the coast of the beach together, holding hands. There was a tall grass between them and the fine coarse sand on the other side. The beach was large and wide. The tide was out, and the entire horizon was clear, and the ocean was calm.

The couple continued to walk north along the beachfront, reaching an intersection with signs pointing in all sorts of directions in two different languages, French, and another language using the Latin alphabet.

"What language is that?" Diana questioned.

"Probably the local Celtic language," Tristan replied. "Charlemagne said that this area is like the Quebec of France. They're an ethnic minority compared to the Germanic-Latin people of north and south."

"Celtic…" Diana responded, "is that like Ireland? Scotland?"

"Uh… it's a little more complicated than that. Ireland, and I suppose Scotland and Wales too, are homes to people who descended from Celts (although years of British and Viking conquest may have upset that in Scotland and Ireland), but the Celtic people actually are believed to have originated from Central Europe and used to live in all of France in what was known as Gaul by the Romans. Gaul wasn't a unified land, but one made of various tribes of Celtic people. Of course, the Romans conquered the land and assimilated these people. Then the Germanic Franks took over, and so on…. The Welsh people are probably the last remnants of the Celts, because Scottish and Irish people share closer lineage with the English due to years of being together. I wouldn't be surprised if the same were true of the Bretons. All remains for these three groups is their culture and language."

"You know a lot about the Celts," Diana remarked, "did Charlemagne share all that with you?"

"Actually, no," Tristan responded. "My name, 'Tristan,' is Celtic, which makes sense given that my dad was Scottish-Canadian, and 'Merrick' is Welsh."

Diana looked at Tristan's reddish-blonde hair as they reached a narrower seawall path with rocks beneath them, replacing the sand of the beaches. There was an amalgamation of whitewater around the rocks, which were ripe with algae.

"Most Celts look like me too – white skin and red hair," Tristan responded, "and the closest example of what they looked like is from the Statue of the Dying Galatian, which depicts a Galatian (a Celtic people who used to live in modern day Turkey)."

"I wish I knew something about myself, but all I can surmise is being English," Diana replied, shrugging.

Tristan smiled and kissed her on the cheek.

Charlemagne and Judith arrived intown and proceeded to walk down the sidewalk of *Avenue des Druides*, holding hands. They passed an ice cream store and then a toy shop, reaching a surfboard rental shop before they crossed the street. They went past a farmer's market and passed a restaurant, sensing the smell of food inside with the chatter of patrons. From here they passed a bakery and then a souvenir shop. On the other side of the street was another souvenir shop, but with a more Atlantic theme, next to a clothing shop.

"Oh, Charles," Judith said, moving her hands to embrace Charlemagne's side, "forget about this research and let's spend the rest of the week exploring France. I enjoy this."

"Sorry, but I need to do this," Charlemagne replied, "besides, this research gives us an excuse to be in France. You can't complain with that, right?"

Judith sighed and let go. She then looked to Charlemagne apologetically.

"I suppose so," Judith remarked. "I just want to fantasize – that's all."

Charlemagne smiled to her. They continued to walk, eventually reaching a bookshop. Charlemagne entered and browsed the books, spending a considerable amount of time to Judith's annoyance.

"Ah, they seem to have all the French classics," Charlemagne acknowledged, "*The Hunchback of Notre-Dame* and *Les Misérables* by Victor Hugo. His less famous novel, *The Man Who Laughs*, and my father's favorite, *Phantom of the Opera* by Gaston Leroux. Gustave Flaubert's *Madame Bovary* is also a classic. If these novels weren't in French, I would buy Diana copy of *The Hunchback of Notre-Dame*, or *Notre-Dame de Paris* as it's referred to in French, in the least… a novel of almost a thousand pages would last her a good week."

Charlemagne walked away from the classics and towards the history books. He spent a few more minutes searching before purchasing a simple book before exiting. The couple then continued to walk through the town together, resting at a café. The rest of the day went much like this for both of the couples.

Act 2, Scene 4

The next morning, Charlemagne parked the family sedan in a small parking lot surrounded by the neighboring forest. There were several other cars parked around the area. He got out of the car and went to the trunk to retrieve his backpack, including a set of two spades. Charlemagne gave on to Tristan to carry and then the family set off forward towards a trail into the forest.

"We have a little bit of a hike before us to reach the alignments," Charlemagne remarked, "and after the five-hour drive from Orleans, I believe I need it."

Charlemagne led them from the parking lot towards the dirt trail. Trees surrounded them on the left and right as they walked from the parking lot. It was cool out and less than an hour past noon. The family walked down the path, passing some passerby walking dogs on leashes. The trail was less than a kilometer and consistently straight.

At the end, the family reached a beach with cliffs on either side, replacing the forest. The beach went forward and then extended on either side, going in front of the cliffs. The beach was rocky, but not because there was no sand or sand replaced by pebbles, but because the beach was disorganized with various rocks and shell pieces littered throughout atop of the dark sand. The surface of the beach was also inconsistent and not smooth. The tide was out and there was a lot of space with people on the beach with their dogs. On the left, the cliffs were steep, but not tall with overgrowth and grass growing atop the mound, but on the right, the cliffs were rockier and steeper.

Diana and Tristan looked out to the beach and then over to the horizon, towards the rest of the Atlantic Ocean. The horizon was crisp and clear with no clouds forward and simply the ocean before them. Charlemagne looked at the notes that Dr. Dumas had given him and then proceeded to walk forward, towards the beach before going right and down along the coast. The family followed with Judith having the most trouble navigating over the rocks. She was not dressed for a hike in her formal casual top and white pants. She was also wearing moccasins.

Charlemagne continued down the beach until he reached a canyon inserting into the cliffs with a natural dirt path leading down towards a signpost. He walked over and looked to the left where there were steps going up to the top of the cliffs. He began to go upwards each long step. Once at the top of the cliff, the family was able to look around them and even farther along the coast. Behind them were trees that went into the forest below. Near them was a signpost that read, '*Attention! Falaises abruptes!*'

The coast continued along to the right like the peak of a very low mountain. The side of this mountain leveled off behind into the forest but cut off to the beach to steep rocks. Charlemagne continued along the peak until they reached the rocky grounds of the cliffs with the forest directly behind them on a plateau. The family continued along this cliffside, reaching narrower space as bushes overtook them on either side and eventually blocked off the view of the water.

"My, this space reminds me of the cliffs of Harlech over near the university…" Charlemagne remarked, turning to Judith, "do they not?"

"No, they do, now that you say it… a little more peaceful than the university as there are not a lot of people here, but still similar," Judith replied, "also, no islands on the horizon here."

The family eventually reached a dead-end, which caused Charlemagne to force himself into the bush and go into the forest. Charlemagne led them through the forest, which was dense and thick for the first half before easing out towards the end. Ahead of them was a clearing of a medium-sized meadow in the midst of the forest. The grass was tall, but not as tall as the megalithic standing stones set out in two aisles before them.

"Welcome to the Quiberon Alignments," Charlemagne stated.

To the left, at the end of the aisles, was the edge of the cliff and horizon ahead, while on the right, was a large hill surrounded by bushes and trees. Charlemagne walked over to the hill with his shovel, looking down the aisle of standing stones to the horizon before going to the base of the hill with the others.

"The entrance into the tomb should be around here," Charlemagne remarked, poking his shovel into the grass, "the Gauls designed their tombs like most Celtic tribes so that the entrances faced the sunset during vernal equinox, or spring equinox. It's believed that these 'menhirs' were used for burial procedures by Druids, or Celtic priests, but there is no evidence to support that idea or refute it just as there is no real evidence on who set these stones here."

Charlemagne inserted his shovel into the hill and began to dig.

"Give me a hand, Tristan," Charlemagne requested, starting to dig. "We have to dig into the hill to reach the entrance of the tomb. The Celts would bury their nobles in these mounds known as tumulus where they would construct burial tombs within."

Charlemagne and Tristan continued to dig while Diana took out her camera to film.

"I have no idea what to expect as Dr. Dumas' notes were not very specific, but only gave us this location," Charlemagne said, taking a moment to breath. "However, since this is an untampered tomb (hopefully) there will most likely be specimens inside to take samples of."

"How long is this going to take?" Judith questioned.

"Uh, I'm not sure," Charlemagne replied, looking over to her. "It shouldn't be much digging… hopefully."

Charlemagne and Tristan dug for close to an hour. Judith lounged in the grass, absorbing the sun on a towel while Diana filmed the stones as well as the coast. Not before long, Charlemagne ran his shovel into some stone. He then began to clear the space around, discovering a small square tunnel entrance.

"Jackpot," Charlemagne acknowledged, removing a little bit more dirt before setting his shovel on the ground.

Charlemagne set his feet into the hole and got onto his knees. He looked into the hole and saw a long tunnel ahead. Charlemagne then stood up and reached into his backpack for a flashlight. He then knelt down again and lit the flashlight into the tunnel, reaching into a small chamber in the back, but no sight of remains.

"Right, who wants to go spelunking with me?" Charlemagne questioned, looking over to the kids and Judith. "Thought so. Wait here then."

Charlemagne stood up again, retrieved his backpack, brought it around his shoulders and then proceeded to crawl into the tunnel. He brought his feet around and then crouched down the small tunnel. Charlemagne shined his light on the walls of the entrance tunnel, seeing an array of swirly megalithic artwork as he reached the central chamber. On his left and right were separate entrances into secondary tunnels going into secondary chambers as well as immediately ahead of him. Charlemagne looked at the composition of the walls and saw that megalithic standing stones composed them for the most part with slabs of stone composing the roof. The ground was made of loose stones and rubble in almost gravel-like state. The chamber ahead of him was simple, round and did not contain any remains.

Judith sighed from outside and looked to the kids with crossed arms.

"I'm going back to the car – I'll have more entertainment doing some work than waiting around for Charles to take a couple of samples from some ancient bones. Anyone is free to join me too."

Judith then proceeded to leave the kids, causing Tristan to shrug and climb down into the hole to join Charlemagne. Both of the kids entered the megalithic tunnel, joining Charlemagne in the central chamber.

"Just so you know, Judith left to the car," Tristan remarked to Charlemagne as he looked to them.

"She might get lost – one of you go with her," Charlemagne ordered.

"She won't get lost," Tristan remarked.

"Thank you for volunteering," Charlemagne replied. "Go and make sure she doesn't."

Tristan groaned and left. Diana looked to him and then looked to Charlemagne.

"This tomb is larger than I anticipated... I'm beginning to hypothesize that its entrance was buried because early Christians found it too bothersome to destroy so they simply buried it in hopes of forgetting it existed. I'm going to need some help – follow the right tunnels and I'll follow the left. If you find anything, come back and let me know. If I'm not here, join me in the left tunnel."

Charlemagne handed Diana a flashlight.

"Sure thing," Diana replied, going into the right tunnel.

Diana reached the right secondary chamber and saw another tunnel to her left, going further underground. The walls of the stone transitioned into cobblestone instead of large standing stones the deeper Diana went, reaching the tertiary chamber on the second sublevel. The next tunnel was on the left. Diana shined her light and saw Charlemagne at the other side through the central chamber ahead.

The two reunited in the anterior chamber and looked down towards a posterior tunnel going further down.

"Well, this was less dramatic than I hoped, but perhaps for the better. Let's keep going," Charlemagne remarked, going down the tunnel with Diana behind.

At the third sublevel, the chamber did not break off into three more tunnels, but there were three chambers on either side with the remains of three people in each of them. Diana looked at the items accompanying the deceased with little interest and not looking too impressed. The skeletons were dressed in cloaks with artefacts around them. The items ranged from weapons, perhaps a shield, and then vases and other jewellery.

"Perfect," Charlemagne said, dropping his backpack on the ground, "it's time to get a sample."

Charlemagne entered the first tomb and saw the skeletal remains of an unknown Celt. The deceased was dressed in a purple robe and had jewellery attached at the wrists in the form of bracelets and neck in the form of a necklace. Charlemagne dropped to his knees next to the corpse and set down a case with some tools inside. He put on some latex gloves and then applied a respirator mask over his face. Charlemagne then picked up a file and removed a rib from the corpse. He proceeded to file the rib, cleaning off the bone and causing dust to drop down.

Diana put on a mask as she saw the dust through the light of Charlemagne's lantern. She then sat down and watched. She looked at the loot in the tomb and then looked over to Charlemagne.

"There's not that much treasure for a supposedly unpillaged tomb," Diana remarked to him. "What's up with that?"

"I never said it was 'unpillaged,'" Charlemagne replied. "I said it was untampered with – as in, there would be skeletons inside. It was more than likely that the tomb would be pillaged like the ones in Egypt."

"Maybe Tristan should have stuck around," Diana said. "He would have been more interested in this than I am."

"There's nothing quite interesting about cleaning a bone," Charlemagne remarked, filing the bone down so that there was only a clean and polished layer.

Charlemagne then set the file down and changed it for another one. He had various files with him. He also produced some waxy paper that looked like a coffee filter and set it down. He held the bone over the paper and proceeded to file into it, causing dust to fall onto the paper. Once there was a neat pile, Charlemagne put down the bone and his tool to pick up the paper and fold it. He then pointed to his backpack and asked Diana to bring him a rack of test tubes.

Diana brought it over and Charlemagne had her open one. Charlemagne then had the dust go into the tube before he shut it. Once the contents were in the test tube, he closed it off and cleaned up his tools.

"Great, three more to go and then we're done," Charlemagne remarked, going back to his items.

"What then?" Diana asked.

"Then, we go to our next stop," Charlemagne replied. "Dr. Dumas suggested I visit a catacomb in Bordeaux."

Act 3, Scene 1

Diana stood atop a set of round steps in front of a large column with a statue atop, Le Monument aux Girondins. There were three other female statues beneath the column with carved letters that read, '*A La Memoire des Girondins.*' The entire monument was surrounded by a space enclosed by stone balustrades. On the left and right of these rails were fountains. Diana took a picture of the monument, focusing on the female figure atop of the column before zooming out to the statues beneath.

Tristan watched from her side as she took photos, looking up to the grey cloudy sky and then the stone floor at their feet, which was wet from the rainfall that had fallen earlier. He then turned around and down to a set of two tram rail lines that span around the front of the plaza. Behind these lines was a grass clearing with tall deciduous trees at least twenty meters tall. Behind these trees was a road and in front of this road were buildings that, like most of the structures in Bordeaux, were uniform and consistent in their traditional architecture. The buildings closest to them were made of a simple sand-grey stone with white windows that were arched on the first floor, rectangular on the second, and squared on the third. Some of the structures in Bordeaux had dormer windows on the third or fourth level, but the type of architecture was rhythmic and set a tone for the portside town.

Diana came down the steps, causing Tristan to follow. The couple then walked around the brick walkway to the fountain on the left, which was semicircular in its outline with a pond before the black iron railing around the perimeter. In the center of the fountain was a statue of three nude figures, the one on the left was a male on his back, reaching out to the one on the left, which was a female. They were separated by a stone fish in the water with the third figure atop, riding the fish. The third figure was that of a male child. Behind these figures was the larger statue of four horses rearing towards the pond water alongside various other figures surrounding a woman. Water splashed out from this statue. The statue was very chaotic. Diana took a picture of the family-figures, the horses behind and then of Tristan standing in front of the statue. The couple then moved around, looking outwards towards the empty stone plaza behind the statue where there were two poles or columns towards the center of the end. The plaza was surrounded by trees. They came to the other fountain, which was less chaotic.

Instead of the male-female-child figures, the three figures in the water were three males, one on his back, the other on his stomach and the third on his knees with his head down and being covered by his arms. There were four horses rearing outwards from the water, but there were less figures behind them with a central figure being a female with a staff in hand. Diana took her pictures and then walked over to Tristan, taking his hand and then walking over the stone plaza. The floor of the plaza was gritty and had various small rocks atop of it, giving it a rough appearance.

At the end of the plaza were some small steps reaching some rails in the grass. Behind the rails and grass was a double-lane road, which then led to a park on the other side on the coast of the Garonne River. The couple crossed the street and made it to the promenade with a simple railing at the edge of the river. They continued to walk down the side of the walkway, reaching another plaza with an extremely shallow pond next to it. The couple walked up the steps and looked down the long artificial pond. Across the street was another, larger plaza surrounded by some important-looking structures on the left and right, wrapping around the corner before being separated by alleyways with a smaller, but equally tall structure in the middle. The exterior surface of the structure was made of a beige brick and the rooftop of grey slates. In front of the middle structure, towards the lip of the plaza was a circular fountain.

All three structures were three-stories tall and symmetrical. The larger L-shaped structure had a pediment at the side closest to the street and on the side immediately adjacent facing inwards to the plaza. The pediment followed a colonnade of four columns on either side of the façade that went down to arches of the exterior, which housed white-framed windows. The roofs of the structure were slanted, which provided space for dormer windows. Atop of the roof, above the pediments were bell-shaped towers with spires shooting outwards. Behind the colonnades were white-framed windows on the second floor and smaller squared, white-framed windows on the third floor. The structure in the middle, behind the fountain, was similar, although smaller. The façade consisted of windows in the same organization, a colonnade, and pediment above with slanted rooftops that went to a bell-shaped tower and spire. Each tower had a squared rail-guard around it.

Tristan took a deep breath and then looked to Diana.

"I like this town," Tristan said, "even if it is one of the larger ones, the architecture really sets it apart from Orleans or Paris."

The couple then walked down along the sidewalk and back towards the promenade by the river, continuing their walk through the town.

• •

Later that evening, Diana and Tristan reunited with Charlemagne and Judith to have an early dinner at a luxurious restaurant in the heart of Bordeaux, in front of a roundabout with a statue fountain in the center.

Judith studied the menu, looking at the various different types of wines offered.

"Oh, Charles, split a bottle with me, please," Judith insisted. "It would be a shame to not pay for an entire bottle here."

"Sorry, but I don't think I should drink tonight if I'm to go out after sunset," Charlemagne responded.

"Oh, honestly," Judith remarked. "We've come to town most known for its wine in all of France, and you decide not to drink...? A little drink won't make you drowsy or drunk now, will it?"

Charlemagne looked at her with sarcastic eyes.

"What makes this region so special for its wines?" Tristan questioned.

"We're in the Medoc region," Charlemagne responded, "although it isn't ideal for growing wines, it is well-known for being a wine growing region. At the start of the first century, the Romans introduced wine to the local people and slowly viticulture took off. To this date, it is one of the largest economies of the region."

Diana and Tristan both looked at each other.

"On the subject, wine is one of the reasons I'm here. Dr. Dumas told me that 'Cabernet' could have originated from the people of this region as it is a Medoc term. He hypothesized that 'Cabernet' came from the hybridization of the Late Latin terms 'Caput' and 'Nigrum' – Late Latin being a variant of Latin spoken between three-hundred and six-hundred A.D. In English, the words together mean 'black head,' and as you might know from Jacques' rants last Monday, Cabernet Sauvignon is a blackish grape (the grape being the head) that creates a blackish-red wine. Whatever 'Sauvignon' really means, is beyond me."

"What the origin or your name having to do with wine, and the fact that you'll be heading out to do some grave robbing later in the night, is beyond me…" Judith mocked, "especially since it can be put off until tomorrow seeing that this is your last stop."

"Possibly our last stop," Charlemagne corrected, "and I told you already. I have my Celtic samples, but now I need some Roman and Frankish samples. The Basilica of Saint Severin not too far from here holds catacombs that house some of the oldest graves in all of France. It should have enough bodies to satisfy my… oh, *garçon!*"

Charlemagne looked to the right as the waiter appeared at the end of his last sentence. He ordered for the family in French and then left them alone. Charlemagne drank a simple cup of coffee to keep him awake, while Judith was presented a bottle of expensive wine. She looked at the wine she had bought and studied it in her glass. She then brought it under her nose and attempted to waft the scent up her nostrils, inhaling the smell with a deep breath. From there, she brought her lips to the glass and tilted the glass up, taking a bit into her mouth where she then proceeded to swish it around her mouth with pleasure. She then swallowed gave a sigh of relief.

"Marvellous," Judith exclaimed. "Viticulture is truly an art that has been perfected in this region!"

Charlemagne looked to the kids and then over to Judith.

"Pour me a glass and let me try…" Charlemagne remarked, "you're teasing me."

Judith smiled and poured Charlemagne some wine from her bottle. Charlemagne brought the wine glass to his eyes and then smelt it. He went through the same process of tasting the wine as Judith before handing her the glass.

"It's good," Charlemagne acknowledged, "… very good."

"Very good?" Judith questioned. "You're awful at tasting wines."

"When do I get a taste?" Tristan asked. "What's the drinking age in France?"

"Eighteen," Charlemagne responded, picking up the wine menu "same as in Alberta."

Charlemagne looked through the menu and at the various types of wine. Within a couple of minutes, the waiter returned with their food, setting down plate after plate of their chosen entrees arranged in a decorated fashion, or as Charlemagne described, in a *nouvelle cuisine* approach.

For Charlemagne, his squared plate contained a piece of meat cut into threes and sprinkled with a brown sauce. The meat was red in the middle and brown on the sides. It was accompanied by three asparaguses. Judith ordered a white fish wrapped in a black seaweed. It was set atop of a greenish suspension, which itself was sat atop of a reddish sauce. Two carrots were layered atop of the meat along with some small green leaves.

For Tristan, the waiter laid down a roast of beef laying atop of a translucent brown sauce, some sliced mushrooms and roasted potatoes, and some asparaguses on the side. For Diana, a rectangular plate hosting spaghetti strewn into three balls with pieces of chicken resting atop. The pasta had a greenish pesto-type aspect towards it and there was a drizzle of sauce atop.

Once the waiter was done setting the dishes, he bowed and said, *"Bon appétit!"*

Act 3, Scene 2

Charlemagne and Judith sat in the front of the family sedan, looking out the windshield and towards the *Place de Martyrs de la Résistance*, which was a small grass park next to the Basilica of Saint Severinus. The park was empty, and it was late into the night. There was close to nobody around and only the occasional car and pedestrian passed behind them every couple minute or so. The neighborhood they were in was quiet, semi-residential with apartments and the occasional store or two on the ground floor of these apartments along the road.

Across the park, to the side of the church, was a set of concrete stairs going into the earth, surrounded by iron rails. Charlemagne kept his eyes around this general vicinity, drinking a cup of coffee.

"Charles, what are we doing here?" Judith questioned.

"What are *we* doing here? What are *you* doing here, my love?" Charlemagne responded. "I told you that I didn't need any company, but you insisted on joining me."

"I'm here trying to talk you out of this – this is insane," Judith stated. "You can't just break into a late antiquity tomb and expect to find any actual bodies still down there."

"Well, that's where you're wrong," Charlemagne remarked, opening the car door. "You act as if I haven't done this before. I have, so will you kindly wait here for me?"

"Charles," Judith scolded, looking over to him as she left.

Charlemagne exited the car and then closed the door behind him. Judith rolled her eyes and opened her car door. She then stood up and looked over to Charlemagne as he started to walk forward with a backpack around his shoulders. He was dressed in a black suit and had donned black leather gloves over his hands. Judith was dressed just as she was at dinner, but with a dark brown overcoat and her purse.

"Charlemagne, stop," Judith warned again. "You don't need to do this."

"Do what? All I'm doing is a simple investigation," Charlemagne replied, shrugging as he turned to her. "Now, keep your voice down before you attract attention – do you *want* me to get in trouble?"

Judith rolled her eyes again and then went after Charlemagne as he continued to cross the park to get to the staircase. Charlemagne looked around to make sure there was nobody watching him in the near area before he then looked down the staircase to the rectangular iron gate leading into the catacombs. Above the gate were two signs, the larger one above read '*Site archéologique Saint-Seurin*,' while the one below read, '*Nécropole Paléochrétienne*.'

Charlemagne brought his backpack down to the ground and began to rummage through it. He produced a screwdriver and a hairpin. He then huddled by the lock of the door while Judith turned her face to look up the stairs. Charlemagne fiddled around until a click could be heard and he unlocked the gate. The gate then opened with a loud creak, granting the couple access through. Charlemagne turned around and brought the gate to a close, but did not lock it. He then turned around and looked into the tomb he had entered – the darkness within, which forced him to produce his bright handheld spotlight flashlight to give them some light. He handed the spare to Judith and the couple then walked inside.

"Since when have you known how to pick a lock?" Judith questioned Charlemagne.

"It's a little skill I picked up from Diana," Charlemagne responded.

From where they had entered, the couple walked four steps down to the smooth stone floor. The stone around them was less smooth and some of it was rough and jagged. To their left was a statue of a cloaked figure and to their right were three sarcophaguses with pyramidal tops. In front of them was another sarcophagus, but with a smoother and rounder top. Behind this sarcophagus was an entrenched grave with a round top in the ground, but with a rough edge.

At the opposite-side of this room was an archway leading into a small room with another sarcophagus. This room was blocked off by a rope that went either side of the archway. The necropolis continued with an arch on the left, which came after three steps that went up to a small tunnel, which went down another three steps to another part of the tomb.

 The room on the left of the entrance was larger with various sarcophaguses along the back of the wall, blocked off by rope. Charlemagne looked at all of the available graves but frowned.

"They're all empty… I'm sure of it," Charlemagne remarked, looking behind him to another archway with blocked off rope. "They've turned this excavation site into a museum."

"Well, what more did you expect?" Judith replied.

Charlemagne walked overt to sarcophagus behind them and lowered his flashlight. He then attempted to open, or raise the top to look inside, but there was nothing there. It was empty. Charlemagne closed the cover, causing a cloud of dust to lift up. He then brought his hands to his hips and shook his head.

"Let's carry on," Charlemagne suggested, walking towards a narrow corridor behind Judith.

Charlemagne led the way forward and came to a small room with steps on the right leading into another small room with a single sarcophagus. Again, rope stretched across the archway. On the left were three steps going to another two steps that led past an archway leading to a staircase with light pouring in from above. The archway was blocked by an iron gate with squared bars. There was also a green light above the archway and another green light in the staircase. A single chair was situated next to the exit and a sarcophagus on the other side against the wall. Charlemagne came to the lock and proceeded to attempt to pick the lock.

Once the lock was unlocked, he pushed the gate forward and entered the staircase with Judith, coming up to the top and into the interior of the basilica. The top of the staircase led immediately towards a tall pillar that formed the vault of the nave, or center aisle. To their left was a mural and above it an old painting as a part of the lateral aisle. The church was lit with candles on candelabras all around.

The nave of the church had two sections, left and right, each with rows and columns of simple wooden chairs leading to the altar. The staircase came out facing towards the altar. It was surrounded by a stone half wall that wrapped around. On the other side of the church was another staircase going down into the ground again. Charlemagne walked down a row of chairs and came to the center. He then knelt down and made the sign of the cross before standing up again.

Charlemagne looked forward and eyed the sarcophagus before the altar, protected behind iron bars made in the shape of an 'S' backwards and forwards.

"I assume that is the sarcophagus of Saint Severinus of Bordeaux, patron saint of this city," Charlemagne remarked, looking at the sarcophagus with focused eyes.

Judith came to his side and looked at the sarcophagus.

"Please don't tell me you want to look inside," Judith responded.

"Saint Severinus was born in the Levant – extracting a specimen from him would not help me," Charlemagne replied, looking to her. "However, the crypt beneath the church might – and we're just a few meters from the entrance."

Charlemagne moved his foot to begin walking towards the other staircase on the left but stopped as he heard the noise of a door opening. He then hurried over with Judith behind him and went down the steps towards the iron gate. Charlemagne quickly began to fumble around with the lock, picking it and then swinging the gate open with a loud creak. Judith and Charlemagne then rushed into the crypt and closed the gate behind them, locking it before stepping back.

Charlemagne and Judith looked towards the gate for several minutes before swallowing their breath as Charlemagne turned on his spotlight again and shined it down the aisle of the arcade they were in.

The crypt was divided between two arcades and a center aisle with a large space littered with various sarcophaguses all around. Special enclaves existed within the arcades and at the end of them were steps going into small nooks reserved for a single sarcophagus. At the end of the central aisle was a large enclave with a central sarcophagus. Behind this sarcophagus were five statues of church figures looking forward. Each figure was a part of the greater sculpture as they were stood in stone ogee archways that went upwards to a cross. Charlemagne looked at the nearest sarcophagus and saw a metal tag on the front of the sarcophagus – it was fairly new and looked as though it was placed in the last century or so. The words were in French, but stated the region the individual in the sarcophagus was born, the rough time period and then where they died and when. For example, the tomb before Charlemagne belonged to a man named 'Drusus Quintilius' from Ostia on the Italian peninsula.

"Excellent," Charlemagne remarked, dropping his backpack on the ground. "Help me open this tomb."

Charlemagne and Judith lifted the heavy sarcophagus lid and opened it in a manner so they could easily close it again. He brought his hands inside and removed a piece of bone from the corpse. He then went about with polishing, scraping off a sample, and then inserting the sample into a test tube. Once finished, he closed the sarcophagus and went to two more sarcophaguses which were clearly labeled with the names of Roman soldiers.

At the third corpse, Charlemagne began to close the lid and pick up his backpack again when Judith stopped him from walking by bringing her hand to his chest.

"What-" Charlemagne questioned.

"Shh," Judith responded, bringing a finger to his mouth.

The two paused and stood in silence of the crypt. Each of them could hear the chatter of two Frenchmen above. The chatter was met with the sounds of footsteps on stone as well as the sudden appearance of beams of light from the entranceway. Charlemagne quickly turned off his spotlight and backtracked to hide behind a sarcophagus as the iron gate creaked open.

"*Je ne vois personne ici*," a man complained.

"*Le vieil homme est fou*," the other replied. "*Regardons autour puis remontons.*"

Charlemagne edged himself to the corner of the sarcophagus and peaked around the corner. There, he spotted two men dressed in blue with duty belts sporting all sorts of equipment, each with baseball caps and ballistic vests overtop blue jackets. A tag on the right breast read, '*Police Municipal.*' The police officers walked forward.

"*Rechercher à droite et je vais rechercher à gauche.*"

Charlemagne's eyes focused on the iron gate, which they had closed. He then looked to the police officers as they split up with their lamps. He then hid his head and concentrated his back against the sarcophagus.

"There's two of them and they're going to search the room," Charlemagne whispered into Judith's ear. "Stay behind me and I'll get us out the way we came."

Charlemagne looked past Judith and over to the aisle between the sarcophagus behind them and the one next to it. A beam of light had just passed. Judith looked around her corner and then went back to Charlemagne.

"There'll be police in the church, surely," Judith remarked to him. "There's another stairwell across from where we entered – it'll probably go up outside."

"I don't know what's to the right of the church – I never checked when I did my research."

"Well, let's find out then," Judith remarked, removing her high heels and stuffing them in Charlemagne's backpack.

Charlemagne looked around his corner and saw the police officer shining his light into the arcade and making an approach towards them. He then leaned over to Judith and told her to move to the other sarcophagus. Judith crawled over with Charlemagne's backpack and then hid there. Charlemagne soon followed.

"I can make it to the end – they're both facing the other way," Judith whispered to Charlemagne.

"Go," Charlemagne affirmed, "I'll follow behind."

Judith stood up and quietly walked over to a column. She hid behind hit, turned her neck as Charlemagne went around the front side of the sarcophagus he was hiding behind as he saw the policeman approaching closer. Charlemagne focused on him as

Judith quietly and nimbly came to the end of the arcade before disappearing out of the crypt.

Charlemagne then turned back around the other side as he noticed the officer making his approach towards him with the other entering the arcade Judith was just in. Charlemagne quickly went around the other side of the sarcophagus he was at and down to the opposite end, going farther from where he needed to go. He kept his eye on the police officer on his side as well as keeping tabs on the other.

The officer closest began to investigate one of the enclaves, which prompted Charlemagne to jump from sarcophagus to sarcophagus, eventually reaching the midway point. The closer officer began to turn around and walk down the arcade, shining his light between the aisles of each sarcophagus as he walked. The other officer was investigating a separate room at the end of the opposite arcade. Charlemagne jumped to each sarcophagus at the other side of the room, eventually coming to the end with his back turned to the entrance.

Each officer finished what they were doing and were now preparing to come to the side Charlemagne was on. He couldn't go anywhere. Charlemagne hesitated and thought of hiding in the room at the end of the arcade, but the officer had already turned and a beam of light was coming down the aisle he needed to cross. Instead, Charlemagne picked up a rock on the ground and sat down. He then threw the rock towards the left and into the arcade, causing it to bounce and hit the rocky ground, setting off an echo in the room. Each officer's flashlights instantly trained on the location of the rock and they stopped for a moment before moving towards it.

"*Ça c'était quoi?*" an officer questioned.

"*Je ne sais pas,*" another responded.

Charlemagne looked down the aisle he previously needed to cross and the officer had walked away from it, letting Charlemagne go down to the end. In the police officer's disorientation, Charlemagne slipped towards the exit and then went up the spiral steps, crashing into Judith. Judith jumped and swiped a hand onto Charlemagne, but the two quickly recovered and rushed upwards to the ground level of the city.

"Let's get out of here," Charlemagne muttered, turning around and stopping as he saw a third police officer shining his light at the couple.

Charlemagne raised his hands and stopped. Judith followed.

"*Arrêtez*," the police officer said anyways. "*Que faites-vous ici?*"

Charlemagne grunted and then let out an exhale.

"*Attendez… vous êtes Charlemagne!*" the police officer noticed, scanning Charlemagne's appearance with his light. "*Que faites-vous ici, Monsieur Cabernet?*"

"*S'il vous plait, je ne suis pas ici à cause d'un crime,*" Charlemagne responded. "*Je suis seulement ici avec ma copine pour des raisons romantiques.*"

"*Le prêtre de cette église nous a appelés parce qu'il pensait que quelqu'un se mêlait de la fouille archéologique,*" the police officer responded. "*Je m'attendais à des vagabonds, mais à la place je vous ai trouvé.*"

"*S'il vous plait… ne nous arrêtez pas.*"

The police officer hesitated for a moment before sighing.

"*Vous avez dit de belles paroles à nous les policiers lors des manifestations… nous avons eu la vie dure entre les suicides et le stress quotidien que la France de Macron nous a donnés. S'il te plait, pars, mais ne nous abandonne jamais – les gens.*"

"*Bien sûr,*" Charlemagne replied, lowering his hands and nodding. "*Amitiés.*"

Charlemagne took Judith's hand and then left with her. They came to a wooden garage door and left by the wooden door on the side, coming to the street and looking both ways on the sidewalk before going down the street to return to the car. Judith hit Charlemagne in the side with a frown.

"Never again, Charles," Judith complained. "The stress of these adventures is not worth it…"

"Oh, come off it," Charlemagne remarked. "We've got a little bit to go towards the car, so let's not stop now that we've caught a big break."

"What did you say to him? What did he say to you?"

"He said he was thankful for what I said at the protests in regard to the police force and army," Charlemagne replied.

"Oh good, your insincere words at that protest have earned us a pass," Judith bitterly remarked.

"My words at that protest weren't insincere, my love," Charlemagne replied. "I meant everything I said to those people. He replied by saying my words meant something to him because the police have had it hard in recent years to the demands of the job in today's society – and from what I've seen since arriving here, I believe him."

The couple reached the street corner leading towards the front of the church and paused there. In front of the church were two police cars and another two police officers. Charlemagne took a step back with Judith and looked to her.

"We can't pass them with this backpack – it'll be too suspicious," Charlemagne complained.

"Well, abandon it and let's go," Judith replied in a strict voice. "Come on."

"I can't abandon it – if I do, then all of this will have been in vain!" Charlemagne argued with her, looking around before eyeing a car behind them.

Charlemagne went to the car, parked on the curb, and stuffed the backpack underneath and near a tire. He then stood up and went to Judith, presenting his arm.

"Right, shall we?" Charlemagne questioned.

Judith rolled her eyes and took his arm. The couple then walked down the sidewalk, along an alleyway and then crossed a street and then another street to reach the sidewalk furthest from the church. The couple continued to walk, passing the front of the church and police officers. The two of them avoided eye contact, but it wasn't enough.

"*Excusez-moi, mais arrêtez-vous la!*" a female officer ordered them.

Charlemagne turned to the officers with Judith and squinted at them.

"*Oui? Comment puis-je vous aider?*" Charlemagne questioned.

"*Oui, c'est lui,*" another officer remarked to his partner.

"*Vous êtes Charlemagne!*"

"*Oui, c'est moi,*" Charlemagne remarked, stepping forward and coming to the other side.

The front of the basilica had a small patio, which led to the parking lot on one side leading towards the park. Two steps dipped down and towards the rectangular doors of the church. On either side of the doors were statues of saintly figures in enclaves of the wall. Above the main doors were three arch-like windows that led up to a clock. At the top of the church was the tower. The structure was made of a similar stone to the rest of the buildings, and it was less than three stories at the central component and then five stories with the tower. All around the patio were concrete posts to prevent cars from driving overtop.

Charlemagne shook the hands of each officer and smiled.

"What are you doing in France, Mr. Cabernet?" an officer questioned.

"Oh, I'm here on business, but have been doing a little tour of all of France," Charlemagne explained. "I was in Brittany and also *Vals de Loire*, but now I'm here in Aquitaine – just a friendly visit with the girlfriend and kids…"

"Where are you going next?" the female officer questioned.

"Oh, I do not know yet," Charlemagne replied, coughing, "but tell me, what is going on here?"

"Oh, it is nothing – just a routine call for some trespassers. The priest who lives here said he heard some noises, so we have to check it out," the male officer answered.

"Oh dear, well, that sounds serious," Charlemagne responded, eyeing a group of hoodlums walking down the aisle ahead and approaching the intersection going towards the car he had hid his bag under. "I'll let you get back to work then…"

"Ah, but Mr. Cabernet, wait," the female officer remarked. "A picture, please…"

The doors of the church opened, and three officers appeared. One of which was the officer that had let Charlemagne and Judith go, while the other two were the ones below in the crypt.

"What is going on here?" the officer who had let them go asked.

"A picture, come, with Mr. Cabernet and his girlfriend," the officer remarked.

The other officers didn't say anything and instead crowded together to take a selfie with Charlemagne and Judith. Once the picture was finished, Charlemagne shook the hands of the other officers and then bid them farewell. He then took Judith's arm and continued to walk back to their car.

"I better not see that photo on social media…" Charlemagne grimaced.

"Oh hush," Judith responded, "you don't get to be mad – I'm mad."

"What are you mad about? You volunteered to come?" Charlemagne replied.

"Are you happy?" Judith asked.

"No," Charlemagne answered, "because of our rush, I missed out on sampling the entire room. All I got were Roman samples, but thanks for asking – we've now exhausted our ideas, which means I have to talk to Dr. Dumas again…"

"Oh, please, just drop all of this…"

Charlemagne ignored her as they reached the car. He opened the car door for Judith, let her in, and then went around to get to the driver's seat. He quickly started the car and then backed up to drive past the church one more time and go towards the alleyway he was at.

The teenagers had gone down the alleyway a fair distance when Charlemagne got out and went to the car he stashed his bag under. He then knelt down, grabbed his bag and went back to the car to toss it to Judith. He then closed the door and went off into the night without another word.

Act 3, Scene 3

Charlemagne stopped the car with Judith at his side along a small road within the large complex he had driven to. Wavy letters on a corner window to his right read '*Université Toulouse*' on one side and then '*Jean Jaures*' on the other. The buildings to his right were white, modern and new and the concrete pathway was clean and a light grey. Another structure was behind him on his right and across the from the former, divided by a pergola, or covered walkway, between the two. The latter structure was also modern but had shades of green in an eco-green design. There were bike racks in front of this building. On the left was a soccer field protected by a perimeter fence and behind Charlemagne on the left was a small plaza at the street corner, which was next to the soccer field on one end and a parking lot on the other. The parking lot was jampacked with cars. There were not many people walking around and it was half-past twelve o'clock according to the clock in the car. The day was bright, and the sun was shining down again.

"Right, you're here," Judith remarked, "now what?"

"Now, I find her," Charlemagne responded. "My dear, I need to ask something from you."

"What is it?" Judith questioned.

"Your final permission to step out of this car and search for her, Dr. Dumas's daughter," Charlemagne replied. "You see, Dr. Dumas' daughter... Manon Dumas, was my ex-girlfriend from over twenty years ago."

"And why would you need my permission to speak to her? Are you afraid of something?"

"Afraid? A little bit in regard to confronting her, but... it's complicated, and it wouldn't feel right if I didn't ask you before seeking her help," Charlemagne explained. "Please."

Judith rolled her eyes and crossed her arms.

"Do whatever you need to do, but keep me out of it, Charles," Judith replied. "I don't want to go on another adventure like we did in Bordeaux, so if she'll help you, then by all means."

"Thank you," Charlemagne said, smiling and taking her hand.

Charlemagne kissed Judith on the cheek and then opened the car door. She opened the opposite door and went around to take the driver's seat. Charlemagne, meanwhile, walked off towards the structure on the right. At the corner of the building was a map of the campus. Charlemagne walked to it, brought his fingers to where he was and then confirmed the location of the department of archeology to be right where he was. From where he was, Charlemagne walked down the right and entered the building. He walked down a corridor and started to pass through, seeing offices belonging to professors in the department of history. The corridor was simple, and walls only held portraits of former students from different years. Halfway, there was a reception desk alongside a small meeting room.

A stairwell at the end of the corridor led upwards to the second floor. Charlemagne entered and continued to walk through to the end, eyeing the names on each door belonging to the professors. He passed another reception desk and then came towards the end of the corridor. Charlemagne stopped in front of the last door, which had a plaque that read, 'Dr. Manon M. Dumas, Ph.D.' He brought a hand up to knock, but stopped himself halfway through, brought his arm down and then took a deep sigh. Charlemagne then knocked on the door with three hard knocks before waiting with a serious face.

No answer came from the door. Charlemagne took a step back and looked around. He then walked back and went to the reception desk where there was a woman on a computer.

"*Excusez-moi,*" Charlemagne stated, "*je cherche pour une vieille amie a moi – Dr. Dumas.*"

"*Est-elle dans son bureau?*" the woman asked.

"*Non,*" Charlemagne replied, "*est-ce qu'elle enseigne une classe?*"

"*Je peux vérifier pour vous,*" the woman responded. "*Quel est votre nom?*"

"*Charlemagne,*" Charlemagne answered, feeling nervous.

The woman looked on her computer and then turned to Charlemagne.

"*Elle est dans une classe en bas, salle mille*" the woman remarked. "*La class se termine dans dix minutes.*"

"*Pas le temps,*" Charlemagne said. "*J'y vais.*"

Charlemagne rushed down the hallway and came to the stairwell. He went downwards and then re-entered the ground floor, going towards the entrance, but turning to the left and reaching a set of double doors labeled, '*Salle 1000.*' Charlemagne stopped outside the doors and could hear the loud lecture of a female voice from within. He took another deep breath and then opened the doors, stepping into the vestibule and looking through the glass window of the doors to the sight of the lecture theater. He then opened the doors and entered through, stopping atop of a set of steps on the left aisle.

The lecture theater accommodated approximately one-hundred to two-hundred seats and sloped downwards with two screens on either side above chalkboards. The professor below was walking back and forth in a calm pace with her hands together. She also had a microphone clipped to the top of her black blouse. The woman stopped as Charlemagne entered and looked to him for a brief moment. Her face went pale, and she looked a little scared, but she quickly disregarded Charlemagne's presence to continue lecturing. Charlemagne took a seat in the nearest vacant seat and listened.

Manon had less fair skin than Judith as well as darker hair. Manon's hair was a sleek medium-brown and styled in an almost bob cut. Her hair was straight, and her cheeks were with rouge. She had eyeliner applied around the perimeter of her pointed eyes whose irises were blue in a colorful dark shade. She had a chiseled jawline and thin eyebrows. Her nose was straight and medium-sized. She spoke with a firm, Parisian accent.

"*En 395 après Jésus Christ*," Manon said, pointing to the projector screen with a laser pointer that displayed a slide with some text, "*Théodose ier mourut en tant que dernier empereur à gouverner un empire romain uni. Les fils et les successeurs de Théodose, Arcadius et Honorius, gouverneraient un empire divis entre est et oust, l'est demeurant sous l'empire byzantine. Aux mains de tribus germaniques, l'empire romain d'Ouest s'effondrerait au bout de cent ans. Ensuite, nous examinerons l'effondrement plus en détail, puis les séquelles de l'empire jusqu'a ce qu'il soit reconstitué en tant que Saint Empire romain germanique par le roi franc, Charlemagne...*"

Manon looked over to Charlemagne as she reached the end of the room and then turned around. She then looked straight ahead of her as she continued walking.

"*... dont le nom vient du vieux français Charles le Magne, ou en langage moderne, Charles le Grand. Bien sûr, il serait un grand personnage, qui dit quelque chose parce qu'il faudrait être un grand homme pour porter ce nom – pas un-ils de pute douteuse.*"

Manon looked over to Charlemagne again at the end of her sentence. She gave a mild glare before turning to her class and stopping at the center of the lecture hall.

"*Bon*," Manon remarked, smiling to her students, "*maintenant, c'est tout pour aujourd'hui. Assurez-vous de faire vos lectures et préparez-vous lors de votre prochaine classe pour parler des séquelles de l'empire romain.*"

Students proceeded to pack up their laptops, notebooks, and other items into their backpacks while Manon turned her back to pack up her things. Charlemagne stayed in his seat while others left. A few students went to the front to speak with Manon. She smiled as she spoke with them, but Charlemagne noticed her eyes point towards him even if for a millisecond. She went to each of them and then saw them off. Once they were gone, she went back to packing her things into her large handbag before bringing it around her shoulder and looking to Charlemagne with a sunken expression.

The two looked at each other for less than five seconds before Manon went off, using the opposite aisle steps to exit the lecture hall theater. Charlemagne allowed her to leave before he stood up. He then exited the lecture hall theater and intercepted Manon as she was about to pass him. She stopped in front of him and looked to him. Manon was approximately three inches shorter than Charlemagne. The top of her head reached his nose.

"*Puis-je t'aider?*" Manon questioned.

"*Oui*," Charlemagne responded, "*tu peux.* Manon... I need your help with something serious."

"Is that so?" Manon replied, walking past him, "what can be so serious that you would come and see me now?"

Charlemagne walked with her and went towards a set of elevators with her.

"I'm investigating my family history," Charlemagne explained, "and I've already seen your father before you tell me to go to him. I've been collecting genetic samples from the ancient people that have inhabited France in order to create a palette to pit my DNA against. With the help of your father, I've been to tombs in Brittany and Aquitaine, but I'm at a loss and have exhausted my sample pool."

"I assume you found Celtic people in Brittany, and what did you find in Aquitaine?" Manon questioned with slight interest.

The elevator dinged and the couple boarded.

"I found samples belonging to Roman legionnaires that served and were posted in Bordeaux," Charlemagne responded, "but I'm still missing samples before I take these samples out of the country to have them tested."

"Celts and Romans? What a waste of time, Charles – always wasting your time," Manon critiques, shaking her head.

Charlemagne flinched.

"What you needed to look for is Frankish samples," Manon explained, "the most likely explanation behind your genealogy is that you are descended from Franks."

"Franks?" Charlemagne questioned as the elevator door opened again.

"Yes, Franks," Manon said again, walking out with him and going over to her office. "Please don't pretend to not know who the Franks were."

"I know who the Franks were – the Germanic people who moved into the region during the collapse of the Roman Empire," Charlemagne responded, "but where do I look for samples?"

The two stopped outside of Manon's office.

"Samples? I know where you can find some good samples. I can take you there – the Toulouse Museum has various specimens from various excavations made over the years. It'll provide a good range of Frankish DNA for you to take home with you."

"You will help me then?" Charlemagne questioned as Manon turned to open her office door.

Manon didn't reply and instead opened the door. She then proceeded to walk in.

"I can leave in a bit and go with you – they won't let you in on your own, so you will need me to join you," Manon explained to him. "Are you okay to wait for a few minutes?"

"Yes," Charlemagne replied, "of course. I'm okay with waiting…"

Charlemagne then went quiet. The two looked at each other. Manon turned her head to face a computer monitor. She then pulled her chair and sat down. Charlemagne turned around and closed the door behind him. He then turned around to face Manon.

"Listen, Manon…" Charlemagne said with hesitation.

"Please, Charles, stop," Manon insisted, showing him her palm. "I do not want to hear this – the words that are about to come out of your mouth. Please…"

Charlemagne stopped and then nodded.

"I want to be clear with you, Charles," Manon remarked, turning to him with serious eyes, "If you have already gone to my father and he knows nothing more, then you being here means that you are desperate and that you truly do need my assistance. I will help you as who I am – a professional on the subject, but also for the sake of Derby who was so kind with me. He doesn't deserve to have his namesake slandered on television. You on the other hand…"

Manon shook her head and looked to her computer. She typed.

"I will help you, and afterwards, I do not want to see you ever again. Understood?" Manon asked.

"Yes," Charlemagne replied.

Act 3, Scene 4

"So, how long have you been with the University of Toulouse?" Charlemagne questioned, looking to Manon as she drove him through Toulouse.

Manon looked back at him with an unimpressed look before replying, "Since I left the University of Paris, which was almost twenty years ago…"

Charlemagne went silent in response. Manon drove Charlemagne from the university campus into the heart of Toulouse whose architecture was dominated by brick structures in a reddish-orange hue between three to four stories tall. The roofs were almost entirely terracotta tile roofs.

Charlemagne looked to Manon again.

"Do you like your work?" Charlemagne questioned. "From what I remember…"

"I enjoy it," Manon interrupted in a brute tone. "Between Paris and Toulouse, I have been a part of the oldest universities in all of Europe dating to almost a thousand years ago, which have contributed to a millennium of academic research and thought. I have no regrets in my decisions and have enjoyed every moment teaching about European history."

Charlemagne went silent again and looked away from Manon. Manon parked her car at the end of a street along the curb and then turned off the engine. Charlemagne and herself then got out of the car and looked forward to a promenade. Manon drove a red SUV.

From where Manon had parked, the two walked down the sidewalk and came to the promenade. There were various birch trees in the middle of the promenade and before the walkway were two separate structures on the left and right. On the left was a white structure with terracotta roofs and on the right was a red brick structure with the same type of roof, but also a colonnade entrance with a sign that read '*Theatre Sorano.*' Between the two structures was another colonnade with an iron gate fence. At either side of the gate were banners and signs for the Museum Toulouse. An entablature above the columns read, '*Jardin des Plantes.*'

Manon walked Charlemagne towards this direction and passed through the gates. The two then proceeded to walk down a stone path headed towards a park but made a detour on the right as they came to a modern refurbished portion of the structure with steel beams and columns and tinted glass windows. A café was on their right from where they had entered, and Manon went through, crossed through the café and came through an arch to enter a squared indoor plaza with an arcade around them.

The ground of the museum entrance was made of a smooth grey stone. In the middle was a lifelike sculpture of an elephant with tusks. On their right was a gift shop while on the left were reception and information desks. On the walls were large monitors that displayed images of various innovations, some particular to France, such as the automobile, stethoscopes, aspirin, the process of pasteurization, and others. Manon stopped in the plaza and rummaged through her purse, producing an ID tag, which she clipped to the bottom of her shirt. She then went around and through the ticket gate of the museum with Charlemagne, going down a corridor and then reaching a set of doors with a card reader. Manon took her ID and brought it to the card reader, causing a light to turn green and the click of a door unlocking. Manon then opened the door and entered with Charlemagne.

The duo had entered a service corridor, which went down and then came to a turn to the left before reaching a set of double doors. Manon brought her ID to another card reader, causing the doors to click open so they could continue and enter the collection storage area of the museum. The warehouse of the museum was long and shaped in a right triangle with the doors the couple had entered being at the sine angle with the hypotenuse being the wall that faced the outside on the right. This same wall had tall static shelves with props, lifelike animal sculptures and models, empty cages and display cases, and other miscellaneous items laying around. On the left were mobile shelves on tracks that went towards the adjacent wall perpendicular to the opposite wall, but parallel to the shelves. Each shelf had a valve on the lateral side, which allowed for the shelves to be moved along the tracks to provide access to the contents within. Along the opposite wall were further shelves, but these were split between thin drawers on the bottom with handles and open space above with more artefacts. The artefacts in the warehouse varied in size. Charlemagne could see that the smaller ones were kept on the static shelves on the opposite wall, while the larger ones, such as statues, ancient boats, furniture, and simple crates with artefacts inside were on the mobile shelves. At the end of the aisle at the cosine angle were a set of yellow doors with a sign above that read, '*Accès Restreint.*' Above them were bright lights hanging from the ceiling alongside vent tubes. There were no windows anywhere.

"I expect the bones are in these drawers over here then," Charlemagne said, pointing over to them.

Charlemagne walked over to the drawers and opened one, revealing a series of model fish inside. Charlemagne frowned as he saw the fish, closing the drawer to open the one below with another series of fish models.

"Well, this is a museum of natural history, so don't look too upset," Manon replied, walking further down the aisle and reading the tags on the drawers. "Here."

Manon pointed to a row of drawers at the further end of the aisle for Charlemagne to take a look at.

"We have Paleolithic, Neolithic, Levant, North Africa, Sub-Sahara…" Manon remarked listing off some of the locations and time frames, "however, no medieval or renaissance."

"Of course," Charlemagne replied, shaking his head, "why would they keep the bones of Franks over the bones of these foreign people?" he added in a sarcastic tone.

"What a shame," Manon said, walking down the aisle with Charlemagne. "I thought for sure we might have more samples than this."

Charlemagne stopped with her at the end of the aisle and then looked over to the yellow doors. He pointed to them.

"What's in there?"

"I don't know," Manon replied, shrugging. "Where are you going?"

Charlemagne had proceeded to walk down and towards the yellow doors.

"Well, if it is restricted, it probably means the more precious specimens are kept in there – not these knockoffs that can be easily stolen."

Manon didn't argue with him and walked to the end of the aisle with him. Charlemagne stopped in front of the door to wait for Manon. He looked at the card reader and then upwards to the CCTV camera pointed down the aisle they had walked. Manon brought her ID to the card reader, seeing its light turn green to provide them access. Charlemagne brought his hands to the doors and opened the heavy metal doors for them to pass through. On the other side of the doors was a simple elevator.

Charlemagne pressed the elevator call button and waited. The elevator doors soon opened and allowed them inside.

The space of the elevator was large. There was a CCTV camera in the corner of the elevator. The doors closed and Manon brought her ID to another card reader, which allowed them to go into the sublevel of the museum. The elevator went down and opened its doors again into another vestibule, but this time with glass doors and walls. Before them were white walls lit by bright LED lights. On either side were glass walls with further shelves inside individual rooms that contained a larger quantity of artefacts in greater diversity. The room was dark and as lights inside were off. Each individual room had a separate entranceway, vestibule, and sliding doors. There were also various CCTV cameras around, pointed in various angles. The corridor ahead of them was short, but in the middle was a four-point intersection.

Manon and Charlemagne entered the primary corridor and went to the first room on their left. Manon picked up a clipboard on the side of the wall and read the manifesto of items. She then set the clipboard back and turned to Charlemagne.

"Nothing," Manon stated, "we'll have to check each room until we find something."

"Let's split up and each take a side," Charlemagne responded. "We'll be faster that way."

Manon nodded and the two set off to check each side. Charlemagne took the right side and went to each room, turning right and going down a longer corridor with more rooms for him to search. He eventually reached the end and turned around to check the opposite side, looking into a room with various skeletons laid on platforms. Charlemagne looked at the manifesto and his face lit up. The top of the clipboard read, '*Bataille de Toulouse (844).*'

"Manon," Charlemagne shouted, waving over to her on the other side.

Manon put back the clipboard she was reading and then proceeded down the hall towards Charlemagne.

"Take a look," Charlemagne said, presenting her the clipboard. "Battle of Toulouse."

"Excellent," Manon reacted, putting the clipboard back.

Manon took her ID and presented it to the first door that led them into the vestibule. The card reader turned green and allowed them inside where there were boxes of white gloves for them on a stand alongside a door panel. Manon looked at the panel.

"It looks as though the room we are about to enter is devoid of oxygen in order to better preserve the specimens inside," Manon observed. "First, we need to fill the room with oxygen for us to breath before we enter."

Manon tapped at the panel, causing a whir of vents to begin to spin. Additionally, the lights inside the room turned on. The two of them stood in the vestibule for close to five minutes until the doors then opened on their own, allowing them to enter. The room had four platforms at the four sides of the room with bones laying atop. On the lateral walls of the room were drawers on one half and shelves atop with additional artefacts, including armor and weapons.

Charlemagne came to the first skeleton and knelt down. He dropped his backpack to the side and began to set off to work. Manon crossed her arms.

"What primitive tools," Manon critiqued, seeing Charlemagne's file. "Did you have nothing else to do this with? Not even a drill?"

"I had to purchase these at hardware stores – there wasn't really any time to make a special order online," Charlemagne remarked, looking to her.

Manon rolled her eyes and took a step forward.

"Do you have anymore? I assume you have more to avoid contaminating each sample. Give me some tools and I'll work on half – we can finish in half the time."

Charlemagne looked to her and then looked back at the specimen he was cleaning.

"There are more files in my backpack," Charlemagne replied.

Manon went to Charlemagne's backpack and took the tools she needed. She then went to her side and knelt down to set to work. Manon worked in silence much like Charlemagne, and they were indeed finished in half the time.

Once they were finished, Manon took off her gloves and stuffed them in her pocket. She then stood behind Charlemagne as he finished his last sample. Manon knelt down next to him and looked at the skeleton on the table. Charlemagne turned around to look at her before going back to work.

"What happened at the Battle of Toulouse?" Charlemagne questioned as he worked.

"Well, after the death of Charlemagne, as you know, his son… Louis the Pious, succeeded and had three sons. Once Louis died…"

Manon paused for a moment.

"Louis had three sons who fought a three-year civil war, which resulted in the Treaty of Verdun and divided the Frankish Empire into three regions. The Battle of Toulouse took place in the aftermath of the civil war as Charles the Bald, one of Louis' sons, sought to have his nephew, who ruled Aquitaine, submit to his rule. The Franks lost the battle and were forced to retreat."

"How tragic…"

"Hardly… the Vikings were a larger sore spot for the Franks than a little rebellion. The division of the empire and the constant Viking attacks resulted in the collapse of the Carolingian dynasty. Luckily, the legacy of Charlemagne, through his son, would continue through their descendent Hugh Capet and the Capetian dynasty, which would branch into the Valois and Bourbon house that would rule France as the Kingdom of France for three-hundred years."

Charlemagne looked at Manon and then back at his work. He had left bone shavings on a piece of wax paper. Charlemagne took the shavings and poured them into a vial. He then closed the test tube and cleaned up his station.

"You will need one more ethnic group," Manon stated. "One more group to complete your palette, then you must take these samples out of the country to have them tested with your own genes."

"What more?" Charlemagne questioned, looking to her. "I have Celtic, Roman, and Germanic DNA, but what more?"

"A control sample," Manon replied. "French DNA from a group of confirmed Frenchmen. Yes, France as a land was once occupied by Celts, then Romans, and finally the Franks who really shaped this country, but in order to prove your experiment works, you will need control samples to compare with yourself. I know exactly where to look as well, but it means I will need to come with you, take time off work, and travel to Marseille."

Charlemagne did not respond. He instead nodded and then looked to her. The lights in the room flickered, but the two ignored it as they looked at each other.

"Where in Marseilles? What would I find there?" Charlemagne questioned.

"Fort Saint-Jean," Manon explained. "I have access to the lower levels and have been asked multiple times to excavate the area but have not had the time. The forts were used by King Louis XVI during the French Revolution to house political prisoners, and then by the revolutionaries to house their own political prisoners. If you wish to find samples of royal and lay French people, then this will be your best option."

"Thank you," Charlemagne responded, closing his backpack. "Truly, I am in your debt."

"No, you're not," Manon replied. "Let us leave and we can speak more of this once we are out."

Charlemagne nodded and the two walked to leave, approaching the glass doors to the vestibule, but it did not open. Charlemagne took a step back from the door and then waved his hand at the motion sensor, but it did not trigger the door.

"Curious," Charlemagne responded, approaching the door to manually open it with his hands.

The door would not open despite the force he applied. He tried once more, but it wouldn't even open in the slightest amount.

"Oh dear," Charlemagne reacted, taking a step back and taking out his phone. "No signal."

"My God…" Manon cursed, "we are stuck…"

"No," Charlemagne denied, looking around the room. "I won't believe that we are stuck."

"In a room with minimal oxygen to breath… how long will that last before we go unconscious?"

Charlemagne stopped for a moment before looking to her.

"A room this large, two people, perhaps two to six hours…" Charlemagne replied, "assuming the oxygen ventilation system has also been affected."

The lights in the room soon went off, leaving them in slight darkness.

"Charles, we need to figure a way out of here," Manon demanded.

"Don't panic, I'm thinking," Charlemagne responded in a strict tone, continuing to look around.

Charlemagne picked up a hand axe from the artefact and tapped the blade into the shelf. It left a slight dent. He then brought it over to the glass and swung the axe at the glass, but all it did was leave a sharp mark in the hardened glass.

"Damn…" Charlemagne replied, dropping the axe.

Charlemagne proceeded to bang on the glass with his fists.

"Reinforced," Charlemagne determined before looking outwards to the corridor outside. "There's nothing here that can produce enough force to break this glass…"

Charlemagne was panting slightly. He closed his eyes and then banged his forehead on the glass. He then opened his eyes and looked forward to the room opposite where there was a mirror in one of the shelves. He then looked to his left where there was a CCTV camera.

"If only there was a way we could get into contact with security…" Charlemagne muttered, looking back to the mirror. "Even if I shined my flashlight, that wouldn't be enough to alert someone that might be watching…. A concentrated beam of light wouldn't be strong enough…"

Charlemagne looked over to Manon as she looked around the room with a nervous expression.

"Manon," Charles said, "do you have your laser pointer?"

"Yes," Manon replied, taking it out from her pocket. "Why? What are you thinking?"

Charlemagne walked over to her and took the laser pointer. He then shined a beam onto the floor, producing a green beam.

"I'm thinking that if I can point this in the right angles, I can redirect a beam to the CCTV camera over there," Charlemagne said, pointing to camera in front of the vestibule. "A normal flashlight on CCTV does little, especially one reflecting off a mirror or any other reflective surface. However, a laser is much more concentrated and deadlier to a lens. It'll surely grab the attention of the right people to come down here."

Charlemagne went to the glass and pointed the laser towards the mirror in the room opposite. He was able to redirect the light towards them, hitting behind them.

"Charles!" Manon complained, shielding her eyes, "you're going to blind us before you get anybody's help!"

"Sorry, you might want to cover your eyes as I figure out an appropriate angle," Charlemagne replied, adjusting his aim.

Charlemagne repositioned himself and pointed the laser towards the mirror again. He was able to get the beam to aim at the side of the vestibule, and from where he was it was only a matter of perfecting the trajectory until he could see the beam affecting the side of the CCTV camera dome.

"I've got it… now let's hope for our sake that someone is watching…"

Charlemagne continued to point the laser where he was for another couple of minutes until he heard a sound come from the outer corridor. He then turned off the laser and stood up, going to the wall to start banging it and shout. Manon joined him and looked to the appearance of two men dressed in black suits with earpieces. On of the men had dark brown hair, fair skin, and an unshaven beard while the other was Sub-Saharan with black hair. Upon seeing both Manon and Charlemagne, the security guards hurried to open the doors and let them out.

"*Merci beaucoup*," Charlemagne thanked upon exiting.

"*D'accord*," one of the guards replied.

Charlemagne explained to them what had happened. The one with fair skin examined the console in the vestibule while Charlemagne gave his story to the other. Upon the end of his story, the guard with fair skin turned to them.

"Apologies, Mr. Cabernet," he spoke in a thick accent, "but it looks like it was a small accident with the system."

"An accident?" Charlemagne questioned.

"Yes," the man replied. "A little accident, but the system is back to normal it seems."

"Has this happened before?" Manon then asked.

The two guards looked to each other and then to Manon and Charlemagne. They then each shook their head. Charlemagne cleared his throat and then thanked each guard. The two then set off to exit, not saying another word to each other until they returned to the car.

"Where am I taking you now?" Manon asked.

"My hotel, I suppose," Charlemagne replied. "Manon, you should know that I'm not alone on this trip – I came with three others. My girlfriend and two adopted children."

"I am aware," Manon replied, taking out a tissue from her purse to blow her nose. "I saw your award ceremony… they mentioned it."

Charlemagne nodded and then entered the car. Manon drove him to the hotel. There, he looked to her again.

"When can you come with us to Marseilles?" Charlemagne asked.

"I have to return to the university and make arrangements with the department head," Manon replied. "I might have to cancel a lecture if they cannot find a substitute, but I will come with you whenever you decide to leave – I assume that is soon."

"I would prefer to head off tomorrow," Charlemagne remarked. "Is that okay?"

"It is better – if we can finish this tomorrow, then I might not need to cancel anything at all," Manon remarked, looking into her purse, and producing a card and a pen.

Manon wrote on the back of the card and gave it to Charles.

"Here is my phone number. I will travel to Marseille in my own vehicle and meet you there tomorrow afternoon – say around one o'clock."

"Good," Charlemagne replied, taking the card.

"Good," she repeated, looking to him.

Charlemagne looked at her and then gave an anxious smile. Manon looked at him with flat face. His smile became more anxious, pushing him to exit from the car. Once he was out, Manon drove off and left him on the curb alone.

"Good," Charlemagne repeated to himself.

Act 4, Scene 1

"*Palais Longchamp,*" Charlemagne said, looking forward to the monument, "a celebration of the accomplishment of water."

"I don't believe water deserves to be celebrated," Judith grimaced, opening her umbrella as a light drizzle of rain began to unfold. "Where is this woman?"

Charlemagne and Judith stood in the middle of the Palais Longchamp, a monument built in the 19th century to celebrate the construction of a canal, which provided drinking water to the people of Marseille. Before them, below the middle of the hill they stood on, was a large brown artificial pond with a step waterfall in front of them going towards this pond. The pond had balustrades at the front with two thick, but short pillars with a feline animal of sort atop. The pillar was at the base of a large iron gate that connected to another short pillar with a horse. There were gates on either side of the pond and these gates led to causeways that wrapped around.

At the base of the causeway, at either side were a set of stairs that led upwards to the summit with balustrade beige stone railings. The stairs and summit wrapped around a natural pond behind the family, which had a cascade pouring from a large fountain statue similar to the one in Bordeaux, but with bulls instead of horses. The bulls surrounded three female figures, and behind this sculpture was a magnificent arch with two pillars at either side in front with two symmetrical statues of figures carrying wheat above them.

A colonnade curved outwards at either side of the archway and came to vaults that led into the buildings on either side, east and west of the park. Besides the fountain were various bushes and a bit of grass around the edges. The grass was separated from the causeway by a low-height rail with benches in front. At either side of the archway, before the colonnade, were smaller arches with balconies in front. Atop of these smaller arches were griffin statues facing east and west. In the center of the balconies were male figures sitting atop of rocks with a trumpet at their lips, looking upwards to the skies of Marseilles, of which were dark grey nimbostratus that covered the entirety of the atmosphere above. Diana and Tristan were in front of the statue with Diana taking pictures.

Charlemagne continued to stand where he was, looking outwards to the five-point intersection in front of the entrance of the monument. The architecture of Marseilles composed of beige walls in majority with terracotta orange ceiling tiles for roofs. There was an absence of dormer windows in Marseille as the roofs were flatter than the other cities. However, some of the structures were taller, with the largest in plain sight being up to seven floors. The entirety of the city held a southern European impression, and despite the current weather, it was warmer than other cities thus far.

"*Bonjour,*" Manon greeted next to Charlemagne.

Charlemagne turned and saw Manon next to him. She was wearing a dark brown double breasted overcoat with a purse in her other hand. Her face was much as it was yesterday with eyeliner at her eyes and blush at her cheeks. Judith turned to Manon and held a plain look. Manon held a neutral expression. Charlemagne cleared his throat and looked to Judith

"Judith, this is Dr. Dumas, my old friend that I told you about," Charlemagne said, "and Manon, this is Dr. Lambert."

"Hello," Manon greeted to her before looking to Charlemagne. "Where are the kids?"

"Over there," Charlemagne remarked, pointing towards the balcony.

Diana and Tristan had spotted Manon and proceeded to come down together. The two women looked at each other and neither extended their hands to shake the other. Judith simply clung to her purse with one hand and umbrella with the other as Charlemagne waited for the kids to arrive. Once there, Charlemagne turned to them.

"Manon, these are my adopted-children, Diana and Tristan."

"Hello," Manon greeted to them with a warm smile, "it's nice to see that Charlemagne has found some humility in his life."

"I told you this would be awkward," Tristan quietly said to Diana as the two arrived.

Charlemagne cleared his throat again.

"Anyways, Manon and I best be off to the Old Port now," Charlemagne remarked. "How about we see each other in that area around six o'clock for dinner? Is that okay?"

"That'll work," Judith replied, keeping her eyes fixated on Manon. "Take care and have fun."

"Yes, of course," Charlemagne responded, walking off with Manon and going down the causeway.

Judith kept her eyes on the two as they went downhill and then disappeared into the town. Meanwhile, Diana and Tristan looked at each other with awkward eyes.

"So…" Tristan said, breaking the silence, "what are we going to do?"

Judith gave a sigh.

"Well, what do you fancy?" Judith questioned, looking over to them. "We have five hours to spare before dinner and an entire ancient city around us."

The rain proceeded to worsen, requiring Tristan to bring his hood up from his raincoat.

"I don't imagine there's anywhere that isn't outdoors," Diana said, walking over to Judith to share the umbrella with her.

"How about a movie?" Tristan suggested. "There's an old cinema that Charles was telling me about, which is said to be one of the oldest in the world – we can go there and see a French film in hopes that this rain settles. Afterwards, we can visit the *Notre Dame de la Garde*, which is a church atop of a large hill that overlooks the city. You can take more pictures, Diana."

"Okay," Diana replied, smiling. "Is that okay?"

"Whatever you children prefer," Judith replied with a tame face. "How about we return to the car and set off for this cinema then."

The three of them left the monument and walked down the causeway. From there, they walked along the sidewalk to reach the family sedan parked on the curb. Diana and Tristan entered the back of the car and sat together while Judith got into the driver's seat. She turned on the engine of the car and set he GPS for the coordinates of this movie theater Tristan had told her about.

From there, they set off on a thirty minute drive through Marseille to reach the other side of a smaller town on the Mediterranean coast. The rain continued to pour down as she drove, reaching a marina with a large parking lot where she parked the car. The marine held a multitude of sailboats and was in front of a long seawall that stretched the coast of the city. The seawall had short balustrades that were less than three feet tall. The sidewalk of the boulevard they had reached was wide on either side with smooth beige stones. From the parking lot, they walked to the wide boulevard where there were palm trees on the sidelines with a simple two-story structure across.

The Eden Theatre was a small building with a simple patio courtyard with tables and chairs. The building was constructed out of yellow bricks with blue framed windows that were covered by opaque white curtains. The entrance of the building had a pediment atop. The roof was just as the other roofs in Marseille, an orange terracotta tiled roof. A thin annex next to the courtyard attached to the structure on the left with white doors and movie posters on either side. A neon sign above the doors said, 'Cinema' but was off. From across the street, the three of them reached the entrance of the theater.

Tristan looked to a plaque inside of the lobby that said the theater was constructed in 1889 and spoke of a man named *Louis Lumiere* who was a pioneer of cinematography. It also said that he cinema theater had approximately two-hundred-fifty seats and was refurbished in 2013. The lobby had white walls with an elevator immediately ahead of them. There were stairs to the right with the back of stairs going to the second floor on the left. A ticket booth was to their left.

The kids chose a random film with Judith, unable to decipher to surmise the plot of any of the films in showing, and Judith paid for the tickets. The two then walked up the set of stairs on the right and came to a small corridor with a set of stairs on the left going downwards and upwards. There were various movie posters on the wall of old films. In addition, there was a framed picture of the theater in its original state. The three of them walked up to the second floor and came to another corridor with various movie posters on the walls between rectangular white framed windows. Behind them were framed pictures of various unknown people in black and white. They looked as though they were actors or directors. At the end of the corridor were a set of two double doors at a slight angle.

Judith led them through the doors and onto the balcony of the main viewing theater where they chose their seats. The ambience of the theater was reddish with velvet curtains in front of the movie screen and red-painted walls.

"Is this fine or do you prefer to sit below?" Judith questioned.

"It's fine," Tristan replied.

Judith looked to Diana.

"It's fine," Diana affirmed.

The three of them sat down where they were and awaited the start of the film.

• •

Instead of playing advertisements like other movie theaters, the Eden Theater started with an educational film about the origins of the theater, which regurgitated much that was on the plaque downstairs. However, with an additional word on the origins of cinematography in France.

The three of them exited the theater after the credits of the film and stepped outside again. The rain had stopped, but it was still fairly cloudy outside. Judith drove them from the Eden Theater back into Marseilles and uphill to the parking lot at the base of the basilica. From where they parked, Tristan and Diana could see that the clouds had dissipated slightly and the sun was poking out and shining down. They walked towards a set of stairs that opened on either side, left or right and converged at a landing with more stairs going up towards the cathedral.

Tristan smiled as he walked up the stairs with Diana and Judith, but his smile faded slightly as he noticed the presence of men in green camouflage with green berets atop of their heads. The men were armed with assault rifles and were patrolling around the parking lot. Tristan let out a sigh and faced away from them.

The stairs reached another landing, which had a bridge that crossed over and spread out left and right with more steps that reached a third landing. The landing connected to stairs that ran parallel to the last set and converging at the final landing before the bell tower. Beneath the bell tower was a small arcade that broke off to the rest of the patio surrounding the church, left and right, with the front doors forward.

The Notre-Dame de la Garde was constructed in a striped fashion with beige and red bricks. At the side of the church were arches against the exterior walls that ran along with arched windows in the middle. Above the chancel was a domed belvedere with arched windows around. At the top of the dome was a cross.

The three of them followed along to the right, reaching low stone walls that guarded them from falling. There was a minor crowd of people outside. Diana and Tristan reached the edge of the patio and could look outwards towards the rest of the city below them. Marseille was a rocky and hilly area to the left, but on the right, it was a large space that stretched out around the coast and valley.

Diana took out her camera and proceeded to photograph the city. Once she was finished taking some shots, she switched modes to film the area, looking out to the coastal city to capture the moment as she stared at a fort at the mouth of the bay of the Vieux Port de Marseilles.

Act 4, Scene 2

Charlemagne and Manon stood at the battlements beneath the *Tour de Fanal* at Fort Saint-Jean. The fort was made of beige bricks and behind them was the squared base of the circular tower. At the middle of the tower were brackets all around with railings above. At the top of the tower were more railings and a dome.

From where the two of them were, they could look out to the Mediterranean Sea as well as the neighboring fort on the other side of the coast with rocky cliffs, to their left. Within the bay was a large marina of sailboats. In the horizon of the city the Notre-Dame de la Garde could be seen on a hill. On the right was a platform dock with a monstrous grey cube atop. The grey cube's surface was a mesh of metal-like capillaries. The cube was connected to the fort by an iron girder. Not too far in the distance, the *Cathédrale La Major* could be seen – a cathedral with two small bell towers with bell roofs at the front and a large belvedere dome with another bell tower at the top alongside a cross.

Charlemagne took a deep breath and looked to Manon. He smelt the smoke of meat being cooked from a nearby restaurant at the fort.

"So, they've turned this ancient site into a tourist attraction too," Charlemagne remarked, looking to Manon who had her arms crossed. "They've also added that ugly thing," he added, looking at the iron cube. "The Museum of European and Mediterranean Civilizations."

"Are you done?" Manon questioned. "I didn't drive five hours from Toulouse to admire the Mediterranean."

Charlemagne looked to Manon and then walked with her. They came to a clearing where there were garden boxes with people planting near them. The rain had stopped, but the skies were still grey. From where they had walked to, the iron girder was more visible for its large size as it came over the fort and hovered over the floor by less than a foot.

"Right," Charlemagne replied, sighing, "how foolish of me. Let's get to work then."

Manon produced a set of keys from her jacket and walked over to an iron gate. She unlocked the gate with a padlock, which Charlemagne observed with focused eyes. Once the gate was open, she allowed Charlemagne to go ahead of her before she entered and locked the gate behind her. She then put the keys away and the two entered a domed circular stairwell that went into the depths of the fort prison.

Within a couple of steps downwards, Charlemagne found himself producing his spotlight flashlights from his backpack and passing one to Manon. The two then guided themselves down the stairwell until they were at least twenty feet below and reached an archway tunnel. The tunnel was narrow and curved. Charlemagne noted that the tunnels had pipes running along the top with fire sprinklers pointed down.

Charlemagne and Manon walked around the curved tunnel and then came to a straight portion that went along for at least a couple of meters. At the end of the tunnel, on the left, was an exit into wider room with jail cells lined against the wall to the left and an aisle ran down the right-side, which the two followed to the end. The cells and space around them were devoid of any furniture. At the end, there was a small stairwell that led them upstairs to a curved corridor once more. At the end of this curved corridor, on the left was an archway exit that came to a circular room.

The room had a circular grate in the middle and a stairway that wrapped around the side of the room and went upwards into the Tour de Fanal. Light poured into the chamber from the above tower and down through the grate into the space below. On the opposite side of the stairs that wrapped around the wall, in the floor, was a wooden hatch. Charlemagne looked around the room, which was like the cells in the former room – devoid of furnishings outside of a random pipe or metal rod on the floor. The hatch in the floor had a metal circular handle engraved into it.

Charlemagne took the handle and opened it, revealing a ladder that went down into the depths of the chamber. Charlemagne went first and came to the bottom. Another archway tunnel, but this one slightly wider and taller, sprouted off from the circular chamber they were in. The ceiling was about average in the chamber, going towards the grate in the middle.

The two entered the corridor and found a modern fire exit doorway on the left with a fire exit sign above. Charlemagne pressed his hand against the door, but it wouldn't open. There was a card reader next to the door, similar to the one at the university. The two continued down the corridor, which was not a long distance, and reached the end where there was a rectangular crawlspace below. Charlemagne shined his light and then got down on his knees. He turned to Manon.

"I'll lead the way, shall I?" Charlemagne questioned.

Manon nodded and allowed him to go first. Charlemagne brought his lantern down and pushed it with him along the crawlspace until they reached the opposite side. The small tunnel led into a small corridor, which turned into a room with a two-meter wall going upwards. A rope had been cast down from the sloped wall already, and there was a sign on the left. The sign stated that further venture was forbidden by the Department of

Underwater and Underwater Archeological Research of the French Ministry of Culture.

"I'm sure that doesn't apply to us," Charlemagne remarked, going to the rope after putting his spotlight away. "Keep the light on for me."

Charlemagne proceeded to climb up the rope and to the top of the wall and landing above. He then took out his spotlight to give light to Manon as she climbed. Afterwards, the two looked behind them to the second crawlspace that went onwards into the fort. Charlemagne led the way and went through.

At the end of the crawlspace, Charlemagne entered a larger room that spread down with various cells on either side. The cells were smaller than the former ones they had seen. The room was not furnished either, although there were loose items left around, such as a hammer in one or bench in another. At the end of the aisle were a set of stairs that went down to a second level of cells. The ground on the second level was dustier and had more rubble. There were shackles attached to certain walls of the cells. Columns and beams had been knocked over, and a tunnel at the end of the aisle was caved in. There was also a corridor entrance on the immediate left from where they had entered. The two went down the aisles and Charlemagne spotted some loose bones on the ground. He went over to them and began to collect sample.

"I'll take it by the location of these bones, I'm most likely collecting noble DNA," Charlemagne remarked, setting off to work.

"How can you even be sure these are human bones?" Manon questioned in annoyance.

"I'll just have to find out," Charlemagne replied.

Once Charlemagne had finished collecting a sample, he stood up and continued into the other corridor on the immediate left from where they had entered. The tunnels led into separate rooms where some had barrels against the wall, tables, chairs, but another had an intricate device inside – a table set against the wall, but with leather cuffs on either side. At the opposite end of the room was a guillotine. Against the wall were shackles.

"I assume prisoners were tied to this table here and tortured…" Charlemagne noted.

"Execution as a practice was outlawed by King Louis XVI almost ten years before the revolution," Manon replied, "however, these were the laws of the monarchy and not of the republicans. Regardless, I assume they would have held the same standards as torture was seen as inhumane at this time."

Charlemagne exited the room and came to the end of the corridor, which led to additional tunnels that went along the fort. The two went on and came to an intersection. At both ends of the tunnels, rubble had caved in and blocked off the rest of the archeological site. Charlemagne shined his light at one end and then at the other – there were some steps going up to the rubble of the latter. Charlemagne followed and came to the end, noting the damage to the walls, but also a small gap above.

"I wouldn't be surprised if these cave ins were caused by the war – the Old Port suffered a lot because of the war," Manon noted.

"Perhaps," Charlemagne simply replied, "I believe I can get in here."

Manon did not reply and simply watched as Charlemagne climbed up and then crawled through the hole. He came to a rubble-filled crawlspace, but pushed through to come to the end, reaching a strange room on the other side.

The tunnels on the other side were wider and larger but covered with skulls and other human bones. It was similar to the catacombs of Paris.

"What do you see?" Manon shouted.

"Bones…" Charlemagne simply replied. "Lots of bones."

Charlemagne proceeded to go down without her, but within less than two minutes, Manon had joined him.

"The extent of the deaths of the revolution…" Manon remarked, looking around with reverence.

Charlemagne reached the end of the corridor, which continued into another corridor. There, there was a pillar with a skeleton attached. Below read a sign with faded writing, 'Mort aux traitress.' Charlemagne broke off a piece of the skeleton and proceeded to clean it. Manon passed him and continued along. Once he was finished, he went onwards to catch up to her. She had arrived at a room with coffins inside. The coffins were simple, wooden and held nothing more. Charlemagne walked over to one to open.

The coffins had been nailed closed, requiring a lot of force to open. Manon helped him and together they opened the sealed casket of skeletons dressed in rags with a scarf around the neck and a black hat. Charlemagne took a sample of the bone and polished it. He did so with each casket, and once he was done, he gave a deep sigh.

"Let's get going," Charlemagne said to Manon as she finished her sample.

Manon handed him the test tube, and he put it in his backpack alongside any remaining rubbish they had produced. Once they were certain to leave, they went the way they came, through the catacombs, the tunnels, and the prison-space to reach the crawlspaces.

Once at the other side of the crawlspace leading to the rope and wall, Charlemagne noted that the rope had been cut down and left on the floor. He frowned at it and looked at the single-story jump down. He then looked to Manon.

"I'll help you down," Charlemagne said, offering his hand.

Manon took it, and the two sat down at the side of the wall. Charlemagne then held on as Manon lowered herself, causing Charlemagne to come to his stomach as he helped her down. Once she was on the ground, Charlemagne repositioned himself to sit and then slid down, crashing into the floor on his side, but rolling his landing. Manon helped him from off the ground, and the two then carried on, exiting the unexplored portion of the fort to come to the short corridor before the circular chamber.

Manon led the way forward, climbing up the ladder to the hatch, and trying to open it. She was unable to get the hatch to open.

"It's stuck," Manon complained.

"How can it be stuck?" Charlemagne questioned.

Manon looked to him and dropped down to give him space. Charlemagne then attempted to open the hatch, but it wouldn't open.

"Another technical glitch?" Manon asked him.

Charlemagne didn't reply and instead looked around.

"I've had about enough of this," Charlemagne instead said. "I don't have time for this rubbish. Do you still smoke?"

"Yes, why?" Manon questioned, taking out her lighter and box of cigarettes from her purse.

"Well, you should quit then," Charlemagne replied, taking the lighter. "It's a filthy habit."

Charlemagne walked over and picked up a stick. He then turned to Manon who gave him a handkerchief from her purse. He wrapped it around the top of the stick and then lit it. Charlemagne then walked into the tunnel and raised the fire stick towards the sprinkler, which was out of reach for him to manually activate.

"What are you doing?" Manon questioned. "Are you trying to kill us?"

"No, I'm trying to get this fire exit to activate," Charlemagne responded, settling Manon. "I'm not having this foolishness from whomever is trying to prank me."

Charlemagne held the torch over the sprinkler for another minute before it set off, spraying Charlemagne with brown, murky water before turning to clear substance. Upon being sprayed, Charlemagne shook himself and then walked over to the door to open it. The door wouldn't open. Charlemagne continued to try opening the door, increasing his use of force until he then smashed his body into it with rage. A puddle had begun to form on the floor in the minute that passed.

"Excellent job, you imbecile!" Manon critiqued. "What now?"

Charlemagne looked to her and then walked over to the chamber. There was nothing there for them to use. He then went back into the corridor and noticed that the crawlspace was now out of sight due to the flooding that had transpired. Charlemagne looked over to the end of the corridor and then back into the chamber.

"Well?" Manon questioned to him. "What now?"

"I don't know!" Charlemagne yelled at her. "I'm thinking!"

"Well, think faster," Manon replied. "What's the matter with you?"

Charlemagne noticed the water to be ankle high at the moment.

"There's nothing here to use!" Charlemagne argued, going to the fire exit door and bashing his body into it. "It's no use."

Charlemagne then returned to the chamber and climbed up the ladder. He bashed his hands into the wooden hatch, but it wouldn't give. Manon looked at him with crossed arms.

"Excellent work," Manon said in a sarcastic tone, "now we can become a part of the archeological dig."

"Don't give me that tone! I'm doing more than you have at this point – all you've offered are snide remarks and sarcasm!"

Manon pushed him back.

"Do not talk to me in that way, Charlemagne," Manon warned. "You are not forgiven for what you had done to me – I will *never* forgive you!"

Charlemagne flinched at her words. He took a step back and turned away from Manon who had turned her own back to him. The water was now at their knees. Charlemagne looked down at the ground and then over to the hatch. He walked into the corridor and was near the sprinkler when he looked to Manon who appeared to be hurt.

"We're going to die here," Manon remarked in a saddened tone. "Your idiocy has seen to that…"

Charlemagne looked to her as he picked up the wooden stick on the ground. Either he saw a tear stroll down Manon's cheek, or it was a drop of water. Charlemagne took the stick and attempted to poke the sprinkler with it to turn off the water. Charlemagne's meddling with the sprinkler caused the pipe to shake before breaking loose. The flow of water increased. Charlemagne tossed the wooden stick aside and then laid his side against the wall, hitting his head into the stone bricks. The water was at his hips now, but the spray of water separated the two to be alone. Charlemagne went to the hatch again and proceeded to attempt to open it forcibly. However, to no success. By the time he climbed down the ladder, the water was at his abdomen. Charlemagne went to the fire exit.

"Charles," Manon said, looking over to him and stepping closer, "if we are going to die here…"

"We're not going to die here," Charlemagne replied. "I'm still thinking."

"If we are, you need to know…" Manon said, taking a deep breath and taking his hand.

Charlemagne turned to face her with a sunken look.

"You have a son," Manon stated.

Charlemagne's face dropped into shock.

"What?" Charlemagne simply responded.

"I was pregnant in the last days of our relationship – I didn't know until the morning of our anniversary. I planned to tell you on our date, but…"

"I never showed up…" Charlemagne said, swallowing his breath and turning to the side.

"I'm sorry, I should have told you long ago, but… you abandoned me. You left me… you didn't say anything, and you never tried to say another word to me."

"Did you abort?" Charlemagne questioned next, looking to her.

"No," Manon replied, "I gave birth, Charles, to a beautiful baby boy," she described, taking his hand, "and he had hair like yours and eyes like mine. He was the dearest little boy… I named him *Louis*. The day I handed him to be adopted was a worse pain than the pain you had made me feel that night atop of the Eiffel Tower…" she said to him. "It's a pain that cannot be forgiven."

Charlemagne looked to her intently.

"It's a pain that I don't deserve to be forgiven for…" Charlemagne said as she brought a hand to his cheeks.

Charlemagne took her hand at his cheek with his. The water was now reaching his torso.

"Like *Louis* the Pious… son of Charlemagne…" Charlemagne said in a quiet tone.

"Or Pepin, your great-grandfather, and Derby *Martel* and *Charles Martel.*"

"*Martel...*" Charlemagne whispered. "Mart... *Marteaux.* Hammer!" Charlemagne shouted, letting go. "Stay here."

"Where are you going?" Manon questioned.

"We are *not* going to die here," Charlemagne assured her, taking off his backpack and going off with his spotlight. "Wait here."

Charlemagne took a deep breath and plunged into the water. He then swam through the crawlspace and reached the other side. He came to the top of the water, threw his spotlight flashlight up and then jumped out to grab the top of the wall. Charlemagne pulled himself up and then with his flashlight, crawled through to the other side. Once in the prison, he rushed to grab a hammer to take with him. The water had risen another half foot in the time it took, but Charlemagne took the hammer to the trapdoor and bashed it through, smashing the wood for them to climb up and out. The wood smashing was heard with the cling of hollow metal.

Once at the top, each of them sat down to take a break. Charlemagne eyed the metal rod he had seen earlier, which had moved from where it was. He kept his eyes on this piece of metal with intent and serious eyes as he panted and recovered.

Act 4, Scene 3

Later in the evening, Charlemagne, Judith, and the kids were driven in a taxicab through Marseilles and along a to the causeway in front of the *Gare de Marseille-Saint Charles*, a train station in the city. The front of the station had two arches with brown French window doors going into the structure and another two arches on the right of brown framed windows that only reflected outwards. To the right of the entrance were tables with benches to sit. Above the entrance was a rooftop that went along to a clerestory with rectangular windows in the similar manner to the ones on the ground floor. The walls of the train station were made of a smooth beige stone, lighter than the floor. The weather was dismal in Marseilles with grey clouds lingering above and the beige stone brick floor wet from the rain that had fallen earlier in the day.

Charlemagne paid the cab fare while the kids and Judith got out to retrieve their luggage. Once Charlemagne had paid, he joined them to take his luggage and close the trunk of the cab to step onto the pedestrian walkway. The four of them moved forward to stand near the exterior wall of the train station next to the door. There, Charlemagne looked around and then pointed over to a pair of elevators on the island past the causeway for drop-off and pickup. The elevator doors opened with Manon stepping out with her own luggage rolling behind her.

"Charles, why is she coming with us?" Judith questioned with slight distaste.

"Dr. Schneider is Manon's colleague, and he is doing us a favor by processing my samples," Charlemagne responded, "between that, and the probability that her life is in as much danger as mine, she needs to come with us."

Manon crossed the street and rendezvoused with the others.

"Good morning," Charlemagne greeted. "Ready to go?"

"Yes," Manon replied in a timid tone, "I parked my car downstairs for the week and informed the university that I will be on leave for the rest of the week."

"Good," Charlemagne responded, "I returned our rented car and took a cab here. Hopefully, we won't be followed into Germany."

Once the five of them were set, they walked into the train station. At the immediate corridor from the entrance doors, on the right, there was a small coffee shop. Ahead was an entranceway into the main body of the train station, and above this entranceway were screens displaying arrival and departure times with a clock in the middle. The clock displayed the time to be roughly a quarter past seven o'clock. The five of them continued and came into the main space of the train station.

The Marseille-Saint-Charles Train Station was large with a triangular ceiling with certain transparent areas that allowed natural light to flood in. The walls behind and ahead had arched windows on the middle level and rectangular windows above. On the wall to the left were arched windows on the ground level in an arcade. In the space ahead were some ticket machines, and beyond this space was a corridor going towards some shops. On the immediate right, against the wall behind the coffee shop were ticket machines and a long aisle platform next to a parked train. At the end of the aisle, at that side of the train station, it was open to the outdoors.

Charlemagne went to a ticket machine with the kids and Judith and proceeded to purchase tickets going to Aachen. He was about to purchase five tickets when he noticed Manon ahead at another machine purchasing her own. Once the tickets were bought, Charlemagne regrouped with her to go present their tickets at the ticket gate, which was a simple podium with an attendant dressed in a red suit with a red officer cap. The five of them passed the booth and went forward down the platform.

The train was already parked next to the platform with various porters dressed in blue bellhop suits moving cargo and luggage. The train was red colored with dark gold grooves and rims around. It had a traditional aspect attached to it, and on the side, was its name, 'Occitanie-Alpes-Rhin Orient Express.' Some staff members, including a chef, were stood outside of the train and greeted them as they passed. Charlemagne brought them to a guard, or conductor, outside of an open door going into a vestibule. He was dressed in a black suit with a black vest and an insignia on the breast pocket. The conductor greeted them, and Charlemagne presented their tickets to him. He took the tickets into his white-gloved hand and then looked at a tablet with him. He refreshed the list on his tablet and then ticked them off.

"*Bienvenue*, Monsieur Cabernet," the man greeted, stretching his arm out and pointing it towards the entrance. "*Nous pouvons prendre vos bagages et les apporter à votre chambre.*"

"*Merci*," Charlemagne responded, taking two keys from the conductor.

The conductor signaled a couple of porters to come and take their luggage from them. The conductor then moved out of the way to allow for the four of them to board before attending to Manon. Charlemagne allowed the others forward while he turned around to look at Manon.

"*Bienvenue, Docteur Dumas*," the conductor greeted, stretching his arm just as he did with the others.

Manon let the porters take her luggage before she went onto the train and followed Charlemagne. Diana and Tristan led the way into a tight corridor with compartments, reaching their assigned compartment and opening the door. The compartment was small and had a cabinet to the right with glasses. The sofa couch on the left had a small table before the window with a lamp. There was a flat screen TV on the wall in front of the couch.

Charlemagne turned around and noticed that he had lost track of Manon. The kids entered the compartment, which drew Judith and Charlemagne to go forward along. The next car over was a lounge of some sort with a bar in the corner, piano in the other corner, and various sofas around with tables with coasters. The two passed this room and went into the next car, which had bedrooms. Charlemagne unlocked the first bedroom and entered a spacious room with two train windows looking out. There were bunkbeds on the right. The beds of each bunk were large. There was a desk on the left-side and a lounge chair next to it. The room had access to a small bathroom. Charlemagne closed the door and came to the next room.

The next room was a suite with a single king-sized bed on the left. On the immediate left was a sofa in front of a table with an armchair on the other side. A large portrait of a train hung over the sofa. On the left was a large shutter door leading into a large bathroom.

"Well, isn't this nice," Judith remarked. "Shall we go look at the bar? Perhaps have a drink?"

"Uh - well, I suppose that would be alright," Charlemagne replied, taking a deep sigh. "It's been a long day after all."

The train whistle went off. The cars began to move.

"Sure, let's go have a drink and enjoy the scenery as we leave – it wouldn't be worth the experience if we didn't admire the scenery and instead slept," Charlemagne said. "I can also go and give the kids their key."

Act 4, Scene 4

Charlemagne and Judith sat at a table in the dining car of the train. Four hours had passed since the start of the train ride and it was now late into the night. Each of them had an empty wine glass and sat across from each other at the inner-most chairs. The tables were set up with white cloths, lamps, and four seats, two on each side. The car was empty besides them. Charlemagne looked out the window on his left and held a pensive, but also saddened look on his face. Judith was looking at herself in a portable mirror that she put back into her purse. She then stood up.

"Well, I believe it's time to call it a day," Judith said, standing up. "What do you say?"

"In a minute," Charlemagne replied, "I have some stuff I have to do before I turn in."

"I'll see you in bed then," Judith responded, grabbing her purse and then leaving.

Charlemagne continued to sit where he was for another five minutes before standing up and leaving. He passed through the three cars behind, which all had compartments. Charlemagne then entered the lounge car with the bar and then came to the sleeping car with the bedroom. He stopped at the kids' bedroom and knocked on the door. He then opened the bedroom door and saw that the room was empty. Charlemagne closed the door and walked back towards the compartment, coming to their designated compartment and sliding open the translucent door.

Diana and Tristan were sat on the couch with Manon between them. Manon had a tablet in her hand and was talking to the kids. Each of them looked to Charlemagne. He noticed that both the kids had faint smiles on their faces.

"Sorry, I didn't mean to interrupt," Charlemagne remarked, putting his hands in his pocket. "What's going on here?"

"Manon was just—"

Tristan stopped from finishing as Diana and Manon looked at him.

"About trains," Diana said, finishing his sentence. "She was telling us about how the French invented trains."

"Interesting concept..." Charlemagne responded, smirking, "but the French didn't invent trains. The English did."

"Ah, but luxury trains were invented by the French," Manon replied, setting her tablet on her lap. "Georges Nagelmackers was a Frenchman."

"Belgian," Charlemagne corrected.

"Walloonian," Manon corrected. "The Walloon are as French as you or me, Charles."

"So, you believe I am French?" Charlemagne asked.

"I never said that I did not," Manon responded.

Charlemagne went quiet. He nodded before looking out into the corridor. He then looked over to the kids.

"Children, will you please give me and Manon a moment alone? We have to debrief about some things we discovered at the fort today..."

Tristan looked over to Diana. The two then quietly stood up and left. Charlemagne closed the door behind him and then looked over to Manon and sat next to her.

"Are you okay?" Charlemagne asked, looking over to her.

"I'm fine."

"Are you not shaken up?"

"No, are you?" Manon replied.

"Someone tried to kill us," Charlemagne explained. "Are you not in the least scared?"

"Of course, I am," Manon responded, slightly annoyed. "Is this what you wanted to talk about? How I am feeling? When did you ever care about how I felt?"

Charlemagne rolled his eyes and sighed.

"I wanted to actually talk about our son," Charlemagne replied in a hushed voice. "I have questions."

Manon sighed. She put her tablet to the side and then crossed her arms.

"What do you want to know about him?" Manon asked. "Where he is? Who adopted him? All I can say to that is that I have not seen him since I gave birth and do not know who adopted him."

"When was he born?" Charlemagne asked.

Manon sighed and said, "September 11 of the same year you left me."

"I didn't leave you," Charlemagne corrected. "I mean, I did, but..."

"What? What excuse do you have for abandoning the two of us?"

"I didn't know I was abandoning you, or even the both of you – I- I had to be in Switzerland – I thought you would have understood?"

"I thought you would have understood by that time too– that I loved you, that you loved me. You didn't. All you cared about was yourself. What was *so* important in Switzerland that you felt the need to leave me?"

Charlemagne went quiet again and gave another sigh.

"Judith," Charlemagne responded, "it was her research team and they were making a pinnacle discovery at the time – the creation of anti-matter – the first of its kind, or so we thought. I thought they would have won a Nobel Prize for their discovery, but for as much as I supported and kept tabs on our research team, I never kept tabs on the rest of the scientific community who had beaten us, but it was not in vain. By her research at the time, we made an important step towards the fusion reactor."

"I hope it was worth it all," Manon simply said.

Charlemagne turned his head and then shook it.

"It wasn't," Charlemagne remarked, looking up. "I came to hold a deep regret – almost two years ago, I came down with a deep depression because I was truly not happy. Some enjoy lives of pleasure and fall in the same holes, but I enjoyed a life of discovery and curiosity and received the same. It was only when I realized what was really wrong, that I wanted to be a father and have children, that my life changed for the better, but it was not the matter of *having* children and *being* a father. I am a man that enjoys discovery, and although one day I might die, the enjoyment I have had in the last year or two have not been in having the children around, but in seeing them live, experience, laugh, and learn. To be their mentors and their guardians – to train them and share in the joys of life – that it is what has made me also happy and given me the resolve to know that when the time comes, I might be able to die happy when my work with them is done."

Manon didn't reply. Charlemagne turned around to face away from her.

"I could have realized that earlier," Charlemagne also said, "had I not abandoned you and our son. We could have shared in this joy together, to have raised our own son in this manner and have been a healthy family."

"Please, Charles, don't hold regret in that," Manon replied. "Diana and Tristan are remarkable children and deserve you – even if you are an ass. Over the last twenty years, what has helped me cope is the thought that although what has happened, happened as it did, our son is alive and healthy with a couple who love him. You also cannot be certain that our lives would be as you imagine. Yes, our son is apart from us, but you have had a second chance, a second life. How can you hold regret with what you have now?"

"How can you be so sure that our son is well?" Charlemagne asked her.

"I have faith."

Each of them went silent for a moment. Charlemagne gave a long sigh and then turned back around.

"Does your father know? Does Jacques know?" Charlemagne questioned.

"No," Manon denied, shaking her head, "not another soul is aware of this fact."

"Shouldn't he know?"

"Are you crazy?" Manon reacted, standing up. "If you tell him, he will never speak to you ever again and hold me with a great shame for giving up the child – I didn't tell him because I didn't want him to lament for the fact that he never met his grandson."

Charlemagne nodded and then turned to the door as he heard a knock. Charlemagne could see a figure on the other side. He walked over to the door and opened it in a rushed manner, looking out and looking with widened eyes as he saw the man before him who grabbed him by his throat and picked him up. The stranger then walked forward with Charlemagne in his grasp.

"*Mon Dieu!*" Manon cursed, standing up and backing away.

The mysterious stranger was approximately six feet four inches tall. He wore a black-brown Sherpa coat with brown wool alongside a combat vest with various gear. He also wore black-brown trousers with kneepads and additional gear at his pockets. At his feet were black boots that gave him an extra two inches in height in the least. Over his face was a black gas mask, leaving only his green eyes exposed to Charlemagne with a hint of fair skin. At the top of his head was a black combat helmet. His hands were gloved.

Manon immediately took something from her purse and then sprayed the man in the sockets of his gas mask, clouding it with the bear mace liquid. The mysterious stranger let go of Charlemagne. Charlemagne immediately followed Manon out of the compartment and down the corridor to escape to the lounge car. Charlemagne closed the door behind them and then ran forward. They stopped in front of the bar and then looked to each other in agreement. The two vaulted over the bar and hid behind the counter-top.

The car door opened and then closed. Charlemagne listened to the sound of heavy boot stomps as the mysterious stranger walked across. Charlemagne peaked around the corner and saw the man wielding an assault rifle and walking with careful steps. He made it to the opposite-side of the car and opened the door. The mysterious stranger then left, letting Charlemagne and Manon stand up and look to each other.

"What is going on?" Manon questioned. "Who is that?"

"I have no idea," Charlemagne responded, "but whoever that is, they want me dead. Go as far as you can and wait for the rest of us. We can't stay here and need to stop this train. I have to go after the kids – wait there, understood?"

"Yes," Manon replied, nodding.

The two split up with Charlemagne returning to the bar to arm himself with ice picks and a bottle of wine. He tied a cloth around the neck of the bottle and then placed it in his jacket. He then went after the mysterious stranger with haste. Charlemagne slowed his pace down as he entered the sleeping car. He hid around the corner and looked forward to where the man had stacked at the side of the children's bedroom door. He knocked on the door, triggering Charlemagne to go forward with the ice picks in hand. The door opened and Charlemagne stabbed the ice picks into the shoulders of the mysterious stranger, causing him to yell out.

The mysterious stranger turned around and hit Charlemagne with the butt of the assault rifle. He fell onto the ground while Tristan looked out to who was there and immediately went forward to tackle him. Tristan pushed the man into the glass window, causing it to shatter and for the assault rifle to drop to the floor. Diana ran forward for the rifle, grabbed it, and then snuck towards Charlemagne. The mysterious stranger recovered from Tristan's tackle and then knocked him onto the ground. Diana pointed the assault rifle at the mysterious man, but Charlemagne took the weapon off of her and moved himself in front of her.

"Get to the front of the train where Manon is," Charlemagne ordered, readying the weapon while the mysterious stranger pulled the ice picks out from his shoulders.

"Let us help!" Tristan insisted.

"Go!" Charlemagne shouted in a harsh tone at them.

Diana helped Tristan onto his feet and the couple then left. The mysterious stranger rushed forward and placed his hand onto the barrel of the assault rifle, tipping it up as Charlemagne opened fire. The rifle shot into the roof. The man pushed Charlemagne back while Charlemagne kicked him. Judith exited from the suite, still dressed and looked down at what was going on. Charlemagne pointed the rifle towards the mysterious man, which forced him to turn back, grab Judith, and pull a pistol from a holster at his leg.

"Oh my God! Charles!" Judith shouted. "Help!"

"Let her go!" Charlemagne demanded.

The mysterious man didn't reply. Instead, he simply breathed from his mask, breathing out with panted breaths. Charlemagne looked at the man and began to weaken his grip. He stood up from where he was and gently lowered the rifle onto the ground, but before he could place it onto the ground, the train came to a sudden stop.

Both Judith and the mysterious stranger fell forward towards Charlemagne who crashed into the back of the train car. Charlemagne threw the weapon at the man and then grabbed Judith's hand. The two then went into the lounge car, the compartment cars, and then through the dining car to escape. At the end of the dining car, Manon was with the kids. She held the car door open as Charlemagne arrived. He pushed Judith forward.

"Go on!" Charlemagne demanded. "Get out of here!"

"What about you?" Manon questioned.

"I'll be right behind you – I'll need to slow him down, however."

Charlemagne produced the wine bottle from his jacket as well as Manon's lighter from earlier. The others vacated from the car while Charlemagne waited patiently with the wine bottle and lighter in hand. The door soon opened and the mysterious stranger entered. At that point, Charlemagne threw the bottle and made direct contact with the man, igniting him into a burst of flames. Charlemagne then withdrew from the car and stepped out onto the grass next to the rail.

Act 5, Scene 1

From where the train had stopped, the five of them ran off into the darkness, reaching a road, which they followed for twenty minutes to come to a small town in the middle of nowhere. Charlemagne's first sight within the town was an old church along the main road, so he went there.

The church did not appear like any of the ones they had seen so far. For a start, it's exterior was constructed out of grey stone bricks with arches at the door. The main body of the church was rectangular with buttresses along the side to support the middle structure, which included a circular window above the main entrance. Above the main structure was a small bell tower with arched slits and a pointed roof with a cross atop. At the corner of the middle structure were circular towers with coned roofs.

Charlemagne knocked on the door before pushing it open. He then led the others inside and closed the door behind him.

"Charles, what are we doing here?" Judith questioned.

"What else?" Charlemagne replied. "We need to hide – and right now, I'm not too confident using my credit card only so this fiend can find us in a hotel to murder us in our sleep!"

Judith went silent and simply groaned. She took out her phone, but the battery was dead.

"Damn," Judith cursed, sitting down. "What then?"

"We'll need to sleep," Charlemagne responded. "This church is our sanctuary for the night – even if it is a protestant one."

"How can you tell?" Diana questioned.

"I saw a sign outside," Charlemagne simply replied. "Come now, each to a bench. I'll look for some sort of blanket we can use – perhaps find some heaters."

Early next morning, Tristan woke up to the sound of Manon and Charlemagne talking. He sat up on his bench and looked over to the front pew where Charlemagne was knelt over.

"I couldn't sleep," Charlemagne answered Manon, "not after what had happened yesterday."

"Nobody was hurt in the least…" Manon remarked.

"Since when did you become an optimist?" Charlemagne questioned her.

"Since when did you become a Christian? Or religious for that matter?" Manon asked.

Charlemagne sat onto the pew and looked forward.

"I had an interesting experience at the end of last summer…" Charlemagne replied, "probably one of the most bizarre, but profound experiences. I can't tell you the details, partly because you wouldn't believe me, but it threw me in a rollercoaster of emotions. The principle ones being fright as well as ease. You and me – the world is bigger than it seems, and there are truly things out there that one cannot expect. I should have known this myself, but there are lots in the world we do not understand. It doesn't mean we can't explain, but it means that there is simply lots that we do not understand and have yet to explain. It was a combination of this experience last summer, which made me feel humble, and the influence of Diana that pushed me. She had myself and Tristan attend Mass every Sunday at our local parish since last May. We're a Catholic family."

"Incredible," Manon simply said.

Charlemagne looked to her. Manon shrugged.

"I'm shocked," she said as well.

"You were one to believe that people change," Charlemagne said to her.

"You taught me that people don't change, but that they shed their skins."

Charlemagne shrugged this time. Manon sat down next to him.

"Where did you go?" Charlemagne asked in reference to Manon leaving the church a couple of minutes ago. "Earlier?"

"I stepped out for a smoke, some fresh air, and to see where you had taken us," Manon replied. "We're in France, near the Swiss border based on a travel sign nearby. Sainte-Blaise in Upper Savoy to be more specific, and only a drive away from Geneva."

"Good," Charlemagne replied, nodding. "We can take refuge in Switzerland. I need to make some phone calls and let my people know what's happened."

"Why do you need to phone 'your people?'" Manon questioned, closing her purse.

"Last summer, I was in Egypt and ran into a lot of trouble – there's an American company known as Zimmerman Corps. whose CEO manipulated me into finding an artefact for him. Two winters ago, I was in Russia on a simple family vacation. Both times, these mercenaries working for Zimmerman threatened myself and the kids. I had my people work on putting together a team of my own mercenaries to protect me, the kids, and all those dear to me. It's an off-branch to our current security force – my own paramilitary. First, I need to talk to my own CEO and ask him if they're ready, if they can get into France, and how fast they can come protect us. I won't let that man come after us again – I won't let anything happen to you or the kids."

Manon nodded to him.

"You know, Switzerland was a refuge for protestants and revolutionaries during the reformation and the French Revolution," Manon said, looking ahead to the altar.

"Interesting that you bring up two different revolutions," Charlemagne replied.

"They're not so different and influenced each other," Manon stated. "The independent thought and rule from the Church, and the independent thought and rule from the king."

"Interesting…" Charlemagne responded.

"If you wish, we can use my credit card to find a better place to stay in Geneva – I don't think I can sleep in a church again tonight," Manon offered. "If you think this assassin is targeting you... or has access to your credit card information."

Charlemagne nodded to her.

"Perhaps not the assassin, but whoever is employing this assassin – whoever that may be. Thank you regardless," Charlemagne said, "but I will reimburse you – including the ticket for the express, which reminds me – I also need to make a phone call to have our luggage brought somewhere for pickup, especially since I left all our research behind."

"Do not worry about your research," Manon replied, opening her purse to show Charlemagne what was inside. "I have it – in case something would happen."

Charlemagne looked at the vials inside her purse. He then smiled to Manon.

"Thank you," Charlemagne said to her.

Manon closed her purse.

"I am going phone us a taxi to take us to Geneva," Manon said. "Stay here."

Charlemagne nodded and allowed Manon to leave outside. Once he heard the door close, looked forward to the altar and cross above it. Charlemagne then stood up and went down the aisle to leave as well.

··

Manon phoned a taxi to pick them up from Saint-Blaise and take them to Geneva. The car ride from the small town they were in was less than thirty minutes but included a scenic view of the French and Swiss countryside at the base of the Alps; the Alps of which could be seen in the horizon with snow-capped peaks.

The architecture of Geneva was similar to Paris with seven story apartments, some with flat roofs, others with sloped roofs. The colors of the buildings ranged from beige to white and crème. The taxi crossed a low bridge along Lake Leman, or Lake Geneva by the locals, which viewed out to the large body of water with mountains in the distance. The bridge had simple rails with the Swiss flag flying on poles attached.

The car turned left and came down a quiet lakeside street. The car then pulled into the curb of the street in front of the entrance of a five-story building with a pediment at the top of the middle half where the main entrance was. The front door had a man in a black suit with an officer cap greeting people. The doors inside were also revolving doors and came into a regal interior. Manon checked in at the front desk while the others stood behind a simple table in the middle of the foyer with a vase filled with purple flowers in the middle. The floor was marble and the walls were white.

Once in his room, Charlemagne went for the phone and proceeded to contact Richard Huxley. He sat at a desk in his room. The room was formal and had a clean, pressed king-sized bed with white covers. The floor was a grey carpet and at either side of the bed were beige end tables with white lampshade lamps. In front of the bed was an armchair, and immediately in front was a desk against the wall. The room had two windows that looked out with grey curtains. The kids' room was similar but had two beds. Manon's room only had one like Charlemagne and Judith's.

Charlemagne sat at the desk as the phone rang.

"Hello?" Huxley answered.

"Richard, this is Charles," Charlemagne responded.

"Oh, Charles, how's the trip in France? Where are you now?"

"I'm in Geneva," Charlemagne answered.

"Geneva? What are you doing there?"

"There's been an incident – two, possibly three incidents..." Charlemagne said to him in a distressed manner. "Listen..."

Charlemagne proceeded to tell Richard of his adventure since Toulouse. Once he was finished, there was a pause.

"What do you need from me?" Richard asked.

"I need you to do me a favor – I need you to have Protection Squad activated at once. Get into contact with Henry Heavner so that he can rally the mercenaries as soon as possible. I want a small platoon deployed and spread out to protect every board member, department head – anyone of high target, including Allodia."

"Are you sure? If the moles find out that these mercenaries are armed with more than their wit, but with firearms and other weaponry, there could be serious repercussions for Cabernet Industries."

"We have no choice – an attempt on my life has been made and with the current rhetoric surrounding my family, I won't have anyone get hurt."

"Very well, Charles," Richard responded. "I'll get into contact with Henry. Be careful until then – the earliest I can promise them to appear is two days from now."

"I'll hold out here in Switzerland until then," Charlemagne replied.

"Please, Charles, while you are there, try to petition the Canadian consulate, Swiss government, or even the United Nations to help you – anything."

"I'll speak with some contacts in those departments to see if they can help, but I doubt it – I have suspicion that these same people might be behind this assassin."

"Okay... I'll get on it."

Charlemagne put down the phone. He then looked to Judith who was frowning at him.

"You're going to talk to the Global Defense Project?" Judith questioned him.

"I have to ask Ms. Black if she will help us," Charlemagne replied, "assuming her masters haven't given us a death sentence."

"Don't be ridiculous," Judith responded, "of course she will help us. We helped her – she owes us."

"I don't think Ms. Black is a believer in that sort of thing," Charlemagne replied, dialing another number. "I'm going to see about having our luggage brought to us now."

"Good – I'd hate to have to wear this for another couple of hours," Judith complained.

Once Charlemagne had finished speaking with customer service, he hung up and sighed. He then went for a shower and returned to the room, dressed in the same clothes. He then heard a knock on the door and went to answer it. Judith was sat in the armchair, looking outside.

Charlemagne opened the door and saw Manon on the other side.

"Charles," Manon remarked, "I have something to tell you."

"What is it?" Charlemagne asked.

"My father," she replied, "he was attacked in his home yesterday – by a group of thugs."

"What? Who? Why?" Charlemagne questioned.

"I'm not sure," Manon responded, "but what if it is related?"

"It's possible... it's very possible..."

Charlemagne told Manon about the journalist that was spying on him as he spoke with Dr. Dumas. He also went on to tell her about how he had contacted his people and that he was going to go talk to some contacts in the Canadian consulate before going to the Swiss government and then the United Nations if need be.

"Let me come with you," Manon suggested, pausing to look over to Judith, "if you are going alone."

"No, that's alright. You can come," Charlemagne responded, turning around. "Judith, would you mind keeping an eye on the children? I don't want them to wander without adult supervision – if you can, don't let them leave the hotel until I return."

"Certainly, Charles," Judith replied, looking over to him from the magazine she was reading. "I'll keep both eyes on them."

Act 5, Scene 2

Tristan woke up dressed and atop of the bed in his and Diana's bedroom. Diana lay next to him. Tristan sat up and then left the bedroom to go into the bathroom. The bathroom had another window on the left and a shower immediately ahead of him. To the immediate left was a bathtub. The shower was large and had glass walls. Next to the shower were counter tops with a sink and mirror. Tristan took a shower and redressed himself in the same clothes he came in. He then entered the bathroom where Diana was sat on the bed, lying on her side.

"What's up?" Tristan asked.

"I don't like how Charles talked to me last night," Diana replied. "It felt… strange."

"He told us to get out of harm's way. He did what he had to do to avoid us getting hurt."

"I could have helped him," Diana argued.

Tristan looked at Diana and then went over to sit next to her.

"Let's go out for a bit and get some fresh air. I had a nap, feel refreshed, and we have a whole day to spend in beautiful Switzerland," Tristan encouraged. "Come on."

Tristan helped Diana onto her feet. The couple then left their room and went down to Charlemagne and Judith's. He knocked on the door.

"Come in," Judith claimed from inside.

Tristan opened the door and looked over to Judith who was still sat on the armchair, but with her feet up on a footrest.

"What's up?" Judith questioned, flipping through her magazine.

"Where's Charles?" Tristan asked.

"Charles went out," Judith replied. "He left me in charge."

"We want to go out – for a bit to get some fresh air," Diana requested. "Is that okay?"

Judith sighed and then said, "I'm sorry, Diana, but Charlemagne asked that we remained here until further notice after what happened last night. I don't want to upset him anymore than he is."

Diana looked to Tristan. The two then let out weak sighs.

"It's alright," Diana replied, "I understand."

"Alternatively, this hotel does have a rooftop swimming pool nearby," Judith pointed out. "There's also a boutique downstairs. Charles only said that you couldn't leave the hotel – he never said anything about exploring the hotel and enjoying your stay. There's lots here for one to not go mad… in the least. I might go get a massage later if you care to join me."

"Maybe later," Diana replied, smiling and looking at Tristan. "I have some money Charles gave me – so do you. We can buy some swimsuits, right?"

"Yeah," Tristan replied, "let's do it."

Diana and Tristan closed the bedroom door and then left to go downstairs to the lobby. They went to a shop attached to the hotel and looked at the clothing in search of swimwear. Diana looked at the options between a one-piece suit and a bikini in various designs. She checked the price tags of various articles and noticed prices to be in two different currencies, euros and francs. She picked up a two-piece swimsuit to bring a price tag to Tristan's attention.

"I think Switzerland uses francs," Tristan replied to her. "I don't think they're in the eurozone. Franc used to be French currency before the euro."

"Do they take euros?" Diana questioned in a hushed tone. "If not, we're screwed."

"I don't think they'd show prices in euros if they didn't take euros," Tristan assured her. "Now help me find a swimsuit because I'm having a hard time."

Diana looked at Tristan's options, which ranged from jammers and briefs to short boxers in different intricate designs. She chose a cyan pair for him and the two then went to pay. They then returned to their room to get changed before adventuring towards the swimming pool on the same level.

The indoor swimming pool was rectangular with a sun roof above it. The water was raised above the marble floor from where they had entered and there was a low glass wall between the water and floor. On the left was the pool and on the right was a hardwood floor with lounge chairs looking out to the lake and rest of the city through sloped windows. On the left were a set of marble stairs that went upwards to a portion where one could either go in the pool or go into the hot tub, which was situated in a nook. At the end of the marble pathway from the entrance was a steam room.

Diana and Tristan were the only ones in the room at the moment. Diana sat down at the side of the pool and waved her hand in the warm water. Meanwhile, Tristan sat on the side of the hot tub as he looked down to Diana before looking towards the view.

"Well, this isn't ideal, but at least we get a view of the city to accommodate for the fact that we can't go out," Tristan said. "Although I'm not sure how that makes up for almost being killed."

"You know, I'm starting to notice what you meant about Judith behaving stricter towards you," Diana replied, changing the subject. "She kind of changed tones when she was talking – it makes me uncomfortable."

Tristan turned to face Diana.

"Relax, she probably either doesn't like me because I'm a hick who refused to allow her to give me my travel vaccinations, or because I'm a dude – either way, I don't really care."

Diana smiled to him and then turned to face the water. She fell into it and then maintained herself, floating and then swimming forward a bit. Tristan looked at her with a quaint smile. Diana suddenly stopped and froze entirely. She struggled in her place and fell into the water, attempting to keep her head above to breath. She screamed.

"Diana!" Tristan shouted, standing up and jumping into the water.

Tristan shouted in pain as his skin touched the water. A violent vibration overtook his body. He grabbed ahold of the glass pane next to him and stretched out his other hand to grab Diana, pulling her towards him.

Tristan took a deep breath as he came to and held Diana close to him. The couple quickly got out of the water and crawled away from the edge of the pool with held hands. The two panted and looked at the water before them – the clear water with only slight ripples from their recent movement out. The room was calm outside of them panting.

"What the hell was that?" Diana questioned, looking to Tristan.

"I think someone just tried to electrocute us," Tristan responded, looking back at her.

• •

Charlemagne and Manon exited the visitor entrance into the United Nations headquarters and came to a clearing next to car gates. The two walked down the clearing to reach the street. Charlemagne brought a hand to his forehead, tilted his head down, and then closed his eyes. Manon brought a hand on his back.

"It's going to be okay," Manon assured him.

"Why am I surprised that they denied our request? Why am I surprised that all of them denied our requests?" Charlemagne questioned.

"They don't want to associate with you because of your ideals," Manon assured him.

"Of course," Charlemagne replied, "some want me dead because of my ideals…"

The two proceeded to walk down the sidewalk, crossing the causeway headed towards the entrance gates. Charlemagne looked over to the *Palais de Nations*, the UN HQ. The main body of the headquarters had five tall pane glass windows like columns at the main entrance with the organization name and logo in English and French. The complex then spread out form the rear into different departments and annexes. The front of the UN consisted of parking spaces while the rear consisted of clearings of grass, which were part of the *Parc de l'Ariana*.

"What an outrage… after all I've done for them," Charlemagne muttered.

"You spoke against the President of France…" Manon replied.

"I spoke for the people!" Charlemagne shouted to her.

Manon stopped walking and looked at him. Charlemagne looked at her.

"Sorry," Charlemagne replied, "I'm sorry, it's not your fault. I- I'm just having a rough month."

The two continued to walk.

"If these politicians gave a damn about their respective people, the world would be a better place," Charlemagne said to

Manon. "Instead, they stand idle as they permit the replacement of the European people."

"So, you believe in it then," Manon replied.

Charlemagne sighed.

"I've had a long trip here in France, have talked to a lot of people, and seen what I was previously blind to – I was just like the elites. I hid in my palace…"

Manon smiled to Charlemagne and said in a soft voice, "You're nothing like the politicians, Charles. You are a populist – a man of the people."

"I care about people," Charlemagne affirmed her. "I care about my people more though. She is my family, and these elites invite strangers into my family's homes and treat the original inhabitants as the problem. Do you think this is how it was during the French Revolution? Three hundred years ago, Robespierre and all the revolutionaries claimed to have spoken for the people, claimed to have been populists and doing what they did for the sake of the people, but look at what has become of the liberal world. Human rights and laws have torn this world into a dystopian vision, and it'll only get worse, much worse…"

"I cannot say, because I cannot place myself in the hearts of these men, but if I had to guess, I would say that they were not selfless – they were middle-class men looking for their own power and influence. Have you ever heard the thesis that compares the French Revolution with the Russian Revolution – two bloody revolutions resulting in two governing systems based on economics?"

"No," Charlemagne replied, "but do tell."

"The French Revolution operated in a similar fashion to the Russian one with the distinct difference of a civil war since France was not a multi-ethnic empire like Russia. The Jacobins has commissars who enforced what was politically correct at the time, they brutally terrorized and persecuted all who disagreed with them in reigns of terrors, granted, the Russian persecutions were larger and worse, but then came the dictatorships – Stalin and Napoleon. Haven't you ever thought it was curious that George Orwell named the pig based off of Stalin, Napoleon?"

Charlemagne did not say anything to Manon. He instead looked aside and then back to her.

"Are you comparing Stalin to Napoleon?" Charlemagne asked.

"Not in the manner you are assuming, but only on a general level – Napoleon was not a sociopath, but a great general who made great mistakes, but regretted them. He was a sentimental man, whereas Stalin was a monster. The point is that they were both dictators, and on a trivial level, two dictators that conquered much of Europe."

Charlemagne and Manon returned to the hotel from the Palace of Nations. The two separated and went to each of their bedrooms. He stepped inside and sat down on the bed. Judith then exited from the bathroom in a bathrobe.

"Ah, Charles, how did it go?" Judith questioned, sitting down. "Any good news?"

"No, it went horrible," Charlemagne replied, staring ahead of him.

"Well, I have some good news…" Judith remarked, opening a magazine she had been reading. "Take a look."

Judith presented the magazine to Charlemagne who looked at her.

"I don't have my reading glasses, my dear," Charlemagne said. "Please, tell me what you've found."

"Well, there's this chateau, or mansion, in Burgundy that apparently used to belong to a noble French family that sprung up during the Napoleonic Era. The article, written by a professor from U.S. wrote it in defence of you," Judith said. "He claims that the Cabernet family may have had Norman origins and originally been known as the 'Cataret' family, changing it to Cabernet during their migration from France after the defeat of Napoleon in 1815. The Cataret family owned a chateau in the Forest of Chaux, which has since been abandoned by the noble family who have been thought to be extinct as there are living relatives, but the house has been preserved as a heritage site."

"Interesting…" Charlemagne simply replied.

"Charles," Judith said with a smile, "we can put all of this madness to rest if you go there. All of this tragedy… we can put it behind us and go home. Imagine that!"

"I suppose it is a small stop from here to Aachen…" Charlemagne agreed, scratching his head. "I don't suppose it'll hurt. I'll call Richard and tell him to have the Protection Squad meet us there."

Charlemagne turned his head as he saw the door open with the kids standing there in bathing suits. Each of them looked terrified and frightened. Charlemagne frowned at them.

"What's going on?" Charlemagne questioned, standing up and going to them. "What happened?"

"Someone tried to electrocute us," Diana simply said to him. "We almost died."

Act 5, Scene 3

The five of them rode a taxi into the Forest of Chaux in the province of Burgundy. The road the taxi drove along was narrow and surrounded by dense deciduous trees. The morale in the car was low as everybody held sunken looks of defeat and slight paranoia. The taxi driver was a Sub-Saharan who had driven them from Geneva for almost a couple hours. Charlemagne had promised him double in cash.

The taxi continued to drive along a winded road before stopping in front of a set of open gates that looked forward to a house at the end of a causeway on the other side. The end of the causeway surrounded a fountain in front of the mansion, which was split between two wings from the main entrance. Each wing was symmetrical to each other with three Versailles windows on the ground floor, balcony above with four columns and windows behind belonging to the second and third floor. The mansard rooftop had dormer windows. The main entrance had simple steps that went towards the main door. On either side of the main doors were columns with statues above.

"Is this it?" the cab driver asked, looking to Charlemagne as he squinted.

"I believe so, but… there a bunch of cars parked at the front of that home."

Charlemagne turned around to look at Judith.

"Sorry, I forgot to mention, but the chateau is hosting a fashion show this weekend starting today – minor inconvenience, but I thought it might provide a distraction for you to go and investigate while I enjoy something."

Charlemagne looked at her with an annoyed face and said, "An excellent idea, but you seem to have left out the fact that there'll be increased security who might prevent me from going into the sections of the house I want to go."

Charlemagne then looked to the cab driver and had him drive to the front of the house. On their approach, he could see a parking lot on the right-side with various vehicles parked. He paid the driver once they were in the front of the house and saw him off. The five of them then walked up the steps, going through the open main doors, and entering the lobby of the mansion. The lobby had a wide staircase immediately ahead with arches on either side leading further inside. On the left and right were additional arches, with the left-side blocked off by security. The right-side seemed to lead into a bar of sort with tables and people drinking. There were approximately two dozen people inside, behind a velvet rope that separated the five of them from the others. There was a loud techno beat of music. The room was also darkened with opaque curtains blocking light from outside and lamps lighting the room from the corners.

"*Puis-je vous avoir des invitations, s'il vous plait?*" the bouncer asked, presenting the palm of his hand.

"*Uh… je suis désole, mais je n'ai pas d'invitations,*" Charlemagne replied. "*Savez-vous qui je suis?*"

"*Je regrette, mais sans invitations, je ne peux pas vous laisser entrer,*" the bouncer reasoned, bringing his hands together and in front of him.

Tristan looked to the side as he spotted a familiar face walking towards them. The man in question was Audric Zimmerman with a cane in his right-hand and dressed in a black suit with a handkerchief in his breast pocket. The top button of his white shirt was unbuttoned, exposing slight chest hair and he was slightly unshaven since the last time they had seen him in Egypt. His brown-black hair was longer as well, but he still appeared to be as young as and defined as he was.

"Well, well," Zimmerman remarked, stopping before the five behind the velvet rope. "It's been a long time, hasn't it? Fancy meeting you all, here. Charles, you don't look too happy to see me."

Charlemagne held a frown and crossed arms as he replied, "How can I? The last time we saw each other, you tried to kill me."

Zimmerman gave a nervous laugh and replied, "What do you mean?"

"Egypt?" Charlemagne questioned.

"Oh, that's right... please, don't let that bother you – it's in the past, isn't it? Besides, I wasn't trying to kill you... I was just trying to get you to help me, help you."

Charlemagne was unimpressed with Zimmerman's excuse.

"Anyhow, who is this friend of yours?" Zimmerman questioned, looking to Manon and shaking her hand. "Audric Zimmerman, pleasure to meet you."

"Dr. Manon Dumas," Manon replied.

"Oh, right," Zimmerman replied. "I've heard about you – what are the five of you doing at Castle Cataret? Here for the fashion?"

"Hardly..." Charlemagne muttered.

"As a matter of fact, Mr. Zimmerman, we are," Judith replied, launching an elbow into Charlemagne's side, "but it appears that we are not on the guest list."

"Oh, that must be a mistake – *garçon*, can't you see these five are my friends?" Zimmerman questioned, looking to the bouncers. "*Mec, ce sont mes amis.*"

"*Je suis désole, Monsieur Zimmerman,*" the bouncer replied, opening the velvet gate for them and allowing them to enter.

"Come, I have front row seats to see my beautiful Vineri on the runway," Zimmerman boasted. "Come."

The five of them walked through the gate and came into the side of the lobby with the rest of the people. Zimmerman brought them through the archway on the right-side, through the reception where there were people surrounding cubes and enjoying drinks. He led them through another archway on the left, entering a large ballroom in the middle of the house. An arcade surrounded the room, supporting a balcony on the second floor that looked down to the center where the runway was.

No models were currently walking the runway, but there was a minor crowd of people sitting down around the walkway. A façade stood at the start of the runway, going around so that half of the room was blocked off. Security guards stood at the halfway points of the arcade, blocking off these sectors. Zimmerman walked them past and brought them behind the scenes. He led them into the left wing of the mansion where there were various makeup desks set up in a room with models brushing up.

Zimmerman stopped at the start of the door and searched around.

"What a shame," Zimmerman remarked, "I can't seem to see my precious anywhere. Let me bring you some seats then – the show will begin soon, and we'll see her then."

Zimmerman led them out from the back of the room and into the main ballroom. There, he stopped and had them sit down at front row seats right next to the runway. Zimmerman sat next to Judith who was between her and Manon. Tristan and Diana sat next to each other with Tristan next to Manon.

"Tell me, what brings you all together in France?" Zimmerman questioned.

"It's confidential," Charlemagne responded, "but I assume you've seen the news."

"Yes, I have – quite the performance and reaction, Charles," Zimmerman replied, keeping his attention at the runway in anticipation. "I'm impressed even if I don't agree with the things you said, but let's not talk about politics. How are the kids?"

"They're fine," Charlemagne replied.

"I don't want to hear that – I want to know what they've been up to, what they're planning on doing after high school," Zimmerman replied, turning to them and then to Charlemagne.

"Please, don't antagonize him," Judith said to Charlemagne, defending Zimmerman. "He's just trying to be friendly to us."

Charlemagne sighed and then looked to Zimmerman.

"The kids are fine," Charlemagne repeated. "Tristan is doing well in school, although, we've had some thoughts about perhaps transferring Diana to a private school to give her some more opportunities to grow. The decision hasn't been finalized yet, however."

"Does Diana want to go to a private school?" Zimmerman questioned. "Does she want to be separated from Tristan?"

"Well, I haven't talked to her, but…"

"Diana wants to be independent and on her own," Judith interjected. "She told me herself – she wants to leave."

"What does Diana want to do after high school?" Zimmerman asked. "You know, from what I know about Diana, I could see nursing to be a good fit."

"I don't think Diana would appreciate nursing. She simply hasn't decided yet," Charlemagne said, "which is why we hope private school might help her decide."

"No," Zimmerman rejected, "it won't. If Diana hasn't decided on what she wants to do after her time living with Charles, then she won't decide on her own at a private school where others will constantly influence her. What's best for Diana is that she remains in Allabrese so that she can continue to grow, mature and then decide for herself what fits her. The kids of today are too easily manipulated in urban centers – Diana will only be corrupted into a useless profession like… a liberal arts scholar or politician… Don't let her waste her potential."

The volume of the techno beat rose. The lights in the room darkened. A dense fog arose from the entrance onto the catwalk and the first model took her steps onto the runway floor. She wore a white dress that flushed out to give her a triangular or cone-like appearance. She wore white stockings and high-heel shoes and had black hair.

"What on Earth is that?" Charlemagne remarked in distaste.

"It's in style," Zimmerman replied. "*À la mode!*"

Charlemagne continued to sit with the others as he watched the models stroll down the catwalk. He continued to watch before becoming bored and disinterested. He looked around and saw there was a large crowd of people sat around. Charlemagne decided to stand up.

"Where are you going?" Zimmerman questioned.

"I'm just going to the washroom," Charlemagne replied, "I'll be back."

Charlemagne brought himself out from the audience and returned to the arcade surrounding the ballroom. He then slipped past a security guard with his back turned to view the models and disappeared into the backstage. Charlemagne looked at the models ahead, lined up to go, and decided to disappear from view and enter a quiet space of the mansion. He entered a corridor but could still hear the sound of the music in the background.

The hallway was elegant, and the floor was designed in an intricate manner with the wooden floor creating a square design. He walked along and reached a display case with a headless, legless and armless mannequin with a diamond necklace. Next to this display case were pillows with rings and bracelets resting atop.

Charlemagne entered the room next to the display case, which was a sitting room with a couch surrounding some carpets. He looked out the window and towards the garden outside. Charlemagne exited the room from the other side and entered another corridor that was perpendicular to the last. He walked down and admired the view of the back gardens from where he was. The hedges were trimmed and flowers in bloom. At the end of the corridor, he reached a square room past a set of double doors.

The room was large and had a circular floor panel with the crest of the family engraved. Charlemagne looked at the display cases with mannequins which bore more uniforms from the Grand Armée alongside rifles with bayonets. A certain mannequin had long black boots, white trousers that went up to a blue coat with gold fringe epilates. The hat was tall, black and had a feather atop with a gold rim. The sword in the display case was long and went to the floor from the belt. On the walls were swords and shields. At the adjacent wall was a display case containing medieval armor. Charlemagne left this room to come to a neighboring one.

Act 5, Scene 4

Charlemagne arrived in the library of the mansion, which was large with tall bookcases that were about three-times the height of the ones at Cabernet Manor. He went down the corridor and arrived at the end where there was another display case with a large hand-drawn map of Europe. Charlemagne turned the corner and went around to the center of the library. The sun was shining into the room and through the translucent curtains. A fireplace at the end of the room held a portrait of a man with blue eyes and dark hair dressed in a Grand Armée uniform. He had skin similar to Charlemagne's, but looked nothing like him.

In the center of the library was a table with maps stretched out and behind display case tables. Beneath the table were drawers with additional maps stretched out inside. Charlemagne went through a few and found schematics of the house and a family tree on the bottom. The names of the tree were handwritten and hard to decipher. Charlemagne carefully brought it out and laid it atop of the glass.

Charlemagne quickly turned as he heard the sound of enclosing footsteps. The assassin from the train appeared and ran down an aisle, heading towards Charlemagne with a sword held like a javelin. He threw it towards Charlemagne, who dodged out of the way for it to peg the wall between two windows. Charlemagne then backed up and ducked down as the mysterious stranger attempted to plant a punch against him. Charlemagne took the sword from the wall and then swiped it down in front of him. The mysterious stranger reacted by retrieving a long combat knife from his right leg. The two then clashed metal with metal before breaking off.

The mysterious stranger took a step back from Charlemagne as the two looked at each other. The assassin stepped forward first and attempted to take a jab at Charlemagne. Charlemagne deflected with his saber. The mysterious stranger jabbed again. Charlemagne swiped and caused him to jump back.

The two continued to clash sword with knife. The mysterious stranger pushed Charlemagne backwards and towards a bookcase with a pedestal nearby holding a vase. Charlemagne held his ground once he was backed up, looking to the side for an exit. He then looked to the vase as he poked his sword forward to cause the assassin to back up. With his other hand, he grabbed the vase and threw it at the assassin, hitting him in the side and providing a distraction for him to escape. The mysterious stranger threw his knife towards him as he ran, but it missed and hit a book. Charlemagne heard it fall to the floor.

Charlemagne came to the armory where he closed the doors behind him and then ran towards the center of the room. The assassin kicked the doors down and looked towards Charlemagne. He lowered his sword as he looked to the assassin.

"I have you beat – I was raised in this art," Charlemagne remarked. "Who are you? Take off your mask and surrender."

The assassin looked to Charlemagne and smashed the glass cabinet next to him. He then pulled an identical sword and lowered it. Charlemagne looked at the assassin with careful eyes. The two then stepped forward and clashed once more, saber with saber before backing off again. The two judged each other before the assassin gave two swings, which Charlemagne deflected. They then broke off again and paced around the room.

Charlemagne took an aggressive approaching, coaxing the mysterious stranger into a corner of the room before stopping. Charlemagne kept his sword up and to his side, while the assassin kept his sword down and behind him. The assassin raised his sword and then took a step forward to swing at Charlemagne from the side before zigzagging to the other side.

The two were brought back to the middle of the room where they broke off and paced once more with their swords pointed at one another.

"I see you've done this before too," Charlemagne remarked. "I'm impressed."

The assassin leaned forward and the two clashed again. He pushed Charlemagne back and into the hallway. They stopped briefly in the middle of the hallway before going at it again. Charlemagne edged himself to the right, bringing the assassin to his right. The assassin then pushed Charlemagne against a door. Charlemagne opened the door with his other hand and then ran into it, turning around and deflecting the wave towards him and pushing the assassin back.

Charlemagne pushed the assassin towards a set of stairs, but the assassin pushed back, attempting to get Charlemagne into the corner of the room. The assassin became more aggressive with his swings, and with it, more reckless. Charlemagne dodged around, swinging his saber around and then taking a step back as he found himself at the edge of a set of stairs going into the basement. He instead took a side step and hopped up onto a set of stairs. Charlemagne then ran up to reach a landing where he turned around to prepare for the immediate swing. He deflected and then backed up the rest of the staircase.

The assassin followed Charlemagne up the staircase and the two clashed swords into the hallway outside, which led into another hallway. Charlemagne ducked down and changed positions with the assassin once more as they reached this hallway, pushing him towards a set of arched French doors that went to a patio balcony on the side of the house. The assassin raised his sword up and then brought it down. Charlemagne deflected. The assassin then changed positions with him and began another aggressive attempt to push him back towards the doors, kicking him into them and onto the patio.

Charlemagne fell onto his back and deflected the incoming attempt on his life. The assassin took several swings at him, each deflected until Charlemagne was given an opportunity to swing his sword and stand up. The mysterious stranger continued to push him back along the patio, pausing and letting the two pant for a moment as they lowered their swords and looked to each other. This time, Charlemagne pointed his sword forward. The assassin deflected and pointed his sword forward. Charlemagne kept his sword up and the two continued, reaching the end of the patio where Charlemagne coaxed the assassin against the wall as he went right. The assassin bashed his body into the arched French window door and found himself in a study. The two continued to clash into the middle of the room before they broke up.

Each of them lowered their swords as they looked at each other and stood still. The assassin took a step forward towards Charlemagne, panting through his mask. The mysterious stranger then lunged towards him. Charlemagne deflected and moved to the right. The assassin pushed him back towards an unlit fireplace, but Charlemagne held his ground and pushed him backwards in his direction towards a desk. The mysterious stranger side-stepped in front of the desk and the two broke off with it in front of them. They looked at each other with focused eyes.

The focus broke off at the sound of loud, noisy cars in front of the house, stopping. Each of them looked for a brief second, seeing a convoy of three light armored utility vehicles (LUV) in a dark blue color appear in front of the chateau. The assassin looked back to Charlemagne and then jumped out of the window behind him. Charlemagne looked at where the assassin was in shock before rushing over to look outside. He was gone without a trace.

Charlemagne took a step back and then went back to the windows on the other side to see the people exiting the vehicle. They were dressed in black tactical gear and one of the members had a familiar face. Charlemagne took a deep breath and then looked forward, above the mantle of the fireplace in the study. There was another portrait of a Cataret family member, but this man was dressed in a grey suit from the mid-nineteenth century. He had fair skin like Charlemagne's, blue eyes, but black hair atop of his head. Charlemagne frowned and stuck his sword into a nearby plant. He then rushed out of the study and went back downstairs.

The main ballroom appeared to be half empty and there were no models on the runway. The music had also settled down to a gentle background beat. Charlemagne came into the foyer and spotted Judith with Manon and the kids in a corner of the room. He rushed over to them, panting.

"Charles, you're all sweaty," Judith remarked to him. "What happened?"

"I'll explain in a bit, my dear," Charlemagne responded, "but it's time we left. Hurry."

Charlemagne led the four of them out of the mansion and down the gravel path to the driveway where the LUVs were parked. The LUVs were of the Cabernet make and of a special *Bayard* model. They had tinted and reinforced windows and seemed impenetrable. The armored mercenaries in tactical uniforms were accompanied with a man in an expansive black suit. The man wore round eyeglasses, had blue eyes and short, neat dark blonde hair. He was of a shorter statue in comparison to the mercenaries with him who stood in front of the armored cars with neutral expressions with each of their arms to their sides and their faces staring ahead.

Each mercenary, or merc, had a beret atop of their head. Their trousers and jackets were black and consisted of a pixelated camouflage pattern in that color. Atop of their jackets were solid black ballistic vests with munition pockets in the front. Around their waists were belts with additional pouches. Some mercenaries had handguns on their belt and others at their thigh. Each merc had an earpiece in their ear that ran down their neck and under their clothing. On the right shoulders of each uniform were shield patches with the symbol of ethnicity of each mercenary. On the left shoulder was the insignia of the Protection Squad, 'P.S.'

"I'm glad you could arrive so promptly, Mr. Heavner," Charlemagne greeted, shaking his hand. "Thank you."

"Sorry, we couldn't have arrived sooner," Heavner responded in a North American accent.

Charlemagne faced the man next to Mr. Heavner – it was the squad leader, Miklos Horvath, Charlemagne's former security expert and bodyguard. Miklos had cut his hair since Charlemagne had last seen him in Egypt. It was short on the sides and the top was buried beneath the black beret he was wearing. His skin was the same darker shade of white common in Slavs and Hungarians. On his shoulder was the Hungarian tricolor. Charlemagne took his hand.

"At ease, Miklos, it's good to see you, old friend," Charlemagne remarked, walking over to the Hungarian as he relaxed from his pose. "Come here."

The two shook hands and then hugged.

"It's good to work for you again too," Miklos responded, patting his back before separating. "Hopefully you can breathe a little easier that we are here, right?"

"I hope so," Charlemagne responded, turning to Judith, Manon, and the kids behind him. "You remember the kids?"

"Of course," Miklos replied, waving to them. "Who are the ladies?" he questioned, looking to Charlemagne as he stuttered. "I'm kidding," he laughed, gently slapping the back of his hand into Charlemagne's chest. "We were briefed about your company. Let me instead introduce you to my team instead."

Miklos turned to the man on his right. Charlemagne stepped forward to shake his hand. The man was clean-shaven as each of the mercenaries were and had olive skin common in Mediterraneans. His ethnic patch indicated him to be Italian. He had shortened blonde hair and green eyes.

"Meet my second-in-command," Miklos said as Charlemagne offered his hand "At ease, Sceafa."

The man relaxed from his position and took Charlemagne's hand.

"Sceafa is an interesting name," Charlemagne remarked.

"It's a nickname, like Attila," Miklos responded. "For use in battle."

"You remind me of someone," Charlemagne surmised. "What's your real name, son? You wouldn't happen to be related to anyone with the surname Medici? Would you?"

"Lukas Scaravetti, and not exactly – you may have known my cousin, Bianca Siciliano, who married a man with such name," Lukas responded.

"There it is," Charlemagne said, holding an empathetic expression, "I'm sorry about your cousin, son."

Charlemagne moved on to the man next to him. The man had fair skin, shortened black hair and blue eyes. He also had a cleft chin. His patch indicated him to be Bavarian.

"This is Naimon," Miklos introduced. "At ease," he said to him and the men next to him.

Charlemagne shook Naimon's hand. The two then moved on to the man next to him. He had skin similar to Miklos, but in darker tone and different hue. He also had brown eyes and dark brown hair. He was older than most of the men here who were in their mid to late twenties or early thirties.

"This is my brother-in-law, Igor, but we call him 'Dracula' because of how much of bloodsucker he is" Miklos remarked, turning to the last man next to him, "and this is 'Holger.'"

Holger had fairer skin like Charlemagne and blue eyes. His blonde hair was almost white. He had a Danish flag on his shoulder. Miklos guided Charlemagne to the three others on the left.

"This is Olivier and Elegast," Miklos said, introducing two men at once.

Olivier had dark brown hair, fair skin, and blue eyes. He seemed to be the youngest with a round clean-shaven face. Next to him was another young man who was tall with fair skin, blue eyes and red hair. Olivier was identified as French and Elegast as Dutch. The two then moved on to the last man. He had light brown, or dark blonde hair, skin like Miklos, but slightly lighter, and blue eyes. His patch indicated him to be Latvian. He was of a stockier build.

"And lastly, this is Lacplesis," Miklos said, patting Lacplesis' back.

Charlemagne shook his hand and then looked to Miklos.

"With the introductions out of the way, perhaps it would be better if we moved along" Henry said, interrupting. "We have orders to escort you into Germany – anywhere specific?"

"Aachen," Charlemagne responded, looking to him "let us get there as soon as possible."

Act 6, Scene 1

The LUVs drove into Nancy and passed the urban and modern sector of the city to reach the downtown heartland. The architecture of this older part of town mostly consisted of beige and white stucco buildings anywhere between four and six stories tall. The roofs were made of red shingles and lacked dormer windows. However, they did have sunroof windows occasionally from house to house. The streets and sidewalks were made of chiseled stone.

Charlemagne rode with Judith in the frontmost vehicle with Miklos driving and Henry on his right. The couple were cuddled in the back of the car. Manon was in the second vehicle with the kids who were with Lukas and Elegast. The third vehicle contained the five other mercenaries on their own. Judith gave a sigh as she looked at the buildings.

"We're on the final stretch," Charlemagne remarked with a pleasant sigh. "Three more hours and we'll be in Aachen to meet Dr. Schneider."

"Oh, Charles, what's the hurry?" Judith complained. "We can go into Germany tomorrow when we're all refreshed – I haven't been able to change out of this outfit since we left that train. Come on, you've been having us work too hard. Let's stay here for the rest of the day, enjoy some sort of family activity, and then set off tomorrow morning for the university."

Charlemagne looked to Judith and separated himself from her. He looked at her strangely as if she had been replaced with another person.

"Strange, two days ago you were begging me to get out of here, but now you seem to want to stay…" Charlemagne said. "What's changed?"

"Our security detail," Judith replied. "I feel safer and as though we won't be kidnapped… I heard that this town has a lovely opera house – we should see when their next performance is and buy tickets."

"A musical performance would be an excellent idea that we could both enjoy – unlike that fashion show…" Charlemagne responded. "I'll see about it – Miklos, change of course, let's stop here for the night and go to a hotel. We'll continue towards Aachen tomorrow morning."

"Of course, Charles," Miklos responded, picking up his radio "*Wir andern unsere Richtung. Bereithalten.*"

"Do you care to join us, Henry?" Charlemagne questioned. "It'll be a delight."

"I'm afraid not," Henry responded. "I'm due in Harlech and have lots of work to do now that this project of ours is in fruition. Lots of management that needs done."

"Pity," Charlemagne replied, "that's quite alright. It'll be a night for just us then."

・・

Later in the evening, Charlemagne looked at himself in the mirror of his hotel room as he adjusted his bow tie of his tuxedo. The room had a king-sized bed with a single, but large window that opened to a balconette. In the corner of the room were Charlemagne's and Judith's suitcases from the train. The room had yellow walls, which in combination with the incandescent lights, gave the room a warm glow. The windows looked out to the Place Stanislas. A heritage site and plaza in the center of town dedicated to a former king of Poland who was immortalized in the form of a bronze statue atop, which was atop of a pedestal. Around the place were additional heritage buildings including the city hall, an art museum, and office pavilion. The buildings were constructed of beige stucco with balustrades along the perimeter of the roofs. Generally, the outer façades consisted of arched white-framed windows on the ground and second floor with smaller arched windows on the third floor. The city hall included a pediment with a clock at the top and the ground floor exterior walls were a darker shade in the form of bricks. The plaza was lit by warm lights originating from the buildings and lamp poles scattered throughout the space.

Once Charlemagne's bow was tightened, he looked down at the open briefcase atop of the dresser before him. The briefcase contained his vials of DNA. He closed the briefcase and locked it. The briefcase required a pin code to access the contents. Charlemagne turned to the side as he saw Judith step into the room from the bathroom. She was dressed in a crème colored dress with pearl earrings around her neck. She also tied her hair in a bun.

"Ready?" Charlemagne questioned.

"Yes," Judith replied, going to the closet to take out a white fur coat she had bought. "Let's go and enjoy the symphony."

Charlemagne and Judith walked out of their bedroom and into the hall. Holger stood outside of their bedroom on watch. He was dressed in a tuxedo suit but retained his earpiece. Miklos had accompanied him and the two had been chatting. Miklos was also dressed formally.

"We're ready," Charlemagne said to Miklos. "What of the kids?"

"Let us see," Miklos replied, walking down to the room next door.

Miklos knocked on the door and in a light voice, asked, "Diana."

Diana looked to the door as Manon finished doing her hair.

"There," Manon said, finishing, "pretty enough to attract Tristan."

Diana smiled and gave a light laugh, "What?"

"Oh, please," Manon replied. "I've seen the way you look at him – you like him."

Diana blushed and then stood up.

"Thanks for your help," Diana simply said, hugging her before going to open the door.

"I'm ready," Diana said, grabbing her coat and exiting.

Tristan stepped out from his bedroom adjacent to Diana's dressed in a black suit with a black dress shirt. He had combed his hair. He walked towards the others as Manon came to the doorway.

"Can I change your mind to come with us?" Charlemagne asked. "We have the extra tickets and it'd be a shame for them to go to waste."

"I'm fine," Manon replied with tired eyes. "I just want to relax a bit and catch up on some emails if possible."

"Suit yourself," Charlemagne responded, "two guards will stay with you in case that assassin appears again."

Tristan looked to Charlemagne and Manon. Manon nodded to him and then walked down the corridor in the opposite direction from where the others went. An additional four mercenaries joined the group and they all went downstairs to the main lobby of the hotel via elevator before stepping out onto the plaza. There was a cold chill, not below freezing, but just at the cusp of being cold over cool.

The group walked down the plaza and came to the main entrance of the *Opera National de Lorraine*, which was adjacent to the hotel. The façade of the opera house was constructed of beige stone bricks with the ground floor being made of a thicker layer with six white-framed arched French windows with a set of double white doors in the middle. Above these windows were seven French windows with golden balconettes before them., and above these windows were smaller arched windows with smaller golden balconettes. At the roof were balustrades with statues spread across. Beneath the balustrade, in the middle of the structure in gold font was, '*Opera National de Lorraine.*' The doors into the opera house were open for them to step into the main foyer through another set of doors behind.

The main lobby was a rectangular room with brown doors with glass panes leading into the rest of the building. The doors were open and there were approximately four men in black suits waiting on the other side, accepting tickets. Charlemagne distributed the tickets to the nine party members with him before they passed through. On the immediate left and right were white staircases going up to the second floor with another set of two stairs left and right, perpendicular to the former. The group went up the first set of stairs ahead, reached a landing that joined together and continued with a staircase in the middle going the opposite direction to reach the second floor.

The stairs then reached a second lobby atop with windows looking out to the plaza. Left and right, going into the structure were corridors with chandeliers and doors at the end. Charlemagne led the group through the doors and into the opera hall. Charlemagne chose seats from the viewing gallery that gave a good view of the stage.

The opera hall was a mix between red and gold with red walls, seats, and curtains, and gold railings, seat rims, and ceiling. The area was decorated with stucco and statues. At either side of the main stage were balconies with two statues on either side. The rest of the stage was out of sight from the red curtains that were approximately ten meters tall.

The Protection Squad sat behind the family. Charlemagne sat with Judith who was next to Diana and Tristan. There was a quiet murmur in the opera hall as people found their seats and it slowly filled.

Approximately thirty minutes passed before the lights in the room dimmed and the curtains rolled open. On stage was an orchestra seated with their instruments behind a plain wall lit by a white light. The orchestra area was lit with lights from above too. A minute passed before a man in a tailcoat suit walked across to stand at the conductor platform. He bowed to the audience who clapped for him and then he turned to his performers. He tapped his baton upon the musical stand before him and then he began with a simple motion of the stick and his hand to produce an audible art.

The song began with the strum of a harp met with the sound of flute in sync. The music was gentle and soft at a moderate beat and went up and down. Twenty seconds into the song, violins joined at the same pace and timbre, replacing the flute. A split second of horns was also heard before the flute replaced the violins. The lights on the blank wall behind the orchestra were a gentle green. At forty seconds, the flute was replaced by violins again with an oboe that came for a brief moment. The music then dropped and the lights flashed yellow. The pace then increased and settled before calming entirely as the flute played with the violins and harp. The tubas were heard for another split second. There was then a volta and the flute played with double basses and the harp at the same tune with the occasional sound of the French horn at an increased presence and occasional joining in of the violins. The piece then finished in a gentle manner that was also sudden. Once the music had ended, the audience erupted into applause.

Act 6, Scene 2

Violins played in a hurried tone, up and down with the occasional beat of a double bass. The lights on the background were orange-red and breathed like a quick heartbeat. At sixteen seconds in, a cello joined at a faster pace before at thirty seconds, the music shifted with the violins and cellos shifting importance at a slower, but still fast pace. The lights were at a darker tone. The music and lights then continued as it was before shifting again like a chorus. A sense of urgency was felt with the music as it played.

The music returned to violins and cellos in the background with double bass making occasional beats. It then quieted down but kept its pace. A harp could be heard strumming as well as the strings of cellos before it then cut out. The audience clapped and the lights in the room brightened.

"*Mesdames et messieurs, nous allons faire une pause de trente minutes, s'il vous plaît,*" a voice said over a PA system. "*Veuillez revenir dans trente minutes.*"

Charlemagne stood up with a pleasant smile on his face. He looked to Judith.

"How about we get some fresh air before the next act," Charlemagne suggested. "All of us – come on."

Charlemagne led the family outside and into the hall. The mercenaries followed them and stood nearby.

"I have to go to the washroom," Charlemagne stated. "I'll be just a moment."

"Me too," Judith replied, "sitting down for an hour and a half can be challenging. Diana, are you alright?"

"I'll just come with you," Diana replied.

"How about you, Tristan?" Charlemagne questioned.

"I'm alright, actually," Tristan responded.

Charlemagne motioned over to the guards. They came over.

"Some of us need to go to the washroom," Charlemagne said. "Can one of you come with me and another two go with the girls? The rest of you can stay here with Tristan."

"I'll come with you, Charles," Miklos replied. "You two, take the ladies to the washroom on the other side."

"Yes, sir," Holger responded, walking forward.

"Now hang on," Judith protested. "We don't need men to protect us while we go fix our makeup, do we Diana? Just stay here and we'll be a second."

"Judith…" Charlemagne said.

"No," Judith replied, stopping him. "It'll only be a moment – nothing will happen."

Judith walked off with Diana down the corridor and into the second floor lobby. Charlemagne and Miklos walked down the corridor and entered that lobby. They then walked to the side and came into a small corridor that led into the washrooms. Like the rest of the structure, the washrooms were regal with white patio tiles and black and white walls. Charlemagne walked to a urinal while Miklos occupied the other. Once they were finished, Charlemagne flushed and went to the sink to wash his hands.

"What do you think of the performance so far, Miko?" Charlemagne questioned. "Certainly France's best pieces – I had a particular fondness for Gabriel Fauré's *Sicilienne* at the start."

"I'm not much of a music expert, Charles, so I cannot really offer much of an opinion," Miklos replied before flushing.

Charlemagne smiled and then turned off his sink. He looked at himself in the mirror before seeing the toilet door behind him open with the mysterious stranger behind him. The assassin brought a carbon wire around Charlemagne's neck and proceeded to strangle him.

"Charles!" Miklos shouted, rushing over and tackling the assassin as he pivoted to put Charlemagne between the two.

Miklos slammed them both into the wall, which was enough to loosen the assassin's grip from Charlemagne's neck to let him fall to the floor in a gasp for air. Miklos raised a fist to punch the mysterious stranger across the face, but he caught it and the two tensed before letting each other go. Charlemagne ran towards the exit and then turned around to see as the assassin grabbed Miklos by his tuxedo jacket and through him into the mirror.

Charlemagne looked around for a weapon to aid Miklos and only found a garbage bin next to him. Miklos kicked the assassin back and into the toilet stall. Charlemagne opened the bathroom door a bit and took a deep breath.

"Help!" Charlemagne shouted before turning back to Miklos as he stood up.

Miklos raised his fists to the mysterious stranger. The assassin then attempted to punch him, but Miklos dodged out of the way and landed a punch in the side. The fight was cut short by the appearance of two guards entering and standing next to Charlemagne. They produced their pistols from their jackets and took aim. The assassin ran off into the toilet stall again and threw a grenade behind him.

Miklos ran from the grenade, grabbing Charlemagne and rushing him out of the bathroom with the others behind. A large cloud of smoke filled the bathroom, but no explosion went off. Miklos and the others returned into the washroom, waving their hands in search of the assassin, but he was gone. Charlemagne stood in the corridor outside of the bathroom and rubbed his neck. He then groaned before hearing screams from elsewhere in the opera house.

Charlemagne looked out into the second floor lobby and his eyes focused.

"Diana!" Tristan shouted from elsewhere.

Charlemagne rushed forward, grabbing Tristan to allow the mercenaries forward before him.

"Let me go!" Tristan complained, breaking free and then running forward into the female washroom.

Charlemagne joined him and saw Judith on the floor of the washroom. The mercenaries were looking around the room where Diana was nowhere to be seen. Charlemagne ran to Judith and helped her onto her feet.

"What happened?" Charlemagne questioned. "Where's Diana?"

"I have no idea – one second, I saw that man, and the next second, I was on the floor and Diana was gone."

"Boss, we have an opening in the ceiling here," Miklos reported, shining a flashlight into an open vent duct.

"Crafty bugger," Charlemagne responded. "They'll still be in the building – find a way onto the roof and spread out! Cover the exits!"

Miklos jumped up and grabbed the ledge of the vent duct, bringing himself up and in.

"Let me come," Tristan insisted.

"No," Charlemagne denied, "keep Tristan here and keep a firm eye on him. I won't have another one get kidnapped."

"Yes, sir," Lukas responded, grabbing Tristan by the arm.

"Let go of me!" Tristan complained as he was dragged off.

Charlemagne walked into the stall and stood onto the toilet. He then looked up.

"Miklos, give me a hand – I'm coming with you."

Instead of Miklos turning around (which seemed impossible) a mercenary stepped forward and gave Charlemagne a boost. Charlemagne climbed into the vent and then followed his old friend through.

At the end of the duct, they reached a tunnel upwards that was impossible to climb up of. Miklos then crouched and looked to Charlemagne.

"Dead end," Miklos reported. "No way through."

"How did they get through with my daughter?" Charlemagne questioned. "How?"

Miklos brought a hand to his earpiece and paused for a moment.

"We've got sights of the assassin in the opera hall – let's hurry."

The two returned into the washroom and then rushed downstairs to come to the ground floor. Mercenaries were rushing towards the stage and the sound of Diana screaming could be heard. Charlemagne and Miklos climbed onto the stage and looked up to where the assassin could be seen with Diana atop of a catwalk. The assassin had Diana over his shoulders as he carried her. Diana was banging her fists into the back of the assassin. Several mercenaries had their pistols drawn, while others were securing a ladder.

"Up – we need to go up!" Charlemagne commanded.

Miklos had already begun to climb the ladder onto the catwalk, running after Diana with Charlemagne behind. The chase led to a space behind the stage with a fire exit door. Miklos jumped down as the saw the assassin open the fire exit door and walk out. He and Charlemagne rushed over, only to wave their hands due to the heavy presence of smoke before them in the alleyway behind the opera house.

Charlemagne could see an LUV different to his with the presence of a driver other than the assassin in the driver's seat. Diana had been thrown into the back and was with another female – Manon. The two of them hit their fists into the reinforced glass of the back of the vehicle as it drove off and away from them.

"No…" Charlemagne whispered.

Act 6, Scene 3

Charlemagne returned to the hotel with the mercenaries and Tristan. They came to the hallway outside of their bedroom and saw Naimon and Olivier on the ground. Charlemagne rushed forward to check on Naimon. He was unconscious, responsive to pain, but breathing and bleeding from his abdomen. The other mercenary was unconscious and unresponsive to pain. Elegast immediately started to begin chest compressions. Charlemagne stood up and looked over to Tristan who was down the hall with Judith.

"Get Tristan out of here and to his room – do not let him out of your sight," Charlemagne ordered in a stressed voice. "Call an ambulance for these two."

Lukas took Tristan away from the scene while a mercenary proceeded to give Naimon first aid. Charlemagne walked down the hall and to his room. The door had been left open and the room had been ransacked. The briefcase that was atop of the dresser was gone. Charlemagne slammed his fist down upon the dresser and took a deep breath. Judith entered the room and sat down on the bed behind him. The two were silent.

Charlemagne left his room and went down the hall to Tristan's room. Tristan was atop of his bed with his knees up. His eyes were red as if he had been crying. Lukas was at the door and looked to Charlemagne as he walked in. Charlemagne dismissed him and then closed the door behind him. He then turned to Tristan and hesitated for a moment.

"We're going to find them," Charlemagne assured him, "no matter what it takes, but I need you to understand that I can't have you placing yourself in harm's way anymore. It's bad enough to lose someone than it is to lose another. The Protection Squad are here to help us and will do what they're paid to do."

"I just want to help…" Tristan muttered. "Please…"

"Tristan, I admire your motivation, but…"

"I know."

"I won't rest until they are found," Charlemagne said, placing a hand atop of Tristan's knee. "I make that promise to you."

Tristan nodded and then kept his head down. Charlemagne stood up as he heard a knock on the door. He went over and opened the door. Miklos was on the other side. Lukas entered at Charlemagne's signal. Charlemagne then closed the door and walked with Miklos down the hall.

"What's up?" Charlemagne asked.

"Good news," Miklos replied, "as it appears, Dr. Dumas' cellphone is wherever the mercenaries are. We are able to track their location and can see that they are moving north towards Sedan."

"If I had to guess, Manon is unable to make a phone call for police but is most likely anticipating us to track her down with this signal," Charlemagne surmised. "We need to move fast – keep three men here with Tristan and Judith with eyes on the two at all times. The rest of us are going after this assassin. Prepare for a fight."

"Yes, Charles," Miklos replied, "I will prepare the men."

∙ ∙

Charlemagne left with four of the mercenaries from Nancy and drove north along the A31 to Sedan on the Belgian border. Charlemagne had little time to get changed but was given a combat rain jacket in case he needed it and a pair of boots. The mercenaries were able to change back into their tactical uniforms as well as able to don smocks. A storm had begun, bringing ounces of rain down to the earth. The LUV drove through on the highway as fast as possible.

Igor, with a heavy-duty laptop, kept track of Manon's location. Somehow, it seemed as if the Protection Squad was gaining up on the assassin as the distance between them shortened. Within three hours, they had passed Sedan as they continued west to *Charleville-Mezieres*, passing through and then coming into the Ardennes Forest. The freeway through the forest was dark with no lights on the sidelines. The forest was not that dense where the road had been constructed, although it was relatively remote. Charlemagne looked out the window of the jeep with a saddened face. He saw a signpost that told him he was now in the Walloon region of Belgium.

"We are almost a kilometer apart from the target," Igor stated.

The LUV continued through the Belgium part of the Ardennes.

"The target is moving off the highway and into the forest," Igor later updated.

"What are they playing at?" Charlemagne questioned. "Do they know we know?"

"Impossible," Miklos replied.

"It should have been impossible for this assassin to have found us in Geneva or on a train," Charlemagne argued. "How is that they found us?"

The LUV continued to speed down the highway before coming to an off-ramp that brought them into a denser part of the forest. The road was narrower and the evergreen trees to the side were closer. Eventually, the road was replaced with a dirt path that they followed. The ride became bumpy as they ventured forward, coming to a point where they were required to stop because the LUV became trapped. He attempted to drive forward, but the car wouldn't move. Instead, the LUV gave an awful sound as the wheel span. Charlemagne could see mud flying around from outside.

"Damn!" Miklos remarked, slamming his fists on the steering wheel.

"Come on!" Charlemagne complained, "if Gerd von Rundstedt can lead a group of tanks through this forest, we can move a simple bloody truck!"

Miklos changed gears and attempted to back up, but it was impossible. A wheel had become entrapped in some mud.

"Enough," Charlemagne told him, "we'll continue on foot."

Charlemagne exited the car and closed the door behind him. He put on his leopard-print camouflage jacket over his tuxedo and brought the hood up. The other mercenaries had similar jackets as well as field caps that replaced their berets. The coats were long and went below the hips for a belt to come across. The belt included suspenders, which allowed for pouches.

Miklos opened the rear trunk and the mercenaries armed themselves with assault rifles. Charlemagne took a rifle before Miklos closed it.

"The good news is that the road is one-way," Igor remarked, readying his weapon and looking at a GPS mounted to his wrist, "and the better news is that they've stopped not too far from here."

"On me," Miklos told the others, lowering his own wrist. "Stick together."

Miklos raised his assault rifle and led the way down the muddy road. The rifles had flashlights that gave them some light. Charlemagne followed them from behind. The rain continued to fall down as they went forward in search of the assassin.

The deeper they went along, the denser the trees as well as a thick fog became. Charlemagne looked around him and held an uneasy look on his face. He started to fall behind, which Miklos noticed. Miklos looked to him and then to the mercenary immediately behind him.

"Lacplesis, take lead," Miklos ordered, looking at his GPS. "Charles and I will cut through and we'll ambush them on the other side."

"Yes, sir," Lacplesis replied.

The two went off, down the road and into the fog. Miklos went to Charlemagne and brought a hand to his shoulder.

"Are you alright?" Miklos questioned.

"I'm fine," Charlemagne responded, taking a deep breath, "it's just that this forest… it's eerie and bring back bad memories."

"What memories?" Miklos asked.

"My grandfather… he died in an accident when travelling through the Ardennes. It was a car accident – this is my first time entering this place since then because I dreaded to ever have to go in here and bring my mind to wonder what it was like. Right now, all I can imagine is that it was just like this night – foggy and raining."

"Take deep breaths," Miklos suggested. "Stay focused and we'll get through this. What's in the past is in the past, and right now we need to look forward to preventing any harm from coming to Diana or Dr. Dumas."

Charlemagne nodded to him.

"Let's move forward then," Charlemagne said, turning to the forest with his assault rifle.

Act 6, Scene 4

Charlemagne and Miklos ventured into the forest together, passing ferns and bushes as well as the tall coniferous trees of the Ardennes. The rain did not cease and the fog did not clear for them. Charlemagne took a moment to breath, which drew Miklos to stay with him.

"Was this worth it?" Charlemagne questioned as he leaned his back on a tree. "Had I known what would have happened had I opened my mouth at the Champs-Elysées, I would never have said anything. I wouldn't even have gotten out of the car."

"You did what you felt was right – you voiced your opinion," Miklos replied. "You cannot blame yourself for this, Charles. You cannot take responsibility for the vile actions of others."

"No good came out of it," Charlemagne argued, "because of what I've done, many more might become hurt. Who knows what hive I've stirred and the backlash it'll have in the future."

"What's done is done," Miklos remarked to him, "and your conscience is clean. If doing what is good were easy, there would be more good people in the world. Saints are not easily made."

"I had to pull you out from retirement…" Charlemagne added with guilt, "put you in harm's way when you could be with your wife and child."

"I volunteered to help, Charles," Miklos replied, placing a hand on his shoulder, "because you are part of my family."

Charlemagne looked to him and nodded. He raised his weapon and the two continued onwards, climbing up a cliffside to come to a perch that looked down and over to a road on the opposite-side. The two hid in a bush. Miklos picked up a pair of binoculars hung around his neck and looked over. He scanned the area and then gave the binoculars to Charlemagne. He looked through and towards the vehicles parked on the road.

There were at least two LUVs parked on the road. Charlemagne could see Diana and Manon in the back of one of them, each with their hands tied behind them. The cars were protected by mercenaries in ponchos with conventional assault rifles. The assassin was nowhere to be seen but could easily be hiding amongst the others.

"I count at least four," Charlemagne said, handing the binoculars back to Miklos. "Are the others in position?"

"Lacplesis, this is Charlie-One," Miklos spoke into his radio. "Are you and Drac in position?"

Charlemagne couldn't hear any response due to his lack of radio and earpiece.

"They're almost in position," Miklos told Charlemagne. "I'm going to spread out and take position to the left. Stay here and wait for my signal."

"Certainly," Charlemagne replied, focusing on the convoy below.

Miklos broke off and disappeared. Charlemagne kept his eyes on the targets, eyeing the ones closer to the LUV with the hostages. All Charlemagne could hear around him was rainfall led by the sudden onslaught of gunfire coming from the bushes. Charlemagne opened fire and aimed for the mercenaries near the LUV with Manon and Diana.

One of the mercenaries was shot to the ground, while the others scrambled into cover. Charlemagne continued to open fire at the one hiding behind the LUV.

Diana peaked her head up as she heard the gunshots outside. She looked to Manon and the two went towards the window that looked to where Charlemagne and Miklos were hiding. All Diana could see was the flash of muzzle fire coming from two of the bushes. She could also see and hear gunfire coming from down the road.

The door behind the two opened and Diana was dragged out by the assassin who turned out to be the target behind the car. Another mercenary raised his assault rifle to Manon.

"Hors de la voiture et debout!" the mercenary demanded.

Manon got out and stood up as ordered. The merc then grabbed her by the neck just as the assassin had grabbed Diana. The assassin also took a briefcase, handcuffing it around his wrist so he could carry it and hold a pistol. Charlemagne watched as the two used them as human shields, protecting themselves as they walked back into the forest.

"The targets are moving!" Charlemagne shouted.

"Move forward!" Miklos yelled, coming out of the forest.

The Protection Squad had gunned down two out of the four targets below and the rest were getting away. Miklos and Charlemagne moved down the cliff and towards the road, taking cover behind the LUVs as the others moved up from down the road tree by tree.

"Watch your fire!" Miklos shouted to the others. "Targets have hostages!"

Charlemagne turned the corner and attempted to see where the assassin and pawn had gone off, but they disappeared into the fog. He ran out and took cover by some trees. He then went forward until he could see them again. A gunshot passed Charlemagne, pushing him behind a tree. The rest of the Protection Squad moved up behind.

Above them, Charlemagne could hear the sound of a helicopter in the distance. He frowned and kept moving forward to keep track of where the targets were going. Diana panted with heavy breaths, struggling as the assassin almost choked her by his grip. She held her hands around his arm, attempting to get out, but her attempts of release were futile.

The sound of the helicopter grew louder as they reached a clearing in the Ardennes. The assassin stopped at the edge to the clearing and began to lay further shots towards Charlemagne and the others. Once Charlemagne could see them once more, he remained behind a bush and turned to Miklos.

"We need a plan of rescue," Charlemagne said to him.

"We're working on it, but need more time," Miklos replied. "I have the other two attempting to expose a flank."

The helicopter flew over them, causing a breeze to pass below. The helicopter began to descend onto the clearing. Charlemagne looked and then saw a cloud of smoke rise around and block his sight.

"Dammit!" Charlemagne shouted, rushing forward.

The assassin dragged Diana across the clearing with his pistol aimed to her head. Diana increased her struggle, thrashing around. All the assassin did was hold her tight until they reached the helicopter. The side cargo doors into the helicopter had opened for him to push her inside. The assassin then reloaded his pistol and took shots towards Charlemagne.

Charlemagne came to the edge of the clearing. Assault rifle fire came from the right side, but it was too late. The assassin was at the helicopter with Diana inside. The mercenary next to the assassin took a shot to the leg, causing him to fall over and onto the ground. Manon fell next to him and crawled away.

Once the assassin had run out of ammo, he switched cartridges and then picked up Manon. He dragged her into the helicopter with him and had a mercenary in the helicopter close the doors for them. The hatch of the transport helicopter closed and then the vehicle raised upwards and flew off. Charlemagne and the others ran into the clearing to watch the direction the helicopter flew towards – northwest. Igor looked to his wrist GPS.

"Do we have a signal?" Charlemagne questioned Igor.

Igor did not immediately respond as he looked at his GPS.

"Do we have a signal!" Charlemagne repeated.

"No… it's died out," Igor replied, "we have no other leads."

"Or so we think…" Miklos said, looking to the mercenary on the ground.

"Do you think he'll talk?" Charlemagne questioned Miklos.

"No – this one is dead already, but look here," Miklos replied, crouching by the body, "in the mud… something written by Dr. Dumas it seems."

Charlemagne walked over and crouched down. He looked at what had been written and gave a deep sigh: *Calais*.

"Calais is a large town," Charlemagne remarked, "we can't possibly know where within the municipality."

"We can in the least go and investigate," Miklos replied to him.

"If I had to guess, I would think that they'd be going to Calais either to hide or travel to England," Charlemagne surmised, "and seeing as their primary objective is me, I would hazard on the former – they're going to prepare something with those two and we'll only have to prepare for whatever it may be."

"Fine," Miklos responded, looking to Charles, "then let's prepare for the worse."

Act 7, Scene 1

Diana woke up in a barred cell within a warehouse. She took a deep breath but stopped herself from breathing too aggressively as if it smelt awful around where she was. She looked to the cell next to her and saw Manon on the ground. The two had been released from their ties and were left in small compartments below a balcony. The ground on their feet was concrete with bits of hay scattered around as if they were in animal pens. There was a sink in the corner, but no sight of a toilet.

The warehouse appeared to have been abandoned and neglected. It did not have much in the way of furniture or objects, but did have overtop windows that allowed light inside. From what Diana could see, there was a thickness of light grey clouds in the sky. She could also hear the sound of seagulls coming from outdoors.

Diana observed there to be a CCTV camera near a shutter door, pointed towards her and Manon and looking at them. She felt uneasy as she saw it and turned around to sit down. She then looked behind her and jumped at the sudden appearance of the assassin. She backed up and stood at the opposite side of her pen. The assassin had a coat similar to his in one hand and a plate in the other. The plate contained a decent-looking breakfast of toast and scrambled eggs.

The Mysterious Stranger lowered the plate into the pen and left it on the floor. He then tried to push the jacket on through for her. The assassin looked at her with focused eyes and then left. He went through a door outside and disappeared. Diana took a step towards the food on the plate. Her stomach growled. She sat down and looked at the food, inspecting it before she stood up and grabbed the coat to wear. Diana was still only in the dress, which had become dirty due to the adventure in the Ardennes.

Once Diana was dressed, she walked over to the sink to wash her hands before looking to Manon. She was asleep on the ground.

"Manon," Diana said in a hushed tone. "Are you awake?"

Manon did not reply. Diana walked over to the plate and sat down to eat. Once she was down, she backed up and sat with her back against the wall and arms crossed. Diana jumped as the door to her left opened again and a group of three mercenaries came around to unlock Manon's gate. Diana looked at the mercs – they were unlike the Protection Squad or Huntsman. They were an ethnically diverse group of people including two Arab-looking men, and a greasy looking white man with an unshaven face and large nose.

"*Levez-vous!*" the large nosed man demanded, banging a baton on the bars to make noise. "*Hâte!*"

Manon woke up. The other two walked in and helped her on her feet. They then dragged her out and towards the center of the warehouse.

"Hey!" Diana protested, standing up and going to her bars. "Leave her alone!"

The door to the left opened again and the assassin walked in. The mercs brought Manon onto the floor and threw a wet towel over her face. Another brought a bucket of water nearby and sat it down.

"*Quel est le code de la mallette?*" the large-nosed man asked.

Manon did not answer. The man asked again in a louder voice before snapping his fingers. The merc picked up the bucket of water and brought it over to dump on Manon. Manon choked as the water fell down upon her. The large-nosed man then had him stop. He knelt down.

"*Quel est le code de la mallette?*" the man asked.

"*Je ne sais pas!*" Manon denied. "*C'est la mallette de Charlemagne, pas la mienne!*"

"*Encore!*" the man shouted, snapping his fingers.

Another gallon of water came down atop of Manon. Manon squirmed.

"*Quel est le code de la mallette?!*" the man questioned. "*Nous savons que les fichiers sont dans cette mallette!*"

"*Je ne sois pas le code!*" Manon shouted. "*Lâchez-moi!*"

The large-nosed man looked to the assassin. He walked over to him and brought a hand onto his shoulder.

"*Ramenons-la dans sa cellule,*" the large-nosed man ordered the others.

They dragged her back into the cage and left her there. The group then left with the assassin being the last, looking at Diana as they went off. Diana went over to the bars that divided the two.

"Are you okay?" Diana questioned.

"I'll be fine," Manon replied in a broken tone.

"What did they want?" Diana asked.

"The pin on Charlemagne's briefcase," Manon responded. "I told them I don't have it, which is true. Charlemagne bought the briefcase – all I did was help him collect specimens."

"Who are these people and why do they want Charles' research on himself?" Diana questioned. "It makes no sense."

Manon did not reply to that question. She instead sat up with her back to the cell and produced her cell phone from a pocket. Diana looked over to the CCTV camera and then back to Manon.

"Be careful – they can see us on camera," Diana warned.

"I have to send a message to Charles so he can set us free," Manon insisted. "Damn, my phone has died!"

"What are they going to do with us?" Diana questioned as she watched Manon attempt to reboot her cellphone.

"Hold us for ransom or as bait," Manon replied in a dull tone. "To be honest, this is not my first time being entrapped because of Charlemagne, so excuse me if I am a little unenthusiastic."

"You also just felt the sensation of drowning, so I'm pretty understanding of your situation," Diana responded to her. "I'm surprised you were able to withstand that."

"Who said I withstood it? I told them the truth, even if it wasn't what they wanted to hear – I can't tell them the right answer because I don't have it."

The door opened and the assassin walked in. He went over to Manon's cage and brought his hand in as if he was asking for the phone. Manon looked to him and threw it over to him.

"It doesn't work anyways, so whatever," Manon remarked. "Just hurry up with whatever it is you intend to do with me."

The assassin crushed the phone in his grip and then tossed it on the ground. He then left the two alone again. Diana watched him leave before looking to Manon. She stood up and sat down in the corner of her cell.

"What are we going to do?" Diana asked her. "How are we going to break free?"

"I'll think of something, hopefully, but our possibilities are limited," Manon replied. "Right now, most of my trust is in *Charles*."

Act 7, Scene 2

Charlemagne sat in an LUV in an alleyway in Calais with the Protection Squad. He was dressed in one of their uniforms and with a ballistic vest. There were only four of them in the car – the same group from the Ardennes. Charlemagne was texting to Judith in regards to herself and Tristan. The two of them were in Calais and at a hotel under protection from the same three that protected them in Nancy.

Charlemagne's phone began to vibrate in his hands. He was receiving an incoming phone call from somewhere with an area code of '3.'

"Someone local is phoning me," Charlemagne told Miklos, showing him.

"Answer," Miklos insisted.

"Are you connected to my cell?" Charlemagne asked Igor.

"One second..." Igor replied, clicking and typing. "Go ahead."

Charlemagne answered and brought his phone to his ear.

"Hello?" Charlemagne asked.

No response came. There was no sound on the other side. Charlemagne brought a hand between his ear and the phone and looked to Igor.

"Are you tracing?" Charlemagne questioned.

"No need..." Igor responded, "the call came from a landline. I have an approximate location at the Port of Calais."

"Let's roll out then," Charlemagne replied.

The LUV engine roared to life and Miklos sped out from the alleyway and onto the streets of downtown Calais. Charlemagne looked out his window as they rode through as fast as they could through traffic. He admired the architecture of Calais, which generally consisted of apartment buildings with red-orange roofs and stucco walls that were typically white or beige but could also be red or brown.

From the center of Calais, the LUV travelled over a bridge that went over the Calais Canal and came towards the dockyards. Igor gave Miklos directions to an entrance point. The LUV parked outside of some gates and then everyone got out with their assault rifles to group up outside of the migrant camp before them. From what Charlemagne could see, there were various tents and containers stacked around and being used as shelters. He knelt down next to Miklos as he lowered a map onto the ground.

"Alright, the target is somewhere within this area – we'll need to pass through this slum to get to the pier," Miklos briefed, tracing a circle around the dockyard. "Remember, we're expecting for the worst so stay sharp."

"Satellite images showed a possible entrance point around here," Igor remarked, pointing to a space in the camp. "From there, we'll have to search each of the abandoned warehouses along this stretch to find the target."

"Let's end this then," Charlemagne encouraged. "Lead on."

The Protection Squad stood up and Miklos led them forward. They entered a ghetto or shanty town with makeshift homes out of shipping containers. At their feet was dirt with litter throughout the sides. The team walked down the main corridor and turned to the side. Various Sub-Saharan men could be seen around, looking at them as they entered and passed.

"Who are these people?" Charlemagne questioned as they came to a corner.

"Macron's new Frenchmen awaiting to escape to England," Miklos replied, turning the corner and continuing down another alleyway. "Let's not make contact with them – we're far outnumbered."

"That'll be the same for the rest of France soon enough," Charlemagne bantered.

The Protection Squad continued down a corridor and passed a gate where there were several migrants playing soccer on the other side. The team reached a dumpster and proceeded to climb over it and hop over a fence onto some concrete on the other side. Miklos then led them forward and down an alleyway where they stopped and got into cover behind another dumpster.

Miklos looked around the corner and then backed off.

"Let these people pass," Miklos cautioned.

Miklos looked back around the corner and continued. The group went to the end of the alleyway and then turned left to come along another alleyway before going right to a dead-end. Miklos stacked up at a set of double iron doors. He then produced some bolt cutters from his backpack and cut through the steel chains around the door handles before opening.

The team filtered into the building and went up a set of stairs to the top where there was a TV on a table playing a soccer match between France and another country. The team went down this hallway, looking into a window on their left which looked into the warehouse space on the other side, and down another set of stairs that went to the other side. Miklos led them back outdoors and into another part of the ghetto ahead, behind a chain-link fence.

"Who owns this area?" Charlemagne questioned.

"I'm not sure," Miklos replied, looking to Igor.

"It's privately-owned," Igor assured them, looking at his GPS. "The telephone call came from somewhere on this property."

"The owner must be housing all these migrants," Charlemagne remarked.

"Most likely," Miklos responded, taking a deep breath. "I can see another warehouse either within or on the edge of this camp."

"Let's punch through then," Charlemagne insisted.

Miklos went forward and knelt down in front of the chain-link fence. He produced a spray can from his backpack and shook it. He then sprayed an oval into the fence before putting the can away and grabbing the space in between the oval he had drawn. He tugged at the fence and broke off a bit of the fence for them to go through. Miklos led them back into the camp and through to the left where they then turned to go right and straight.

"I haven't seen a place like this since I was in Sierra Leone," Miklos remarked.

"You import the third world, you get the third world," Charlemagne frowned as they continued.

The team turned right again and then left once more to reach a set of doors that a part of a building in the center of the camps.

"We'll need to breach," Miklos advised, "stack up."

Charlemagne stacked up behind Igor who was behind Miklos. Lacplesis was behind Charlemagne. Miklos took a breach charge out from his backpack and placed it on the doorknob.

"Breaching!" Miklos shouted.

The door handle exploded, and Miklos kicked the door down. The team filtered into the warehouse and were met with the sight of migrants on stretchers throughout the warehouse. The group scanned the area before continuing forward to the end of the building to exit. Miklos looked forward and could see another building up a head. The team went through the Calais Jungle to reach the chain-link fence on the end. The top of the fence had barbed wire, so Miklos punched another hole to get to the other side. They then dashed across the space between the camp and warehouse to reach the exterior walls.

Charlemagne looked to his left and took notice of the sea close-by. The building on the other side was some sort of former boathouse by its proximity. Miklos went forward and stacked up at the side of a door with the others behind him. He placed a charge on the doorknob and then blew the door handle to kick the door down.

The team entered a vacant warehouse with a pair of cells on the opposite-side. They lowered their weapons as they saw Manon and Diana in these cells. Diana instantly stood up and grabbed the bars on her fence as she saw them. Her reaction was met with the sudden appearance of hostile forces from the opposite-side. The team opened fire at them as they appeared behind cover at the door next to Diana's cell and on the balcony above from an open door.

Charlemagne laid down some fire at the hostiles above them. He then reloaded his rifle and turned to the other side. A pool of blood could be seen on the ground floor near Diana's cell. The team continued to lay fire towards the balcony. The hostiles were supressed from retreating. Miklos killed one of them, triggering the other to attempt to leave. Igor took him down. The team moved up and towards the door that went to the area behind the warehouse. They looked out and saw an open space alongside a shack at the end.

Miklos and Charlemagne went outside and up a set of stairs on the side of the warehouse to reach the second floor. They checked the area and saw it was clear. The team then returned downstairs to inspect the cells that Diana and Manon were inside. Miklos produced his bolt cutters to snap off the locks of each gate. Charlemagne opened the one for Diana and she hugged him as she exited.

"I told Tristan that I would find you," Charlemagne said to her. "I keep my promises…" he added, looking over to Manon in her cell, "… even if it takes ages to fulfill them."

Miklos opened Manon's cell and helped her out.

"Let's get these dames out of here, Miklos," Charlemagne said.

"With pleasure," Miklos replied. *"Ich brauche einen Hubschrauber an meinem Standort."*

"Jawolh," someone over the radio replied.

"Where's the assassin?" Charlemagne questioned the girls. "He wasn't here."

"I'm not sure," Manon replied as they went outside, "but they were going to take us to England by a ferry. I heard it all when they had kidnapped us – there!"

Manon pointed out to the water and towards a ferry leaving port. Behind them, a helicopter flew in and touched down in front. The team helped the girls aboard before Lacplesis and Igor boarded. The two then helped Charlemagne and Miklos aboard.

"That assassin still has my briefcase… and an unsettled record," Charlemagne told Miklos. "We have to go and finish this."

Miklos nodded and went to the pilot to say, "Take us to the ferry ahead!"

"Yes, sir," the helicopter pilot replied, bringing the helicopter up.

Charlemagne sat down on the side of the helicopter with Miklos as they ventured forward, towards the ferry.

Act 7, Scene 3

The helicopter flew over the *Pas de Calais* and towards the ferry. The clouds in the sky over the water was darker and the water had a grey appearance. Charlemagne and Miklos rode together at the side of the helicopter, readying their weapons and spirits for a fight. The helicopter lowered down at a top deck and hovered in place for them to drop down.

Miklos and Charlemagne stood up and held on as though they were surfing.

"You two, stay with the ladies and keep an eye on them – take them back to the coast to join the others!" Charlemagne shouted. "Miklos and I will take care of the assassin!"

"Be careful!" Manon yelled to him.

Charlemagne nodded and then hopped off with Miklos. The helicopter then flew upwards with a flood light to spot for them as they went forward along the portside of the ferry to reach an entrance inside.

The two of them stacked up at the side of the watertight door before Miklos lowered rifle by its sling and turned the valve. He pulled the door and picked up his rifle to walk into the corridor with Charlemagne. Charlemagne gave a thumbs up to the helicopter pilot who then flew off.

"*Wir werden kostbare Fracht abgeben und dann zuruckkehren, um etwas Unterstutzung zu leisten,*" the helicopter piloted informed them over the radio. "*Ungefahre Ankunftszeit, dreizen Minuten!*"

"*Verstanden,*" Charlemagne responded, turning to Miklos in the corridor.

The two turned on the flashlights on each of their rifles before they walked with caution. The interior was dark. The ferry was old and seemed as if it had been abandoned for some time. The corridors had paint falling off the walls and the dirty floor seemed as though carpet had been pulled from where they were fastened. Stains on the wall indicated where furniture and equipment had been pulled off from.

Miklos and Charlemagne came to an area in the front where it seemed as though chairs had been ripped out from where they were in rows and columns facing a window to the bow of the ship. The two then went down the opposite corridor on the starboard side of the ship and went down, checking room by room as they cleared the area. Halfway down the ship, they reached a set of stairs that went downwards as well as connected the starboard with the portside.

Charlemagne signaled for them to continue forward. They searched the rest of the top deck before they came back around to go downstairs, reaching another level. The duo went down a corridor headed towards the bow of the ship and reached a watertight door. Miklos lowered his rifle to open the door while Charlemagne watched their back. Once the door opened, Miklos entered with Charlemagne walking backwards inside. They closed the door behind them. They had entered the bridge of the ferry.

The bridge was livelier than the rest of the boat. There were consoles facing a flat window that looked out to the sea. The consoles and computers were active. Charlemagne investigated them and saw that the boat was set to auto-pilot to travel to Dover in England. Their trajectory had been set on a GPS within the console. Miklos looked to some monitors to the side, which showed the rest of the boat. In the bowels of the ship, in a section that would have been reserved for vehicles, there were hundreds upon hundreds of migrants huddled around with men holding assault rifles walking amongst them. The rest of the corridors of the ship were quiet – there was no trace of any guards or even the assassin.

Miklos tapped Charlemagne on the shoulder and then pointed over to a room behind the bridge. The room was an office with a desk. Atop of the desk was a briefcase – Charlemagne's briefcase. Charlemagne went forward, but Miklos stopped him from proceeding. He decided to lead forward himself with careful steps, stacking up at the door into the captain's office and then carefully entering with his rifle pointed forward. He searched the room and then relaxed as there was no trap for them inside. Charlemagne took the briefcase into one hand.

"Well, that's one objective," Charlemagne said in a quiet voice, "but what about the assassin?"

Miklos looked to him with an unsure face.

"We can either face him, or leave," Miklos said to him, "assuming he is even here to begin with."

"If we do not neutralize him here and now, he will continue to threaten us."

Miklos nodded and the two exited the office to return to the bridge. Charlemagne went back to the security cameras and examined each view. He scrolled through a menu with all the available views and found a blueprint with all the camera positions. He checked each deck and then stroked his chin.

"The engine room does not have any cameras – if I had to guess, he's hiding there," Charlemagne surmised.

"If you think so," Miklos responded.

"We check there, and if we don't find anything, we leave," Charlemagne told him. "I promise that."

"Okay," Miklos responded, "then let's get moving."

Charlemagne followed Miklos out of the bridge and into the opposite corridor from where they had entered. They reached the staircase going downstairs and came to the bottom-most floor before the car deck. The two then followed down the corridor, coming to the rear where they found a watertight door going into the engine room.

The door was already open. Miklos pulled the door so that it was wide open before he entered and went down, reaching the control room overlooking the engines. The room was bright and had consoles ahead with windows that looked inwards. At the back of the room were generator panels that looked like tall grey cabinets. There was no sight of the assassin in the control room.

Charlemagne was not content with what was here. He placed the briefcase atop of a table in the middle of the room. He then went to the door going into the engine room and opened it, going down a ladder staircase to reach the top level of the engine room, which was a balcony around the perimeter that looked down to the bottom-most deck of the boat where the engines were purring away. The room was not as loud in comparison to the Ingstad, the boat that Charlemagne ventured on to get to the Arctic. However, it was warm in temperature and color. Incandescent lightbulbs above gave the room an orange-yellow lighting effect. Miklos followed him and closed the watertight door into the control room so that nobody could leave. Charlemagne walked over to the edge of the railing, which was composed of three metal bars attached to poles scattered throughout. There was a sheet of metal over these bars, making the railings protected. Charlemagne looked down the railing with his rifle. He could not see the assassin.

Miklos stood next to him and looked down. Charlemagne frowned and then turned to him. The two looked at each other before Charlemagne jerked his neck to look up to the beams above him. The assassin jumped down with two pistols in each hand, firing at them. Charlemagne jumped out of the way as the mysterious stranger landed atop. Miklos immediately engaged him in hand-to-hand combat while Charlemagne scrambled to ready his assault rifle.

The assassin jumped over the railing and down to the bottom of the engine room. Charlemagne stood up and joined Miklos as they looked down to where the assassin had fallen. He had disappeared and left behind a puff of smoke. Charlemagne and Miklos spread out along the railing and scanned the space below. The smoke quickly cleared out, but the assassin was nowhere to be seen.

Charlemagne's eyes focused on the movement of a figure below behind some generator panels. The assassin had an assault rifle and laid down some fire towards them. Miklos and Charlemagne took cover and returned fire. The gunfire from the assassin stopped suddenly and the duo looked down to see where he was, but he was gone. The two continued to stand where they had been standing with rifles pointed down.

A couple minutes had passed and Charlemagne lowered his rifle.

"He's not going to show himself – he doesn't have to show himself," Charlemagne stated. "We have to hunt him and he has nowhere to go."

"Let's give him what he wants then," Miklos replied, retracting his gun and moving out. "The worst thing that can happen is that this coward runs away."

Charlemagne and Miklos proceeded to move around the perimeter to reach a ladder staircase that went to the deck below, in the middle between the two decks. The duo continued around to reach the other ladder that went below, but quickly moved into cover as the assassin appeared from the other side, firing his assault rifle. Charlemagne and Miklos kept their heads down and returned fire. The assassin ran forward behind the railing and caught the two on their flank. Miklos rushed forward to grab the assassin's rifle. He then struggled against the assassin while Charlemagne stood up and pointed his rifle towards the hostile target.

The assassin tipped Miklos overboard and onto the steel floor below. He then produced a knife from his jacket and threw it towards Charlemagne, causing him to duck, which gave the assassin a chance to run off, jumping towards the floor above and pulling himself up. Charlemagne opened fire and attempted to get the assassin, but there was no sight of him. Quickly, the assassin then jumped down, over the ledge above Charlemagne, and kicked him back.

Charlemagne fell backwards onto the floor with his rifle atop of him. The Mysterious Stranger produced a pistol from his trouser holster and pointed it towards Charlemagne. Some gunfire could be heard from below from Miklos and towards the assassin. The Mysterious Stranger rolled out of the way and then ran off. Charlemagne saw the assassin hide behind the railings. He leaned forward and opened fire at the assassin who took a simple shot at Miklos. Miklos shouted in pain and fell to the floor. The assassin ducked and sprinted off from Charlemagne who continued to fire as he went down the stairs below and away from them. Once he was spent, Charlemagne reloaded, searched the area and then went around to see to Miklos.

Miklos was on the floor with a puddle of blood by his body. Charlemagne saw where the assassin had shot him – in the thigh. He lowered his rifle and brought his hands over the gunshot to bring pressure to the wound. There was a heavy amount of blood loss. Miklos looked pale despite the warm temperature of the room they were in. He was sweating and panting.

"I'll be fine," Miklos remarked, clenching his teeth.

"It looks like the wound is near the femoral artery," Charlemagne observed. "Keep pressure on the entry point. Do you happen to have a tourniquet in any of those pockets of yours?"

"Yes," Miklos responded, taking a deep breath.

Charlemagne moved Miklos' hands to the wound so that he could get behind him and drag him towards an electrical panel cabinet so that he could sit up. He then quickly applied the tourniquet.

"Don't let him get away," Miklos grunted. "I can handle myself."

Charlemagne nodded and then handed Miklos his rifle. Miklos took it in one hand, propped it against the panel cabinet and then readied his rifle and stepped forward into the ground floor in search of the assassin. He came into a space below the entire ship, which extended from where large boiler tanks were. The space was slightly crowded if not tight. Charlemagne walked with careful steps as he went onwards, looking at the grates below him as well as every possible space that the assassin might be hiding in.

The assassin then jumped out from atop of stand and behind a tall water tank and engaged Charlemagne with a knife in hand. He took swipes towards him, but Charlemagne dodged out of the way, using his rifle to block the knife and then attempt to butt the assassin. The assassin swiped Charlemagne's vest, but did not pierce his body. Charlemagne hit the assassin on the head, which caused him to run off and disappear ahead.

Charlemagne looked at his vest and then forward to keep his eyes for the assassin. He lowered his rifle and took out his pistol from a holster as well as a knife of his own. He kept the two in each hand and continued onwards with still careful steps. Charlemagne came out to a space with a railing in the railing with a rectangular space below. In the space was the propeller shaft sprouting from the main engines ahead. Charlemagne saw the assassin ahead with his assault rifle. The Mysterious Stranger opened fire on him, which forced Charlemagne to take cover and exchange his weapons for his assault rifle.

Once Charlemagne was ready, he stood up to return fire to the assassin on the other side. The two exchanged fire with Charlemagne moving around the side to attempt to get at the assassin's flank. The assassin retreated and went around the other side, running off towards the boat engines. Charlemagne switched his weapons and continued forward to end of the engine room. He came close to the corner going behind the engines and was ambushed by the assassin once more who took Charlemagne's arms and raised them up.

Charlemagne was slammed into the wall and fired a shot into the air. Steam hissed out from a pipe. The assassin had restrained Charlemagne against a wall with a knife almost an inch towards the mysterious stranger's face. Both of them breathed heavily – the assassin let go of Charlemagne before the knife pierced him, but as he did, Charlemagne took the knife and grabbed the assassin by the neck before he could run off again. He then stabbed the assassin in the side, causing him to shout in pain and turn around.

Instead of retreating, the assassin took Charlemagne with both hands and choked him. Charlemagne took his hand. He raised his left up to attempt to unmask the assassin, staring into his green eyes before moving his other hand and lowering his left. He brought his right to the knife in the assassin's side and dug the knife in some more to cause some pain. The Mysterious Stranger slammed Charlemagne against the wall he was pinned against and took a grenade from his belt.

"*Bon Vacances*," the Mysterious Stranger remarked in a gritted accent, words echoed and muffled by the gas mask.

The Mysterious Stranger pulled the pin on the grenade and then dropped so it fell at their feet. Charlemagne grabbed it before it hit the floor and then dropped it to the ground. The grenade was not a smoke grenade. The assassin let go of Charlemagne, throwing him onto the ground. The two then split and went in opposite directions. Charlemagne stood up from where he had been thrown and ran down the platform and hearing the grenade go off as well as a combination of explosions.

Charlemagne returned to the boilers and to Miklos who was dazed. The amount of blood around him had stopped, but he was still unwell.

"Come on," Charlemagne remarked, bringing Miklos' left arm around his shoulder and helping him up. "Let's get you out of here."

Some further explosions could be heard from the corridor ahead, which motivated Charlemagne to quickly go up with Miklos and towards the control room entrance. The door was still closed.

"Hold on," Charlemagne said, bringing both his hands to the valve to turn it around.

Miklos almost fell down the stairs, but Charlemagne was able to unlock the door beforehand to grab him. With one hand, Charlemagne opened the door and then the two walked in with Miklos struggling to keep up as he leaned to the side as if he was about to pass out.

Miklos' weight was too much for Charlemagne who turned to dragging him across the ground. The two passed the table with the briefcase atop. Charlemagne looked at the briefcase and then to Miklos. He took a deep breath and then continued to pull

Miklos, leaving the briefcase behind. Charlemagne carried Miklos upstairs and then looked out to the sight of some lifeboats on the starboard side of the boat.

Vibrations continued to be felt from below the ship. Charlemagne went to another watertight door, unlocked it and dragged Miklos outside to the lifeboat. The boat was white and attached to the ferry with two cranes. Charlemagne struggled to lift Miklos into the boat but was able to by lifting him onto his shoulder and then pushing him into the lifeboat. He then climbed into the boat. Then stood up and looked out of the lifeboat and back into the ferry. Charlemagne then looked down to Miklos before looking back into the ferry once more. Some further vibrations and echoes of explosions could be heard.

"Dammit," Charlemagne cursed, sitting down and then looking for a means to unlatch them from the ferry instead.

Charlemagne broke them off from the ferry and they fell into the water. The ferry continued to sail its direction despite the explosions that continued to be seen from the engine room. The waters were choppy as they floated away. Charlemagne watched the ferry as it disappeared onto the horizon, tipping over to its fate, and leaving Charlemagne and Miklos to theirs as they floated over *La Manche* alone. He proceeded to continue giving Miklos first aid, bandaging his thigh before picking up his radio.

"Bravo One… this is Charlie Actual," Charlemagne said, examining Miklos for his vitals. "I need an exfil at my location as soon as possible – one wounded and in need of medical attention as soon as possible."

"*Jawohl*," the helicopter pilot responded, "on my way."

Charlemagne finished examining Miklos and then gave a deep sigh. He sat back with his legs out on the side of the boat opposite from Miklos, leaning backwards and looking up to the grey sky. He closed his eyes and drifted off, in peace, as it was seemingly finally over.

Act 7, Scene 4

The lifeboat pushed against the sand of the shores of Normandy and then floated back out as the water retreated. The boat then pushed back up against the sands. Charlemagne woke up and sat up. He looked around and at where he was, going over to check on Miklos for his vitals to see that he was alive, but still unconscious. In the least, he was responsive to pain as he murmured in response to Charlemagne placing a hand over his wound.

Once Charlemagne was certain Miklos was alive, he picked him up by bringing an arm around his neck and then falling onto the beach waters together. Charlemagne then tried to stand him up onto his feet once more with an arm around each other's neck and over each other's shoulders to walk across the beach. Although Charlemagne was able to hold this position, due to Miklos' unconsciousness, Charlemagne dragged him and then helped him walk off the beach. The two then proceeded to climb up a grassy hill at the end of the beach, resting atop of the hill as Charlemagne placed Miklos on his back. Charlemagne then crawled a foot away from him and sat down, looking out to the English Channel and taking a deep sigh.

Charlemagne simply looked forward to the channel in silence. He held a saddened look on his face as his eyes examined the shore and its long horizon. The waters were light grey as the sky and calm. The sand of the beaches were smooth and stretched for miles on either direction. There was a perfect solace. A gentle wind in the air. The sound of the tide brushing against the sand. Charlemagne took a deep breath and then lowered his head. A tear rolled down his cheek.

The silence was interrupted by the sound of a helicopter in the distance. Charlemagne looked to the right and saw his helicopter approaching him. He stood up and went further up the hill to wave towards it. The helicopter made its approach towards him and lowered down in the field behind.

Lacplesis and Igor exited from the helicopter and secured the landing zone. Charlemagne waved to them to help him. They rushed forward and went to where Charlemagne had brought Miklos. The two then helped carry him back to the helicopter with Charlemagne behind, holding his rifle in one hand. Charlemagne looked and saw Manon in the helicopter. The two looked to each other.

Charlemagne walked over to Manon and hugged her.

"Is it over?" Manon asked.

"Hopefully so," Charlemagne responded, "but I had to leave behind our research – it's gone now."

"Oh, Charles, to hell with that briefcase," Manon responded, tightening her grip around Charlemagne. "Miklos is safe and the both of you are alive."

"The assassin…" Charlemagne said, "he wasn't our son. I thought he was, but he wasn't. His eye and hair colors don't match ours."

"What?" Manon questioned.

"I thought… I thought our son was trying to kill me," Charlemagne replied. "I know it's silly, but it was a genuine fear because I don't for the life of me know what the true motivates of this killer were. I don't know if it was because of what I said, or if it was possibly something I had down earlier in my life. I thought for sure that this was our son looking to seek vengeance towards me, but alas… no."

"Charles," Manon responded, "our son can never know who we are because there were no clues left to him. I never even met the couple who adopted him, and neither they nor our son will ever come in contact with us."

"I want to find him," Charlemagne said, eyes watering "ever since you told me, I have been itching to go out and search for him."

"Our son does not want to be found," Manon replied. "Let it go."

Charlemagne held a frown and then took a deep breath. He turned his head and nodded. He then looked to Manon, given them some space as he separated each other from each other's grip.

"Can I ask something? I've been wondering.... How did you manage to communicate with us? To call us via a landline to give us your location in that slum?" Charlemagne questioned. "The cell you were in seemed too small for it to be possible."

"But I never communicated with you," Manon responded, "all I did to help was give you the location of where the assassin would take us next – Calais – in the mud of the Ardennes. I thought you deduced the rest yourself."

"Right..." Charlemagne replied, nodding, "anyways... enough of all this. Is Diana okay?"

"Yes," Manon responded, "she is with Tristan and Dr. Lambert."

"Good," Charlemagne remarked, "then let's go join them and return to Paris. From there, it'll be high time for myself and the kids to return home to Canada."

Miklos was loaded onto the helicopter. Charlemagne and Manon joined them. Charlemagne closed the helicopter doors and then sat down to take a deep breath. The helicopter lifted upwards and set off.

Act 7, Scene 5

Diana and Tristan toasted glasses outside on the rooftop patio of an elegant restaurant in Paris. The restaurant itself was atop of the hotel the family were staying at. Tristan was dressed in a crème dress shirt, tucked into some jeans with a burgundy sweater tied by the arms around his neck. Diana was dressed in a dark blue dress with her hair coming down on the right side. Manon had helped the two of them dress.

"Happy one year anniversary," Tristan said, smiling, "we made it."

"Yeah, we did," Diana replied, looking to the side. "It's a shame we couldn't have gone to the top of the Eiffel Tower, but this is nice too."

The couple were sat at a table next to a glass railing, which looked over to the Eiffel Tower. It was past sunset, and the lights of the tower were bright. At the other side of the restaurant was Charlemagne, alone at a table with a small velvet box in his hands. He was fiddling with the box and opened it to expose the diamond ring inside. He then closed it and brought it into his suit jacket as he saw Judith come outside.

"Sorry about that," Judith apologized, sitting down and taking the menu.

"It's quite alright," Charlemagne replied. "If anything, I could be apologizing for this vacation, which turned out so poorly."

"Nevermind that," Judith responded. "You can make up for it in the summer."

"I ordered a bottle of wine from Bordeaux if you're interested," Charlemagne said, changing the subject. "I hope that's alright."

"That'll be quite fine," Judith replied, closing her menu and looking to Charlemagne with a smile. "What's wrong? You look upset."

"I'm... I'm not," Charlemagne responded, producing an artificial smile for her. "I'm only a little exhausted."

Charlemagne's phone vibrated inside his blazer. He took it out and saw that he had received a text message from Manon. Charlemagne put his phone away only for it to vibrate again.

"Sorry," Charlemagne apologized, looking at his phone again.

Charlemagne unlocked his phone and read the text message:

"Charles – be careful around Dr. Lambert. The following was discovered by an investigation of your protection squad."

Charlemagne then looked at the images below. The images were text messages between what was allegedly Judith and an unknown number. The area code was local to Harlech. The messages were dynamic and started with Judith stating to the unknown number that they were in Orleans at a certain address (Dr. Dumas' residence) and then at Carnac in Brittany and going to the Quiberon Alignments. The next message stated what time they left and where they were going next: Bordeaux to visit the Basilica of Saint Seurin. The message afterwards stated the time they were going to the basilica before stating what time they were going to leave Bordeaux to go to Toulouse. The next message stated that Charlemagne would be alone with Dr. Dumas in the University of Toulouse before stating that Charlemagne had messaged her and said that they were going to the Toulouse Museum. Charlemagne continued to scroll through the images – they detailed their exact movements, locations, and activities hence forth to even today.

Manon's text message after these images stated, "The Protection Squad are on their way to the rooftop to detain her."

"Is something wrong?" Judith questioned.

Charlemagne looked to her with a deep frown. He put his phone away.

"No," Charlemagne denied.

The garçon arrived and set down two wine glasses in one hand and carried a bottle of red wine in the other. He proceeded to pour into each glass before leaving the bottle for them. Judith took her glass and raised it to tap with Charlemagne's. Charlemagne picked his up. His hands trembled. The glasses dinged together.

"*Bon Vacances*," Judith cheered with a smile before drinking from her cup.

Charlemagne didn't drink from his and simply stared of into the distance upon her words. His hands trembled more. He grew pale and set down the glass.

"You look uneasy," Judith observed. "What's wrong?"

Charlemagne took a deep breath and swallowed.

"There appears to be some sort of plot here," Charlemagne stated to her. "I'm sorry this may be difficult for you, but in truth, it's difficult for me too. We need to have a serious discussion about something..."

"What is it?" Judith replied with a worried, but innocent look.

"The Protection Squad – Manon, just messaged me a series of screenshots that allege communication between yourself and an unknown number originating from Harlech. The details of the message suggest that you've been feeding someone information as to my whereabouts from Orleans to now."

"Oh, don't be ridiculous, Charles," Judith responded, laughing it off. "Why would I do such a thing?"

"I don't know," Charlemagne replied.

"Why would I try to kill you?" Judith asked.

"I don't know – but please explain to me how it is that the Protection Squad – the people I am paying to protect myself and the kids, would frame you!"

Judith stuttered.

"Nobody else knew I would at the Toulouse Museum other than yourself and Manon. Nobody else knew that I would be at the Saint-Jean Fort in Marseilles or that we would be boarding a luxury train to Germany! Nobody knew we had escaped to Geneva!"

"I'm not having this," Judith deflected, taking her purse and standing up. "I won't have you blame me for our misfortunes! If there's anyone you should suspect, it's this hussy!"

Judith walked off and went inside the restaurant. She rummaged through her purse as she attempted to escape. Charlemagne followed her and stopped her by the elevator. There, she produced a pistol from her purse and turned to point it at him. Charlemagne raised his hands up.

"It was you," Charlemagne said, looking at her.

Judith was red-faced and held a deep frown.

"Why? I loved you, so why? Why have you done this?" Charlemagne questioned her. "What was your motive and plan behind all this?"

"Revenge," Judith simply stated, "from the beginning to the end, it was all about revenge for what you had done to Barry and me."

"What?"

"Last summer," Judith explained, "was the first time I had seen him since the divorce. My beautiful Barry… it brought me so much pain to see him, because it was a reminder of the loss of our children, our miscarriages – the family we could have had together. All that could calm me down was the thought of making things right. Our relationship, Charles, was a fabrication and part of this plan to get revenge. I became your girlfriend – and I would have continued until the day you would propose to me, become your wife, and then inherit what was yours. My conspiracy with this assassin – it was unrelated and just simple business."

"Just business? Your motives sound a lot more than just business," Charlemagne replied.

"Charles, I'm the mole in Cabernet Laboratories. I've been the mole since the beginning. I was the one that got into contact with Nero Medici. I was the one that allowed the Fusion Reactor to be stolen. The GDP had nothing to do with it as you thought. I told the assassin where we were going throughout France. I was the one that attempted to kill Tristan in Geneva, because he needed to die for Diana's sake. Regrettably, when I had snuck into the maintenance room of the pool to electrify them, I hadn't realized that Diana would be the one swimming (thinking she was inept at swimming). I instantly undid what I had done and failed. Regardless, it was all me."

"You can't inherit what I have – you're not my wife. You're not even my common-law partner," Charlemagne replied. "Why try to kill me?"

"You self-absorbed idiot!" Judith shouted. "The assassin's objective was never to kill you. If anything, I pleaded to him that you be spared for my own plan, but he saw you as an obstacle to what really needed to be done. The true objective was to collect important files thought to be in the possession of Dr. Jean-Baptiste Dumas before being given to his daughter, Manon. The files of which produced by your grandfather, Derby Cabernet."

The elevator doors opened with Lukas, Brandan (Elegast) and Lacplesis on the other side.

"Stop right there!" Lukas shouted, pointing his rifle to Manon.

Manon grabbed Charlemagne and held him at gunpoint.

"Back off!" Judith yelled back at them. "I will shoot!"

Judith snuck away with Charlemagne, exiting the inside of the restaurant and going back outside to a corner of the patio. Diana and Tristan saw what was happening and stood up. The Protection Squad ran out with their rifles pointed. Brandan separated himself from the team to stretch his arms out to prevent the kids from doing anything. Lacplesis and Lukas maintained their guns pointed towards Judith.

"Don't shoot!" Charlemagne yelled to them. "Tell me, Judith, if the assassin wanted these files, then what was your plan with me?"

"Simple – I would marry you and then you would have a tragic accident. I would inherit your fortune, Diana, and everything else that you owned, and I would give it all to my love – to Barry after I would die."

"Suicide?" Charlemagne questioned.

"Cancer," Judith responded, "the cancer that you gave me after all the years of researching fusion technology. I was diagnosed with ovarian cancer last autumn – I have less than a year left."

"Your work for me didn't give you cancer…" Charlemagne denied. "We employed the safest techniques…"

"How would you know? You didn't even know that the fusion reactor was leaking until all those ghosts appeared!" Judith shouted. "For all I know, you and countless others could have had their lives shortened because of their work for you. My work for you is why I couldn't hold my children… It's why the lining of my uterus failed to hold them. It's why I lost them. I'm barren because of the years of intense radiation working for you."

"And what are you going to do now?" Charlemagne questioned. "Your plan has failed – it's over."

"If it's over for me, then it's going to be over for you too…" Judith responded.

Charlemagne looked forward as Igor and Holger arrived with Manon. The rest of the Protection Squad pointed their weapons while Manon looked in shock with Charlemagne being held hostage. Judith looked at Manon and tensed her brow.

"Die, you harlot!" Judith shouted, pointing the gun towards Manon and pushing Charlemagne forward.

Judith took shots at Manon who was tackled onto the ground by Brandan. Charlemagne fell to the floor as the rest of the squad opened fire at Judith. The glass railing behind her shattered and Judith fell overboard to her certain death. Charlemagne shouted but was stopped from going towards the ledge by Lacplesis and Lukas. Charlemagne was in tears.

Diana and Tristan watched in horror before Igor proceeded to escort them away. Charlemagne and Manon were brought to their feet. Manon hugged Charlemagne as he cried. Holger and Lukas stayed with them while Brandan and Lacplesis went to the elevator with Igor and the kids. Diana and Tristan watched Manon attempt to reconcile with Charlemagne and held sunken as well as shocked looks. Judith was surely dead.

Epilogue

Charlemagne stepped outside of the *Saint-Etienne-du-Mont* church in Paris as the bells tolled. He crossed his arms and took a deep breath. Less than a day had passed since what had happened on the rooftop. He looked at a sign outside of the church, "In Memory of Dr. Judith Athena Lambert," it said on one line, and the dates below, "November 20, 1964 – April 29, 2019.' Charlemagne sighed and then looked away and towards the city. His ears twitched as he heard steps behind to his left.

On his left was Judith's ex-husband, different to how he had last seen him in Kennte – shaven and with shortened hair, but with the same glasses. He was also dressed in a black suit like Charlemagne. Charlemagne looked to him and stepped forward to shake his hand.

"I'm so sorry," Charlemagne said to him, "about everything…"

"It's alright…" Barry replied, looking out to the city with him. "It was well within your rights. We had divorced."

"She never even loved me though… She loved you all this time, even after the divorce…"

Charlemagne explained to Barry what had happened on the rooftop. All Barry could do in response was to take a deep breath.

"She was never the same after the miscarriage," Barry remarked.

"She never stopped loving you," Charlemagne insisted, "even if her mind had devolved and corrupted because of the psychological pain…"

The two then went quiet as they admired the scenery. The sun was setting across the city and the skies of Paris were orange-yellow as reflected in the clouds.

"If you want, there's an open position for you at Cabernet Laboratories…" Charlemagne said to Barry. "I've missed you and would be happy to see my old friend back in his old position… in fact, given what has happened, it would help a lot to have you around again, Barry."

Barry looked to him and nodded.

"Sure," Barry replied, nodding "I can do that."

"Thank you…"

"Anyways, I'm going to go inside," Barry responded. "We'll talk later."

'Of course," Charlemagne replied, nodding to him.

The two friends shook hands and then walked inside the church together. Charlemagne looked to the side and saw Dr. Jean-Baptiste Dumas hiding in the shadows. Charlemagne stopped and allowed Barry to go in to see his ex-wife as he looked to his old mentor. He walked over to him with an apologetic look, limping. He held two oversized envelopes in one hand and a cane in the other.

"Why didn't you tell me?" Charlemagne asked him. "Why didn't you tell me that you had something of my grandfather – something that might have explained to me why someone was attempting to kill both Manon and me?"

"Manon understood – and for the sake of your life and hers, you couldn't know. She understood that and the risks when I sent her the files."

Charlemagne took a deep sigh and looked up to the stained-glass window. There was a depiction of the Mother Mary with Joseph and Jesus as a baby in the stained-glass window. Charlemagne then looked to Dr. Dumas.

"Here," Dr. Dumas said, handing him one of the envelopes, "your grandfather gave this to me before he died. I did not want to give it to you – seeing more harm come from it than good, but you seem to understand now as he did, so it might be time."

Charlemagne took the envelope and read the title on the front, 'Derby Files.' He then opened the envelope and slid out the first sheet. The sheet contained a family tree of the Cabernet household with Charlemagne as the youngest generation and going all the way to Sennett Aenis Cabernet (Sennett Aenis Witzendorff) as well as his birthdate, June 18, 1850, and birthplace, Klimbach, Elsass.

"Elsass... Witzendorff?" Charlemagne questioned. "What is this?"

"Your grandfather's most cherished work... his final work," Dr. Dumas explained. "Read the files and you will understand, Charles. Your family has a complicated history, but your ancestor, Sennett was born in Alsace and fought for Napoleon the Third during the Franco-Prussian War. His earlier ancestors had served Napoleon Bonaparte himself, but before that, they were Germans who were thrusted between two countries and a feud similar to that of brothers. After the collapse of the second empire and establishment of the Third French Republic, your forefather fled to England – the youngest of a family of nobles who would be incorporated into German Empire – and seek a new life in Canada. To honor his family's French history, he changed his surname from Witzendorff to Cabernet, and immigrated to Lennox, south of Harlech where he met his wife, Ambrosia Stassen. The two established the vineyards that produced the fruit and seed to create Cabernet Industries. His wine was popular nation-wide, and like that, the Cabernet legacy grew. His son, your great-great-grandfather, Lycidas Rerir Cabernet, took his father's fortune and invested it into real estate and then manufacturing, lumber, mining and other trades during the Laurier Boom. His immense wealth was further expanded during the Great Depression and Second World War by your great-grandfather, Pepin Waelsing Cabernet, who expanded Cabernet Industries into weapons manufacturing. His daughter, Alcmene, was meant to inherit the Cabernet fortune, but she abandoned it to marry and American businessman. Instead, his youngest son, Derby – Derby Cabernet who was raised in England and fought for the Allies during the Second World War, inherited the Cabernet fortune and married the daughter of a disapproving Lord Mountbatten, Ophelia, and gave birth to your father, Everest. Everest would become a father at the young age of fifteen when he impregnated your mother, a young Austrian peer of his at his boarding school. Everest, being so irresponsible, would dump the responsibility of raising the young child, yourself, onto Derby and Ophelia. What you don't know about Derby, however, is the resentment your grandfather had in his part in the war – a resentment that would be magnified if he saw the state of Europe today."

Charlemagne looked at the family tree and then to Dr. Dumas.

"From Everest, to you, and to your own son with my Manon," Dr. Dumas said.

"You know?" Charlemagne questioned, looking at him.

"Manon told me this morning over breakfast – she was in tears, and while it pained me to know the fate of this young boy, it pains me less to know of the beautiful creation between the two of you. What a splendor joy, Charlemagne – a child!"

"Wait…" Charlemagne remarked, flipping through the sheets of paper. "According to these papers, my family *isn't* French, but German. Why did you tell me that you knew I was French when you knew I wasn't?"

"But Charles, you are French!" Dr. Dumas insisted, "you see, the French and the Germans are brothers of the same

Germanic background, and had you tested your blood like I had asked, you would have been positive for Frankish blood because the Franks were a Germanic tribe. Any Germanic man can transition to become French from German, and likewise in the opposite manner. The blood, Charles, the blood is what matters, because from violence and blood, all culture and people are born. What difference is your blood from that of a man in Berlin or a man in Paris? None. A big difference is the blood of an African or a Turkman – these bloods are incompatible for assimilation into our nation, because these are not our people. The French nation is a Germanic nation – the country of the Franks! Your name, Charlemagne, comes from the name of the Germanic Emperor who united all Germans! A beautiful nation! This is what both your grandfather and I understood – this is what he would have wanted you to understand… Your child, a beautiful child, was born out of the marriage of a French woman and a German man – a child of both people, but of one race and blood."

Charlemagne looked to him with confusion.

"Then what was so special of these papers that an assassin would pursue yourself and Manon for them?" Charlemagne questioned. "Was it because of my comments? Because these papers would prove the media wrong?"

"No…" Dr. Dumas replied, calming down and gaining a more serious look.

Dr. Dumas handed him the other folder.

"The reason why an assassin was summoned for these folders and to even possibly have to kill you, is in this," Dr. Dumas said, pointing at the second envelope. "It is with regret that I also address this… the nature of your grandfather's death."

"My grandfather died in an accident…" Charlemagne said.

"No, Charles," Dr. Dumas replied, "your grandfather was assassinated in a vehicular accident that was deliberately caused because of information he had uncovered in regards to a certain rootless international clique…"

Charlemagne looked to Dr. Dumas in shock. He then attempted to open the envelope.

"What are you going to do about your son, Charles?" Dr. Dumas questioned, stopping Charlemagne from opening the envelope.

"The only thing I can do," Charlemagne responded, looking to him. "I'm going to go looking for him."

With those words, Charlemagne opened the envelope and took out the sheets of paper inside. He then proceeded to read what his grandfather had forwarded and meant for him to read; a report passed on from grandfather to grandson.

"All of us need an identity which unites us with our neighbors, our countrymen, those people who are subject to the same rules and same laws as us, those people with whom we might one day have to fight side by side to protect our inheritance, those people with whom we will suffer with when attacked, those people whose destinies are in some way tied up with our own."

– Roger Scruton

www.ingramcontent.com/pod-product-compliance
Lightning Source LLC
Chambersburg PA
CBHW051425170626
46809CB00006B/2321